Betting on Love

By the Author

The Artist's Muse

Betting on Love

Visit us at www.boldstrokesbooks.com

Betting on Love

by

Alyssa Linn Palmer

2015

BETTING ON LOVE

© 2015 By Alyssa Linn Palmer. All Rights Reserved.

ISBN 13: 978-1-62639-242-7

This Trade Paperback Original Is Published By
Bold Strokes Books, Inc.
P.O. Box 249
Valley Falls, NY 12185

First Edition: February 2015

THIS IS A WORK OF FICTION. NAMES, CHARACTERS, PLACES, AND INCIDENTS ARE THE PRODUCT OF THE AUTHOR'S IMAGINATION OR ARE USED FICTITIOUSLY. ANY RESEMBLANCE TO ACTUAL PERSONS, LIVING OR DEAD, BUSINESS ESTABLISHMENTS, EVENTS, OR LOCALES IS ENTIRELY COINCIDENTAL.

THIS BOOK, OR PARTS THEREOF, MAY NOT BE REPRODUCED IN ANY FORM WITHOUT PERMISSION.

Credits
Editor: Ruth Sternglantz
Production Design: Stacia Seaman
Cover Design by Sheri (graphicartist2020@hotmail.com)

Acknowledgments

Many thanks to the following people, without whom this book could not have been written: Cathy Pegau, critique partner extraordinare; Anthony Bennett, who took me riding on his Kawasaki Ninja and made sure I at least sounded like I knew what I was talking about when it comes to motorcycles; my family, for all their support; the Calgary Association of Romance Writers of America (CaRWA), for their support and help; and Ruth Sternglantz, my fantastic editor.

For AWB.

PROLOGUE

Cardston, Alberta

Elly laid the lease down on the kitchen table, over the cracked Formica that had seen her through her entire childhood and then some. Everything here was familiar, the worn coziness of the farmhouse, the pots hanging over the stove, the clutter that dotted the counters, the table itself, and the living room. She hadn't had the heart to clean it all up, to move it from where it had stood for years while her parents puttered about, oblivious to most of everything.

"I can't believe you're not staying." Jack leaned over the table, pulling a ballpoint pen from the pocket of his dark blue chambray shirt, clicking the top. He read through the lease, muttering to himself as he went along. "Eleanor Gladys Newton Cole hereby leases the land, as cited in schedule A, to Jack Collins, for the period of one year…" He reached the last page and signed with a flourish. "You sure about this? You don't have to go just because I'm leasing the land."

She wasn't sure, not really, but she wasn't about to tell him that. "I need to find a job again." When she held out her hand for the pen, he passed it over and she signed her name below his. "The diner wouldn't pay enough to keep up with expenses here."

"Not even with tips?" Jack scrubbed a hand over his short-cropped blond hair. It was early in the season yet, but his skin was already windburned from being out of doors, working the fields.

"Not even." It wouldn't have been enough, even if she hadn't been saving. A few months' worth of expenses for a tiny apartment in the city. With luck, that would be long enough for her to find a proper job. She'd had such trouble with the recession; graphic artists weren't exactly in high demand.

"You don't have to do it all alone, you know." Jack bent his head and Elly stepped back, so his lips just brushed her hair. Undeterred, he laid a hand on her shoulder, giving a gentle squeeze. "Your dad always reckoned we'd join our two farms."

"I know, but it just isn't for me."

Jack dropped his hand and gathered up the lease. "I'll check on the house while you're gone, make sure everything's in order. And I'll file this soon too." He held up the lease that he'd rolled up into a white tube.

"Thanks." She wanted to say more but knew he'd take it as an invitation. Even having seen her with Alex, practically a movie-star-romance kiss on the porch, Jack still had hopes. But he was never going to be a gorgeous, dark-haired biker girl who could kiss her breathless. She put her hand in the pocket of her jeans, feeling the worn piece of paper there. Maybe she'd get up the courage to finally phone Alex. Her fingers tensed. It had been months; Alex would have forgotten her by now. She regretted not calling. Even now, she couldn't get Alex out of her mind, couldn't forget that incredible night.

"You've got my number." Jack went to the door, pushing open the screen. It rattled and squeaked. "I'll get that fixed too."

Elly lifted her hand in a halfhearted wave and watched as he thumped down the steps to his blue pickup. That was that.

What if she had called Alex? Their night together had been incredible, passionate like nothing she'd known. Yet she'd held back. A girl like that…she'd surely have someone back in the city and wouldn't want a country girl. Better to leave that night as it was.

When Jack had pulled out and back to the road, roaring off toward his farm, she turned and went up the stairs to her room under the eaves. A light breeze blew through the room, bringing scents of freshly turned fields and clean air. She took a deep breath. She'd miss this. Her suitcase sat open on the bed, almost full. It held all of her city clothes, the ones from her previous job, the clothes she hadn't had much opportunity to wear in the last year. Waitressing at the diner while taking freelance jobs didn't leave much call for skirt suits and pretty blouses. She took down the last few shirts from their hangers, the chambray soft under her hands. She'd take this much of the farm with her, at least.

She closed the suitcase and lifted it off the bed. Time to go.

Chapter One

Calgary, Alberta

Alex slowed as she came up to the traffic light, the Kawasaki Ninja purring under her. She put her foot down and let the motorcycle idle as she waited for the light to change. She usually avoided coming through the city's downtown core, preferring to take the ring road for as long as possible, but today she wanted to get home in time to take a nap before she headed out to Parry's for the usual Friday karaoke. Will would be meeting her, and she needed to have her wits about her. Between the two of them, karaoke was practically a contact sport. She smiled to herself, letting her gaze move over the cars in front of her.

A young woman crossed the street several meters ahead, and Alex admired the slim legs in their professional skirt. She started, then leaned forward. She knew that slim, almost boyish figure, those strawberry-blond curls. Her gloved hands tightened on the handlebars. It was her, the girl from the farm. Elly.

She still dreamed of that girl sometimes, of the single night they'd spent together, on the bed under the gabled ceiling, the cool breeze from the summer storm drifting in from the open window, teasing their bare skin… The girl had been gorgeous. She'd never thought to see Elly here, two hundred kilometers away, in the middle of the city. If she'd been closer, they might've had a thing. Maybe Elly'd be up for an evening if she was just visiting. Alex wasn't one to turn down a chance, not after their last evening together.

Elly glanced over, eyeing the bike. Alex lifted her hand and waved, but there was no sign of recognition. As soon as the light changed, Alex shifted gears and zipped forward, cursing the slowness of the car in front of her. She pulled off to the side, coming to a stop beside Elly, who wore not the jeans and chambray shirt from the farm but a suit, looking like the perfect office worker. If it hadn't been for those curls, Alex might not have recognized her at all.

Alex pushed up the visor, but still Elly showed no recognition, stepping back with a startled look. Alex fumbled with the chin strap and pulled off her helmet, letting her dark hair fall free, exposing her face to the bright afternoon sunlight.

"Hey, stranger," Alex said, her voice a bit huskier than usual. It had been at least a year since she'd seen Elly, and though she'd said she'd get in touch, she'd never quite made it.

"Hey." Elly stepped to the curb's edge, coming alongside the bike. She looked nervous, but a shy smile crossed her features. "Nice bike. What happened to the other one?"

Out at the farm, Alex had ridden a Harley, but wanting more speed, she'd traded it in for the Kawasaki. "Sold it," she replied, patting the handlebar. "I like this one better." She cleared her throat. "You never called."

A delicate wrinkle appeared between Elly's brows as she frowned. "You never called either."

That was true, but it had seemed a waste of time to call a girl who didn't live close by, and who seemed to have sequestered herself in the middle of nowhere. She'd had Jan, and Will, and others since to occupy her time.

Not wanting to get into details that would only get her pickup line shot down, Alex said, "I wish I had, but I lost your number." She gave Elly an apologetic smile. "You busy tonight?" She watched Elly, watched the thoughtful expression flit across her face. No smile, no indication of interest. Elly had been so up for it, a year ago. Alex shifted on her feet, feeling the slight slope of the road.

"Not really. What did you have in mind?"

Alex wanted to punch a fist into the air. Instead, she squeezed the brake. "We should go for a drink. It's karaoke night at Parry's, and the beer is cheap."

"Karaoke?" Elly shifted from foot to foot.

Damn. That wasn't acceptance. "It's fun. Trust me." Alex cradled the helmet in her arm, hoping to convince her. "I'll come pick you up. Where do you live?"

"Just a few blocks over, on First Street. Number 5-1-0-4. It's one of those low-rise apartment buildings."

"How about eight? Would that work for you?"

"All right."

"Wear jeans," Alex said. "No skirts."

Elly gave her a puzzled glance. "What for?"

She chuckled. "A bit awkward, straddling a bike in a skirt. Trust me." She patted the seat behind her.

"But…" Elly looked pale, even in the afternoon sun.

"Eight o'clock." She smoothed her hair back, out of her face, and slipped her helmet on, buckling the strap under her chin. She studied Elly closely. "I'll bring a spare helmet for you. I think it'll fit."

Elly nodded, still seeming hesitant. "All right. I'll be watching for you."

"You'll hear me coming." Alex grinned. "See you later." She steered the bike back out into the traffic, feeling the breeze on her cheeks through the open visor. She darted through an open space between a midsize truck and a sedan and zipped through the next green light, heading up the hill and toward home.

5-1-0-4 First Street, she recited in her head, several times over until she knew she had it down. Will would understand, after all. The two of them were alike, and he wouldn't be hurt if she passed him up tonight for a babe like Elly.

❖

At home, Elly dropped her messenger bag to the floor just inside the door and set her keys in their place on the shelf by the door. She'd usually change into yoga pants and a T-shirt, but now she had plans, a first for a Friday evening in the city. Being here alone, even though she'd lived in the city before, made her nervous. So many people, so many chances for something bad to happen. She wasn't paranoid, but she rarely went out after dark if she could help it. She toed off her shoes and headed to the kitchen, opening the fridge to browse. There was enough time for a proper meal, but she had little motivation to cook. She put on water for pasta, and a second pot for sauce. That would do.

It was almost exactly what she and Alex had eaten that night.

While she waited for her dinner, Elly went into her bedroom and tugged open the closet door. She chose dark-hued skinny jeans, one of her favorite pairs, but when it came to choosing a shirt, she had no clue. She'd never been to Parry's. Was it a pub, or fancier? Or more casual? Nearly anything would have worked at the diner for a night out, but it was different here. Finally, she chose a black blouse with fine white polka dots, a compromise between casual and dressy. She set the clothes on the bed and went to have her dinner.

At five minutes to eight, Elly paced her living room, glancing out the picture window every few moments. As the time had wound down, the tension had ratcheted up and she wished she hadn't eaten. Her stomach churned, and it wasn't just from the nervousness of being on a motorcycle. She wouldn't know anyone at Parry's aside from Alex, and she hated meeting new people. Or rather, she hated meeting an entire group of friends when she was so obviously the outsider, unsophisticated and so, well, rural.

She heard the growl of the motorcycle as it turned the corner onto her street and she snatched up her coat and purse, then headed out resolutely, locking the door behind her. When she came down the stairs and out the front door, Alex had backed the bike into a spot between two cars, bracing the back wheel against the curb. The kickstand came down and she dismounted, swinging a leg over. She still wore her chaps, and from behind, they hugged her jean-clad bottom. Elly swallowed against the dryness in her throat. Her heartbeat sped up.

Alex lifted the visor on her helmet. She grinned. "The helmet's going to flatten your hair a bit. Sorry about that." She unlocked a case on the back of the bike, flipping it open and taking out a gray helmet with black painted streaks. "Hopefully this fits you all right."

Elly took the helmet from her, feeling awkward and inexperienced.

"What's wrong?"

Elly licked her lips. "Just…I've never been on a motorcycle before. Ever."

Alex took the helmet from her, grasping it by the chin straps. She pulled the straps wide. "Hold it like this, slide it over your head." She mimed the motion, then handed the helmet back.

Elly lifted the helmet over her head and tried to slide it on. It stuck. She could feel her cheeks flushing, burning as she lifted the helmet off. Her hair was mussed, the strawberry-blond strands sticking to her forehead. "I think it's too tight," she said, pushing the hair off her forehead with her forearm.

"It's supposed to be tight," Alex said, taking the helmet from her. "Let's try again." She lifted the helmet up and slid it down over Elly's head. This time it worked. Elly fumbled with the visor, and Alex took her bare hand in her own gloved one, directing Elly's fingers to a small plastic tab. Elly pushed against it and the visor slid up with a click.

"I don't think I can do this."

"Why not?" Alex adjusted the helmet, tugging down gently on the chin piece before she took the straps and clicked them into place under Elly's chin. "You're doing just fine."

The helmet seemed to press in on her head, around her crown and against her cheeks, and Elly fought back a sudden sensation of claustrophobia. The visor was up; she could breathe, but her chest felt tight, and her stomach still churned. "What if I fall off?"

"You won't." Alex put an arm over Elly's shoulder, turning her toward the bike. "You'll be right behind me, and you can hold on here"—she took Elly's hand and placed it over the slim handles that lined the sides of the tandem seat—"or you can hold on to me. I won't let you fall. I promise."

"No, I can't." Elly took her hand off the handle and fumbled with the strap to the helmet, stepping back from the bike.

"It's perfectly safe," Alex said. "I promise."

Elly took off the helmet and held it out. "I'll take my car, follow you there." With those words, her stomach seemed to calm, the roiling subsiding.

Alex took the helmet back, letting it hang by her side from one hand. "You're sure? It honestly isn't that bad. And I'll go slow. It's not too far to Parry's."

"I'm sure. Maybe eventually, but just…not tonight." Elly pulled her car keys from her purse. "Shall we go?"

❖

Even though Elly followed her in the car instead of riding on the back of her bike, Alex took it slow all the way to Parry's. She wanted to zip through the intersections, speed up on the straightaways, but she kept carefully to the speed limit. It felt like the longest ride ever by the time she turned into the parking lot at Parry's and pulled into a spot. She killed the engine and put down the kickstand, swinging her leg over the bike. Elly pulled up in a free spot beside her. Alex pulled off her helmet and pushed a hand through her hair as Elly got out and came up beside her. Hooking her fingers around the open gap left by the visor, she let the helmet swing by her side and held out her free hand to Elly. "Come on, let's go. You'll love this."

Elly gave her a hesitant smile and Alex stifled a frown. She hadn't thought Elly was this shy; she hadn't been, at the farm, after their first kiss. But now, it was as if they'd only just met. But she reached out her hand and their fingers intertwined like they'd always held hands. Alex wanted to take her back to her apartment, undress her slowly, and taste the sweetness between her thighs.

"Bellerose!"

Will stood at the door of the bar, smoking a cigarette, and he waved, holding his own helmet. Alex waved back. Too late to turn around now. Maybe Elly would loosen up.

❖

The man that had cried out Alex's last name was tall, his dirty-blond hair spiked into a casual fauxhawk, hanging down over his forehead. He was cute, the sort of guy that Elly's friends in school would have had taped to their bedroom walls if they'd come across him in their teen magazines. She felt immediately frumpy and boring next to his easy bad-boy cool. He flicked the cigarette away as she and Alex came level with him, bending to kiss Alex on the lips. It was a casual kiss between friends, but Elly felt the jealousy rise in her. She wanted Alex's lips on hers, not his.

"Who's your friend?" he asked, looking her over, his deep-set blue eyes seeming to take in every inch.

"Elly, this is Will. Will, Elly."

"Nice to meet you." The greeting came automatically to her lips.

"Likewise." Will held out his hand, his grip surprisingly gentle, though his callused hand dwarfed hers.

"Is it the usual crowd?" Alex asked, holding her helmet under her arm.

"Same old," Will said. "Vanessa's being a right bitch though, as usual. But she has a new girly girl, so maybe that'll mollify her a bit tonight."

"Christ." Alex turned to her. "Vanessa's a bit of a drama queen. She acts like she owns the place. She'll probably want to sing some Christina Aguilera, or Britney Spears, or something. All that pop crap."

Elly didn't know what to say to that. "Oh." She knew the names but was more used to country songs.

"C'mon in," Will said, pushing open the door and letting them precede him. "I've saved us a table."

The bar was much like any other she'd ever been in: the carpet a bit worn where thousands of feet had tracked across it, the booths ranged along the wall, the tables in uneven rows across the floor, filled with an assortment of people, though they were mostly women. At one end, a small stage had been set up, large speakers flanking a microphone on a stand. A man with long hair tied back in a ponytail flipped through a book of songs while another man, his beer gut nearly protruding from his bowling shirt, talked animatedly. A waitress squeezed by Will as the three of them made their way to a booth in the back. The table beside them let out a whoop as the waitress set down a pitcher of beer. Elly held on to Alex's hand, though she loosened her grasp when she realized how tight her grip had become.

Will slid into the booth, moving aside a biker jacket in blue and white. He patted the bench beside him. "I don't bite."

Elly sat down beside him and Will shifted over farther as Alex sat down beside her, shedding her own jacket. She passed her helmet over to Will.

"Toss that on your jacket, would you?"

"You didn't put it with the bike?"

"No space," Alex said. "Elly's helmet's in there." Elly felt herself flush again. She'd chickened out, and she felt again that embarrassment, of being the hick among the city folk.

"Ah." Will gave her a glance, then flagged down the waitress. "What'll you have? The usual for you, Alex?"

"Yeah."

"Pitcher of Keith's," Will told the waitress, "and a…?"

He looked over at her and Elly tried to think of a drink. "Vodka cran?" she said.

"Sure, honey," the waitress said. "Be right back."

"Not beer?" Alex asked.

Elly shrugged. She'd never much liked beer, though Jack had tried to convince her, time after time.

"She's a pretty girl, Alex," Will said, reaching over and tugging on a lock of Alex's long black hair. "Not a crazy biker like us."

Alex chuckled. "Don't scare her away." She squeezed Elly's hand. "I've known Will for years."

"I'm like a brother to her." Will rolled his eyes.

"Some brother," Alex quipped.

"Says the girl who called me when she ran out of gas on the highway last weekend," Will replied.

"I misjudged the distance between here and Longview. It happens." Alex flicked his arm.

Watching their back and forth, their easy teasing, Elly didn't know what to say. When the waitress brought their drinks, it gave her something to do with her hands. Will poured two pints of beer and slid one across the table to Alex.

"Cheers," he said, lifting his pint. Alex lifted hers, and Elly echoed their toast.

Alex laid an arm over Elly's shoulder and pulled her close, her perfume, a jasmine scent that Elly thought might be Chanel, tickling her nose. "I'm so glad I saw you again," Alex said, her voice low, intimate.

Elly leaned in, turning her face toward Alex. "Me too."

Their kiss was sweet, gentle; Alex tasted of the beer she'd just drunk, but Elly didn't mind at all. Her mouth was soft, with just enough pressure that Elly parted her lips, letting Alex flick her tongue inside. A shiver raced through her and she wished for more.

"You'll become a biker though, I'll bet," Will remarked when they broke apart.

"Oh no." Elly shook her head.

"Never?" Will looked doubtful and Alex turned a puzzled glance on Elly.

"I don't think so. It reminds me of Jack, a guy I know back home—he was a great trick roper, and one day, just for fun while he was riding, he saw a porcupine, figured he could rope it."

"And?" Will took a gulp of his beer.

"He did it, but he ended up with porcupine quills in his best rope and in his hands."

"What does that have to do with anything?" Will sounded annoyed, but Elly mastered her courage.

"Sometimes things that start out a good idea don't end up that way. Just like riding a motorcycle."

"There aren't any porcupines when you ride with me," Alex said. She glanced at Will and chuckled. "Unless Will rides with us, of course."

"Smart-ass," he said, making a face at her. Elly tried not to smile. With his hair the way it was, she could imagine Will as a porcupine.

"Good evening, everyone!" The bellowed greeting, amplified by the speakers, startled her. The man in the bowling shirt grinned at the crowd. "Who's the first to get up here?"

A buxom blond woman, her hair teased in a style reminiscent of Dolly Parton, flounced up to the stage. "Y'all know I always go first, Bruce," she drawled, and the man handed over the microphone good-naturedly. "This is something I've been working on."

The man with the ponytail tapped a few keys, and Elly heard the beat of insistent percussion. Beside her, under her breath, Alex groaned. Will took a deep swig of his beer.

Elly didn't recognize the song, but the woman onstage clearly knew it, belting out the words with confidence, sashaying across the stage, winking suggestively to a woman who sat nearby, sipping a froufrou cocktail.

"That's Vanessa," Alex said, her warm breath brushing Elly's ear. "The first song of many."

"Do you sing?" Elly asked.

"Sometimes. You?"

Elly shuddered. "Never."

Will leaned forward, his elbows on the table. "Never?" he repeated, grinning. "You have to on your first time. Everyone does."

"No."

"Everyone does. It's a rule."

"She doesn't have to if she doesn't want to." Alex stuck her tongue out at Will and Elly felt relieved.

"Whatever." Will refilled his pint.

Alex dropped her hand onto Elly's thigh, and she relaxed back into her seat. The song ended and Vanessa stepped down from the stage to applause. Another woman took her spot, flicking her hair back over her shoulder, planting her feet firmly on the stage, her legs wrapped in slim-fitting leather pants.

"What do you like to sing?" Elly cut her gaze back to Alex.

"Pat Benatar, Stevie Nicks, that sort of thing," Alex replied. "Joan Jett, sometimes."

"Don't forget Marianne Faithfull," Will added. "She does a great Marianne," he said to Elly.

"'Broken English'?" Elly asked. It was the only Marianne Faithfull song she remembered, picturing the blue album cover.

"And 'Sister Morphine.'"

"You should sing that one tonight," Will said, motioning to Bruce, who strode over.

"You going to sing?" His cologne wafted over the table, a strong scent of Old Spice.

"Not me, but she will." Will cocked a thumb at Alex. "'Sister Morphine'—you have it, right?"

"We sure do," Bruce said. "I'll get Ron to set it up next."

"Dammit, Will, I'm not ready."

"Sure you are," Will said.

"You can always say no," Elly ventured. Alex shrugged, then sighed.

"Better now, before Vanessa has her second go. She'll hog the stage after she has a couple more drinks." Alex stood, her leather chaps creaking.

"Break a leg."

Alex planted a kiss on her lips. "Plug your ears."

"Really?"

"Not really." Alex grinned and wove her way around the tables to the stage. Catcalls followed, and Alex flashed a rude gesture to a spiky-haired woman near the bar, who whistled again.

"They dated once," Will said. "Sort of. Jan never really got over her."

Elly glanced at him. "Why're you telling me?"

"Just thought you should know." Will shrugged and leaned back, lifting his pint. Elly wanted to say something more, but the music started, and her gaze was drawn to Alex, who swayed in place, waiting for her cue. When she began to sing, Elly was entranced.

The song was softer than she'd imagined, starting with a quiet guitar, and becoming an almost country-song-like ballad. Alex didn't even watch the screen as the words scrolled by, each phrase highlighted in garish yellow. Her hands wrapped around the chrome of the microphone stand and she leaned forward, looking up from under her lashes at the crowd. Her throaty voice caressed each word, delivering it to the audience like a gift. Elly shivered.

When the song ended, there were catcalls and applause, and Will shouted, "Go, Bellerose!" pounding his hand on the table. Alex grinned and gave a short bow before hopping down from the tiny stage and making her way back to her seat.

"What did you think?" Alex asked breathlessly, sliding into the booth next to Elly.

"Brilliant." Will answered before Elly could say a word.

"You always say that," Alex said to Will. "Elly?"

"You were fantastic." Elly knew her words were weak; they didn't come near to explaining how she really felt, how Alex had captivated her.

"Vanessa's fuming already," Will noted with amusement. "I'd say that's compliment enough."

Alex chuckled and Elly glanced over at the blonde, who sat at her table, pouting. "Does she always do that?"

"If things don't go her way," Alex said. "She'll get over it, or not."

"You should sing one," Will said, nudging Elly's elbow.

She shook her head. "Oh no."

Will gestured to Bruce. "Bring us a book, my man."

Bruce lumbered over with a well-used black binder. "Up next, Will?"

"Nope, it'll be her turn in a few. Just need to find a song."

Bruce set the binder in front of Elly. "Just let me know what you want to sing."

"I really don't," she said as Bruce headed over to another table to take their request. Her hands and feet were cold as ice and anxiety made her stomach flutter. She was going to make a fool of herself. But at Alex's disappointed look, Elly opened the binder.

The songs were arranged alphabetically by artist, and she browsed aimlessly, not having a clue as to what she could sing. She liked music, but she didn't know much of it by heart, not enough to perform it. Genesis, Geri Halliwell, Madonna…She slowed, running her gaze down the list. Madonna wouldn't be that hard, would it? She'd sung some of the songs when she was a kid and still knew them well, or better than most.

"Found one?" Alex asked, leaning closer. "Madonna, awesome. Her stuff is classic. You'll get everyone singing along."

"I'm not sure which one to pick," Elly said. A fast song would be hard for her to keep up with if she lost the pace, but a slow song would mean her voice would be on full display.

"'Material Girl'? It's a bit silly, and fun." Alex tapped the page.

"I don't know. Maybe 'Crazy for You' instead?"

"That was a good movie," Will commented.

"Movie?" Alex voiced the question Elly only thought.

"Yeah, *Vision Quest*. Didn't you ever see it?"

"You saw a movie with Madonna in it?"

"It's a wrestling movie." Will sighed. "Now I know what to subject you to next weekend."

"Have you seen it, El?" Alex asked.

"No, hadn't even heard of it," she replied, giving a regretful shrug, looking at Will.

"We'll all have to watch it next weekend, then," Alex decreed. She waved Bruce over. "Elly wants to sing 'Crazy for You.'"

Bruce scribbled it onto his list. "That's a good one. You're up four—no, five—songs from now."

Elly picked up her glass and downed the rest of her drink. Oh God. What had she gotten into?

CHAPTER TWO

I don't think I can do it."

Alex heard the quaver in Elly's voice. "It's a three-minute song, it'll be over before you know it. Don't worry." She clasped Elly's hand, feeling her cold fingers. "I'll get you another drink." She rose from the table and went to the bar. The bartender, Eric, gave her an appreciative glance.

"Good song," he said. "What can I get you?"

"Vodka cran," Alex said, leaning on the bar.

"Who's the new girl?" Jan said from behind her. Alex turned. Jan's cheeks were flushed, her pixie cut emphasizing her thin face. A dozen silver hoops glinted on each ear.

"Elly." Alex knew Jan was pushing for gossip, as she always did. That had been why they'd broken up a few years back, that and the neediness Jan exuded. Even now, she edged closer, her arm brushing against Alex's.

"Never seen her around," Jan said. "She new in town too?"

"Pretty new." Alex didn't really know, but she assumed as much. Elly had seemed too at home on the farm to really be a city girl.

"I don't know what you see in her."

Eric put the drink on the bar. "Five fifty."

Alex took seven dollars from the zipped pocket of her chaps and handed it over. "Keep the change." She picked up the glass. "See you later." She heard Jan make an irritated *hmmph* as she left.

Vanessa's girlfriend passed her and got up on the stage as Alex returned to her seat. She placed the drink in front of Elly, who swapped out her empty glass for the full one.

"I don't think this will help," Elly said, but she took a long drink anyway. Her cheeks were pink, and Alex thought she was cuter with that flush. It made her eyes bright and reminded Alex of the way Elly had looked in bed.

The opening bars of Avril Lavigne's "I'm With You" played over the speakers, and Alex turned her attention to the woman onstage. She was young, how Vanessa liked them, looking soft and fairylike in a pale pink dress and delicate sandals. Her blond hair was back in a braid, but when she began to sing, her voice caught everyone by surprise. Strong, confident, completely unlike her image.

"Wow," Elly said.

"Yeah," Alex agreed. She glanced over at Vanessa, who grinned triumphantly at her girlfriend's stunning performance. The cheers and catcalls were loud when the woman stepped down from the stage.

"I bet Vanessa picked her just for her voice," Will remarked, draining his pint and pouring another.

Alex laughed. It sounded ridiculous, but it was just the sort of thing Vanessa might do.

"Would she really?" Elly sounded incredulous.

"She might have," Alex answered.

"You're up next," Will said to Elly as Metric blared from the speakers.

"Already?" Elly gulped her drink.

"You'll be awesome," Alex said. It was just Parry's, just the usual crowd. Elly would be fine. She rose to let Elly out of the booth as the Metric song finished.

Elly looked up at her. "Do I have to?"

"You'll be all right," Alex assured her. Elly slid over on the bench seat and stood, running her hands down her thighs. She looked pale as the polka dots on her shirt.

"Break a leg," Will said, raising his pint. Alex slipped her arm around Elly's waist and gave her a squeeze.

"Be Madonna," she suggested. "Forget about all of us."

❖

Elly gave her a hesitant smile. "I'll try." Her heart pounded in her ears as she walked to the stage. Her mouth felt dry, even though she'd just had a sip of her vodka cran. She was going to sing in front of a bunch of strangers. Shakily, she stepped up onto the stage and took her place behind the microphone. Why was she doing this?

Bruce's assistant, Ron, gave her a thumbs-up. "Ready?"

She nodded, though she didn't feel ready at all.

The keyboard and percussion opening to "Crazy for You" began, and Elly licked her lips. Then came what she supposed was the horn, though it sounded more like another synthesizer. She looked at the screen, and it was her cue.

The first line came out shaky and weak as she hadn't sung anything in a long time, but the second line was stronger, and by the end of the first verse, she'd picked up the melody, and coming into the chorus, her body relaxed. Her grip on the microphone stand loosened and her voice rang clear on the ballad, the interior of the bar fading into the background as the joy of singing overtook her self-consciousness.

When the song ended, she came back to herself, feeling her cheeks heat at the applause. She moved away from the microphone and, with little ceremony, stepped down from the stage, heading back to her seat, sinking onto the cool vinyl with relief.

"El, you were great!" Alex hugged her. Elly rested her head on Alex's shoulder, reminding herself to breathe, willing her heartbeat to calm. It was over, and she'd never have to do that ever again. She reached for her drink and had a sip of the tart cranberry juice, wetting her dry mouth.

"You did well," Will said with an acknowledging nod.

"Thanks."

"And you're up soon, right, Will?" Alex said.

"Two more songs," Will replied.

"Will likes a challenge, so I picked the song," Alex confided to Elly in a stage whisper.

"That's brave," Elly said, taking another sip of her drink. Just the thought of getting up there again sent a shiver through her.

"I can sing anything," Will stated.

"Cocky," Alex teased.

"You know it, babe." Will winked and rose, swaggering over to the bar.

"Does he really not know what he's going to sing?"

"I picked it from the book and whispered it to Bruce. Will has no idea," Alex explained. "But he likes the challenge. And he's a good singer."

"So what did you pick?"

"You'll see." She gave a mischievous grin.

Bruce came to the microphone. "Oy, Will, get down here." Will said something to the bartender, who laughed, and made his way down to the stage.

"What am I singing?" Will asked, stepping up beside Bruce. The man motioned to his assistant, who hit a button.

Elly didn't recognize the song, but it was apparent that Will, and the entire bar, did.

"Oh, man," he groaned. "I'll get you back for this one, Bellerose."

Alex cackled.

"What is it?" Elly asked.

"Britney Spears's 'Stronger.'"

Elly choked on her vodka. "You didn't."

"I did."

Will's low tenor filled the room, and it was strange to hear a man singing a song meant for a woman with a much higher-pitched voice. Alex mouthed the words along with Will's singing, and it was apparent the song was a familiar one for both of them. To hoots of laughter from the crowd, Will straddled a woman in the front row, hamming it up as he sang the chorus, then left her, tweaking the braid of another woman, and then sidled up to Vanessa, giving her a pouty kissy face. Vanessa made a gagging motion and Will flounced off, winking to Alex as he went back onstage to finish the song.

The whistles and jeers drowned out the applause and Will blew a kiss to the audience. "I'll be here all night," he promised, provoking laughs. He sauntered back to his seat. "You'll have to try harder than that, Bellerose."

"That sounds like a challenge, William." Alex stuck out her tongue at Will, who made a face. Elly watched their teasing, feeling as if she was their audience of one.

"It sure is, Bellerose," Will replied. "I'll find another song for you before the end of the night. And it won't be Marianne Faithfull."

"Do your worst." Alex finished her pint and lifted the pitcher, pouring another glass and emptying it.

"Your round," Will said.

"I'll get this one," Elly said. She needed another vodka cran.

"A girl after my own heart. It's Keith's."

"You don't have to," Alex said.

Will apparently ignored Alex and slid the pitcher across to Elly. Elly rose, adjusting the strap of her purse to keep it from sliding off her shoulder. She hooked the pitcher with a finger and carried it up to the bar.

"Another?" the bartender asked.

"Of Keith's," Elly confirmed, "and a vodka cran."

"Done." The bartender smiled at her. "Well done on that Madonna song, by the way."

"Thanks." Elly felt her cheeks flushing again. The bartender propped a pitcher under the tap and let it run, glancing over as he made her vodka cran. He placed her glass on the bar and finished filling the pitcher.

"That'll be twenty-two dollars," he said. Elly dug into her purse, pulling out her wallet and taking out a five and two tens. He handed her the change and she placed a couple of dollars in his tip jar.

"Thanks again," Elly said, putting her wallet back.

"Want help with the pitcher?" he asked.

Elly gave it an experimental heft and found it heavier than she'd expected. "That might be a good idea," she agreed.

The bartender came around the bar, lifting the pitcher easily. "What's your name?"

"Elly Cole."

"I'm Eric," he said. "Good to meet you." He didn't say anything else, but when he reached the table, he plunked down the pitcher. "Any more than this, and you two need to give me your keys. Got it?"

"I'm only having one more," Alex said, lifting her pint. "Will can have the rest."

"You driving, Bellerose?" Will asked.

"I am, and Elly has her car." Alex shifted over on the bench and Elly tucked in beside her. "But we'll call you a cab."

"No threesome on the bike?" Will waggled his blond eyebrows. "I'm disappointed."

"Hell no, you perv." Alex chuckled, resting her arm on Elly's shoulders. Elly loved the touch, the warmth of Alex's caress. "It's just me and my girl tonight."

❖

It was late when they came out of the bar. Will staggered into a waiting taxi, and Alex took Elly's hand, leading her toward the bike and her car. The wind had picked up and it blew her hair back. Alex could feel the chill in the breeze and knew it'd be a cold ride home. Cold, but worth it.

"What shall we do next?" she asked, stopping beside the bike. She placed her helmet on the seat and let go of Elly's hand. Elly zipped up her jacket, burrowing into its warmth.

"Home, I guess," she said. "I didn't think it would get this cold."

"Yours or mine?"

Elly hesitated.

"Let's go to mine. It's not too far."

Elly nodded. "All right." She pulled her keys from her purse. "I'll follow you. Again." She smiled faintly.

"I'll take it slow." Alex walked to Elly's door, taking the keys from her and unlocking it, pulling it open. Elly's cheeks went a charming shade of pink.

"Thanks."

"Anytime." When Elly had taken her seat, Alex bent down, stealing a kiss. "I'm just up Bow Trail, just a few kilometers." She straightened and closed the door, then stalked back to the bike. Elly started her car, and Alex straddled the bike, turning the key, holding down the clutch and pressing the starter. The bike growled, then settled into a rumbling purr. She let it idle for a few minutes, then glanced at Elly, giving her a nod.

Elly nodded back.

Alex walked the bike forward out of the parking spot, checking for traffic before she shifted into gear and gently eased up on the clutch. Alex took the turn out of the parking lot the way she always did: fast. She loved it on the bike, the feel of its power between her legs, the wind buffeting her, the intimacy with the journey that she never felt in a car, but above all, the speed and power that were hers to control.

There were hardly any unbroken stretches of road between Parry's and her place, much to her ongoing dismay. When she accelerated up the hill on Bow Trail, she snapped down her visor for that brief few moments of speed, and she wanted to be out on the highway, pushing the bike to the max. Not in the dark, of course, but tomorrow she would. She had to work, but she'd have enough time for a short ride. She glanced into her mirror, saw Elly's car behind her, and smiled.

Alex turned the corner, shifting down into first gear as she drew up in front of a small bungalow, white with fading blue trim. The upstairs, her place, was dark, but a warm light glowed through the blinds of the lower suite. Hopefully the woman that lived there, Louise, had kept the television to a reasonable volume. Reality shows weren't conducive to romance. And she wanted Elly, wanted her bad. Bad enough to want to do it right this time, to charm her with pretty words and a glass of wine, to make up for the uneasiness of Parry's.

Elly'd managed to relax, in time, but Alex hadn't missed the hesitation, the nervous fidgeting she tried to hide. Even Will had noticed, and he'd leaned over to her when Elly went up to sing.

"You sure about her? She looks like she'd bolt at a loud noise."

"Of course I'm sure," she'd retorted. And she was. Mostly. If not, then one time was better than none.

She killed the engine and flipped down the kickstand, dismounting. Elly met her on the sidewalk and she led Elly up the front walk and the three concrete steps to her front door, unlocking it and pushing open the somewhat weather-beaten wood. Inside, the place was spare: the living room held a black leather sofa and chair, a plain black coffee table, and a flat-screen TV with a home-theater system, DVDs stacked on a shelf behind it. Alex took off her helmet, placing it on the bench in the hallway where she always did. Elly took in what she could see of the house.

"It's not much," Alex said, waving a hand. "But the TV is great for movies. We could watch one if you want."

Elly smiled. "Show me the rest of your place. It's much bigger than mine."

"Not much to see," Alex said. She bent and pulled off her boots, shoving them under the bench. Elly toed off her shoes, revealing delicate feet, the pink-painted nails showing through the thin stockings. Alex hadn't remembered that about Elly, couldn't recall if she'd worn any nail polish at all when they'd first met.

"I'm sure there's lots to see," Elly said, moving past Alex and glancing left and right down the hallway before looking back at her.

"What do you want to see first?"

"Kitchen first, for a glass of water, then whatever else you want to show me." Her cheeks pinkened and Alex chuckled, coming level with Elly.

"I can think of a few things."

CHAPTER THREE

The water was cold, and it went down easy. Elly's head buzzed from the vodka crans, but she didn't mind. She held the half-full glass as Alex gave her the grand tour.

"Kitchen, not my favorite room as I can't cook to save my life." Alex waved a hand. "Out that window is the next-door neighbor, Ryan, who always smokes up. I rarely ever open the windows on this side—I hate the smell of pot smoke. He's a nice guy, though."

"Ew."

"And that door goes to the downstairs apartment. Come back this way, there are more interesting places to see." Alex led her back down the hallway. "You've seen the living room. There's two bedrooms, though one's sorta my catchall for my bike gear." She opened one door and Elly spotted the shine from another helmet's visor in the light from the hallway. "And this is my favorite place."

Alex opened the door opposite, letting Elly precede her. Instead of hardwood flooring, Elly's chilled toes hit soft carpet. The light flicked on and she blinked, letting her eyes adjust. The room was spare, like the others, but the bed itself was large, spread with a fluffy white duvet and plump pillows. A dramatic sketch of a nude woman sprawled on a blanket that was not much more than a squiggly line hung in a frame over the headboard.

"Mary did that for me, in art school," Alex said, noticing her interest. "About ten years ago."

"She was your girlfriend?" Elly walked closer. The piece was gorgeous, the woman's gaze catching her eye, her languorous pouting sensual.

"Not really," Alex said. "We just hung out sometimes." She took the glass from Elly's hand and set it on the bureau behind them. "I'm glad I ran into you, though. Who would have thought?"

Elly turned toward Alex. "I hadn't," she answered as Alex slid an arm around her waist.

"This calls for a celebration." Alex's lips brushed hers, gentle but not the least bit tentative. Elly responded and Alex deepened the kiss, her tongue flicking into Elly's mouth, making Elly's knees weaken. She wrapped her arms around Alex's neck and gave herself over to the kiss, barely noticing as Alex shifted them back toward the bed. Her knees hit the side, and she sat abruptly. Alex chuckled.

"Pushy, aren't you?" Elly managed to say before Alex kissed her again.

"But you like it."

Alex stood between her knees, and all she could look at was the silver buckle of Alex's leather chaps, how it rested snugly over her jeans. Reaching out, Elly pulled the belt free of the chrome-plated tongue, taking her time, loving the feel of the leather in her hands.

"Hold up," Alex said. She bent and unsnapped the bottom of the chaps, catching the zippers and pulling them up. The leather sagged loose around her legs. "That's much easier."

Elly finished unbuckling the belt and the chaps fell to the floor at their feet. Before she could speak, Alex's fingers were at the buttons of her polka-dot blouse, making quick work of them.

"Gorgeous," Alex breathed, parting the soft panels to expose Elly's delicate lacy bra.

Elly rested her hands on Alex's hips, drawing her closer, tilting her head up in invitation. "If I'd seen you in chaps last time, I think I would have melted on the spot."

"Is that so?" Alex leaned down, kissing her again, her hands cupping Elly's breasts through the lace, her thumbs brushing over the nipples.

"Yes," Elly replied between kisses. She fumbled with the button on Alex's jeans and managed to get it undone, pulling her shirt from the waistband, finally baring skin.

"I'll wear them for you more often," Alex murmured, drawing in a breath as Elly placed butterfly-light kisses over her belly. Elly loved that sound and wanted to hear it again. She inched Alex's jeans down over her hips, her mouth following their path, over the plain black bikini underwear she wore. She heard the rustle of Alex's shirt and felt the cotton as it brushed her on its way to the floor. Hooking her fingers into the edge of Alex's underwear, she tugged the briefs down, baring the trimmed dark curls. Alex cupped the back of her head gently and Elly leaned forward again, her tongue darting to the soft folds, tasting the sweet musk that was wholly Alex. Going to her knees beside the bed, she took Alex into her mouth, teasing and tasting until Alex swayed above her.

"I knew I should have come back to the farm," Alex said breathlessly. "Come here, El, come up." She pulled Elly to her feet beside the bed, pushing her shirt off her shoulders and undoing the clasp on the front of her bra. Her hair tickled Elly's stomach as she bent to tongue her nipples. Elly drew in a quickened breath, cupping her hands at the back of Alex's neck, urging her on.

Alex undid her jeans, and the rush of cool air raised goose bumps as she tugged down the jeans, which stuck tight around Elly's knees.

"They always do that," Elly said, bending to help.

"They're delicious on you, so worth the extra effort," Alex replied, lowering herself to one knee to get a better angle. She pulled off Elly's stockings while she was there, then rose, nudging Elly onto the bed.

Elly felt the duvet against her skin, soft and cool as she sank into it. Alex urged her down and she fell back onto the bed, her arms outstretched.

"This feels familiar," Elly said, remembering the time before. But the bed hadn't been as comfortable; the lumps of her pile of quilts had not been enough to hide the sag of the old mattress.

Alex trailed kisses down Elly's sternum, raising more goose bumps. "It was like a dream, before." She traced over the dampness on Elly's matching lacy panties before slipping a finger beneath, into her wetness. "You missed me, didn't you?"

"Yes," Elly admitted. She had missed Alex, but she'd never thought this would happen again. Alex had become a fantasy, safe in her remoteness, her ideal form. Real life was different. She didn't want to think of that now, real life. Real life meant dwindling savings and no job, the persistent ache of homesickness. Elly pushed it all aside. Right now, there was just Alex, for what it was worth. For tonight, if nothing else. Alex wouldn't be one to follow her back to the farm; she was too at home here, the city her playground.

"What are you thinking of?" Alex lifted her head.

"Thinking of what I want to do to you," Elly replied. Alex and her. Tonight. "I want you."

Alex chuckled and slid up the bed. "You have me, babe."

They kissed again, and Elly wrapped her arms around Alex's neck so they were skin to skin.

Alex pulled back, her dark eyes regarding her. "So, what did you want to do to me?"

Elly skated her fingers down Alex's spine, feeling each vertebra, and slid over her rounded yet muscled buttocks. Alex shifted, bringing her leg up to hook it over Elly's hip, opening herself to more. Elly took the invitation, dipping her fingers lower, teasing Alex's curls, then into her wet heat.

Alex gave a low gasp and squirmed, shifting farther, inviting Elly to go deeper. Elly closed her eyes, concentrating on the feel of Alex, stroking inside, feeling the flutter of muscle, the tensing of Alex around her fingers. Alex moved her hips, the rhythm steady and quick at first, then more erratic as time went on. Elly withdrew for a moment to get a better angle, and Alex made a sound like a whimper.

"I'm not done yet," Elly murmured, sliding her hand between them and taking up where she'd left off. But this time she pressed against Alex's clitoris in small circular motions.

"Oh God," Alex muttered, her eyes closing, her forehead resting against Elly's on the pillow. Elly felt the full-body shudder begin, and Alex cried out, tightening around Elly's fingers, her thighs closing over her wrist.

When the shuddering subsided, Alex rolled onto her back, freeing Elly's hand, sprawling against the mattress, her limbs limp. Her chest rose and fell, and she opened her eyes, turning her head to look at Elly.

"That was incredible," she said, her voice huskier than usual.

"We had a year to make up for," Elly replied, trailing her damp fingers over Alex's ribs.

Alex squirmed and seized Elly's hand in a gentle grip. "That tickles."

"Good." Elly wiggled her fingers and Alex laughed, turning back onto her side, nudging Elly over onto her back with a well-placed knee.

"Your turn," she said, rising to her knees in front of Elly. "Payback time."

Elly saw Alex's mischievous smile as she bent her head, then her dark hair covered her face, draping over Elly's stomach and thighs. Elly felt fingers tugging at her underwear, and she lifted her hips off the mattress so Alex could pull the scrap of fabric down and off. Gentle breath warmed the skin of her thighs as Alex lingered, dropping kisses. Then she felt her legs being parted, and a tongue lapped at her, darting and flicking, teasing her oversensitized flesh. Her hands fisted the coverlet.

"You taste good," Alex said, raising her head for just a moment. She replaced her tongue with her fingers, watching Elly's reaction.

"More," Elly pleaded, locking her gaze on Alex, who gave her a satisfied smile before she bent her head again.

Alex didn't remove her fingers, pressing up hard into Elly's G-spot, tonguing her clitoris as she did.

It had been so long.

Since that night a year ago, though she'd never admit it to Alex.

The muscles of her belly quivered, and thoughts of Alex and the farm fled her mind as the sensation increased, bringing her so close to the edge.

"Alex—" She managed Alex's name, but that was all. The orgasm overtook her, and she squeezed her eyes shut, her head flung back against the pillow, her mouth open in a gasp.

❖

Alex lay back, listening, her eyes open in the dim light from the lamp as, next to her, Elly took a deep breath and seemed to settle deeper into the soft mattress. Her body felt the languor from her earlier orgasm, but there was a tension creeping in, needling at her. Elly shifted nearer, her leg brushing Alex's, her hand resting over Alex's stomach, warm and soft.

Alex went perfectly still.

Elly didn't seem to notice, just shifted nearer again until she was snuggled right in.

Each touch ratcheted up her tension, and she knew she wasn't going to be able to sleep. Cuddling was too much, promised too much. Even with Will, she hardly ever cuddled, nor did she ever need to.

Alex moved out from under Elly's embrace, sitting up in bed. Elly blinked sleepily at her, surprise on her face.

"I'm sorry, El, but you can't stay over."

Elly's look of surprise changed to hurt, but Alex pushed forward. She always slept alone at night, always, and she knew she'd spend the next six hours tossing and turning and watching the clock. The only one she'd ever been able to fall asleep next to had been Heather, and look at how that turned out. She hated being vulnerable.

"But you did, at the farm." Elly sat up in bed, holding the sheet over her breasts, her curls mussed.

Alex cut her gaze away. "I know, but that was necessity." She could tell Elly the reason why, but that was too much information. "I have a hard time sleeping, and I need to get up early tomorrow."

Elly pushed back the covers and turned, sitting on the edge of the bed. She bent to scoop up her jeans and underwear. "No problem." When she glanced back, Alex was sure her eyes were moist.

"It's not you, El." Alex slid over on the bed until they were thigh to thigh.

Elly gave a short nod. "Promise?" Her voice wavered.

"Promise," Alex answered easily. Elly could be anyone and her answer would be the same. Even she and Will didn't spend the night together, not unless they were too blitzed to drive.

"All right." Elly blinked and her expression relaxed. "I've had a hard time sleeping lately too. The city's so loud compared to back home."

"Especially where you are," Alex agreed, glad to be on a new topic. "You are right down in the thick of things."

"There are lots of sirens," Elly said. "And loud bikes." She nudged Alex in the ribs.

"Not mine," Alex retorted with a laugh. "You're thinking of all those Harleys, not the Ninja."

"A bike's a bike, isn't it?" Elly asked, picking up her bra and putting it on. "They're all loud."

"You have a lot to learn," Alex said. She grabbed her underwear and slid it on, and then pulled her T-shirt over her head. "We should go for a ride sometime, and you can see the difference."

"Maybe." Elly buttoned up her shirt and stood. Alex stood with her. "It's dangerous, though, especially riding in Calgary. I don't even like to drive in the city, which is why I'm living where I am."

"Really?" Alex could hardly imagine choosing not to drive, or not to ride.

"Really." Elly's cheeks went pink, and she left the bedroom, heading back to the front door. Alex followed her.

"You just need more practice, maybe."

"I'm hoping I'll figure out some way that I won't have to," Elly said, bending to put on her shoes. "I still keep hoping that this won't be long term. I hadn't really planned to leave the farm, you know."

"Calgary's a great place to be," Alex said. "Lots of clubs, everything close by, lots of action. Way more fun than being out in the middle of nowhere."

Elly slipped her purse strap over her shoulder. "I love it there."

"We'll just agree to disagree," Alex replied, not wanting to leave their evening on a sour note. She didn't like to burn her bridges, and maybe she'd see Elly again. That was a rare thing, especially lately. No one held her interest long.

"You might like it, if you tried it for more than a night," Elly said. She opened the front door, pausing on the threshold.

"Good night, gorgeous," Alex said, leaning in for one last kiss.

Elly kissed her back, pressing close one last time. Promising. "Good night, Alex."

Chapter Four

As soon as she hit the highway, Alex accelerated, shifting gears. She'd be late meeting Will; they always had a bite to eat at the Tim Hortons in Cochrane on their way to the mountains. It gave them both a bit of time on their bikes and got what Alex's grandmother used to call the sillies out of their systems. And she had a case of them today, as she always did after being with someone the night before. That urge to get on the open road, just her and the bike.

She hadn't expected to see Elly; she'd given her up for a good memory, and last night had been an impulsive invitation. She didn't regret it, but yet, twice with the same person? It was hardly like her these days, and she wondered what she'd been thinking last night, considering a third time. That was practically a relationship. Elly was cute, at least, charming in her quiet way, so different from the usual women she dated, the extroverted sorts, just like herself.

A few hours of riding would clear her head, just in time to go to work.

Alex slowed and turned off the highway, heading into town. She drew up into the parking lot and saw Will waiting for her, leaning against his bike, his helmet in the bright colors of the Italian flag hanging from the handlebar. The space next to him was free, so she pulled in and killed the engine, pushing up her visor.

"Late night, Bellerose?" Will teased. "I've never known you to be late to our ride. You're always the one hassling me for not being able to get out of bed."

"I had company, as you well know," Alex said with a shrug, taking off her helmet.

"Don't tell me you let her stay over." Will straightened. "Coffee's on you, since you're late." He sauntered into the coffee shop and Alex followed. The line moved swiftly.

"What can I get you?" the older woman manning the till asked.

"Extra-large double-double, and a maple-glazed doughnut," Will said.

"Same," Alex added, taking out her wallet.

They took their coffees and settled at a table.

"So, is she your new love?"

Alex snorted. As if. "Why do you ask that?"

"She stayed over, didn't she? You hardly ever have anyone stay over," Will replied. He took a huge bite of his doughnut.

"She didn't stay over. No one does. Don't go reading too much into it." He should know her better than that. It had been years since she'd gone with anyone for more than a date or two. She sipped her coffee, taking a much smaller bite of her doughnut than Will had.

"Of course not." Will winked. "I'll only just jerk your chain over it awhile."

Alex stuck out her tongue. "Finish your coffee. I only have a few hours before I have to head back. I'm working tonight."

"I'll come by, harass you."

"As always."

"You'd miss me if I wasn't there," Will said. "I know it." He stuffed the rest of the doughnut into his mouth.

"You have the weekend off?"

"Mmm-hmm." He swallowed. "Then next week it's Monday to Thursday daytime, with a three-day weekend, and off and on after that."

"That's not very consistent."

Will shrugged. "Such is the life of a contractor. They need me when they need me."

"And you'll ride the rest of the time."

"Naturally. Thinking about going out to British Columbia for a bit. Prettier out there. And maybe I can find some work too."

"I'm jealous." Alex finished her doughnut and downed the rest of her coffee. "Let's go. The day's not getting any longer."

Will rose when she did, finishing off his coffee. They tossed their cups in the trash and headed back to the bikes. "Want to do the

Minnewanka Loop today?" he asked. "It shouldn't be too busy yet, given that it's so early in the season."

"You can buy the ice cream."

"Done. And lunch in Canmore on the way back."

Alex put on her helmet and swung her leg over the bike. "Highway 1A to Canmore, then the Trans-Canada," she remarked. "Try to keep up." She started the bike and rolled away, putting it into gear. Behind her, she heard Will mutter something, and she smiled to herself. He'd catch up, but she'd give him a merry chase first.

Will caught up sooner than she'd expected, cruising up beside her in the line to get across the Ghost Lake dam, down to one lane thanks to construction.

"What's that you were saying?" he asked after he'd pushed up his visor.

"You wouldn't have caught up otherwise," she replied.

"So you think."

The flag girl turned her sign and they started their slow progression along the road, bumping and jolting over the rough pavement. Alex kept her bike just ahead of Will's, itching to get back up to speed and pass some of the slow-moving RVs. A bit farther down the road, free of the traffic jam, she saw her chance, and she accelerated swiftly, crossing the broken yellow line and zipping past a lumbering old Winnebago, a powerless compact car, and a pickup truck weighed down with a fifth wheel. She spotted a truck coming up in the lane ahead and pulled back into her own lane. Slowing slightly to get back close to the speed limit, she laughed to herself. Will was stuck back behind the Winnebago, and the road was empty, just the way she liked it, the rolling foothills stretched out before her.

❖

Elly rubbed her eyes, the computer screen blurring in front of her. Half a dozen resumes sent out and she was exhausted. It felt like she was casting a single needle into six haystacks and hoping for someone to see the glimmer. But, if these were anything like the other needles, they'd fall unnoticed. She'd had fewer than ten interviews in the almost two months she'd been in Calgary, and none of them had borne fruit.

If she didn't find something soon, she wasn't sure what she'd do. She dreamed of going back to the farm, but that could only happen if she had some sort of miracle. And not a miracle named Jack Collins. His lease would pay most of the land bills and help keep up the house, but that was it. All those weeks ago, when she'd sat in the town diner after her last shift, still trying to figure out how to make things work, the widow Mrs. Calderwood had kindly suggested that she ought to sell the land. Just the thought of it had made her feel ill.

"It's hard to make a go of it alone," Mrs. Calderwood had said, commiserating. "But then you could get a house in town, like I did. And maybe some young man would snap you up."

Impossible. Not that Mrs. Calderwood hadn't meant well, the comment about the young man aside. She couldn't sell the land. It was in her blood, had been in the family for generations, since the Hudson's Bay Company had sold it to her great-great-grandfather. Her parents had shown her a copy of the original grant of title many times, and she remembered always looking at it with a sense of awe that they'd lived there so long.

She knew she couldn't give that up. It was home.

Elly scanned the list of jobs and found one more to send an application to. Administrative assistant, financial sector. She could be an admin assistant. How hard could it be? She filled out the form and attached her resume, sending it into the ether. Then she set her laptop aside and rose from the sofa, stretching. The sun reflected off the window of the building across the street, hitting her in the eyes. She blinked and squinted. She hadn't thought it was that late.

In the kitchen, she made herself a bowl of mac and cheese, feeling too tired to do much else. She'd go to bed early tonight, to make up for last night. She hadn't slept much once she'd gotten home and crawled into bed. Alex had been standoffish, nothing like the first time they'd been together, last year. There had been the grand gesture on the front porch, being bent over Alex's arm and kissed like a lover in an old movie, and there had been tenderness as she left. Elly wasn't sure what to make of it. Had she read Alex totally wrong?

Her phone vibrated on the coffee table and she hurried from the kitchen, scooping it up. She answered without looking at the number.

"Hello?"

"Elly, it's Jack."

"Jack…hi." Elly tried to keep from sounding disappointed. If only it had been a recruiter, or Alex, even.

"Just wanted to call, see how you were getting on with things," Jack said companionably. "Are you liking it in the city?"

"It's all right." She hesitated to tell him more. He'd only try to convince her to come home.

"No job yet?"

"Not yet."

"You should come back. I talked to Gus at the café and he'd be willing to up your wage another fifty cents an hour."

"Jack, you really shouldn't have." Elly squirmed in discomfort, thankful he couldn't see her.

"Should I tell him you'll be back soon?" Jack pressed.

"No, I'm afraid not," she replied after a long pause.

"I see."

"How's the farm?" Elly asked, changing the subject to something more pleasant.

"Same as it always is," Jack replied. "Beautiful at this time of year, with all the crocuses coming out, and the clover."

Elly closed her eyes against the prick of tears, imagining the sight, knowing it from years past. She felt a pang of loneliness. If she were there, she'd at least be at home and could pretend she wasn't alone. She knew every inch of the farmhouse, had explored every cranny as a child, and its creaky floors and mismatched carpet were as familiar as her reflection in the mirror.

"El? You all right?"

"Yeah." She bit back a sigh. "Just tired."

"Take care of yourself, yeah?" Jack sounded concerned.

"I will, Jack. You too. Say hi to your mother for me."

"I will. 'Bye, now."

Elly hung up and slumped down on the sofa again. She glanced at the bare walls of her apartment and realized she could not stand to look at them all evening, on her own. If only she knew more people in town. Parry's wasn't too far away; she could drive there in a few minutes. Seeing Alex might brighten her mood.

❖

At the front door of the restaurant, Elly's courage wilted. She stepped inside, looking up the hallway toward the hostess station, and turned to the door of the lounge side, where Alex had taken her the night before. Music and muffled conversation came through the smoked glass and she rested her hand on the handle. Taking a deep breath, she opened the door and went in.

The lounge was almost as crowded as it had been the night before, though the karaoke setup had disappeared and tables were in its place. At first glance, Elly didn't recognize anyone, but when her gaze hit the bar, she saw Alex. She headed over and found an empty chair, lifting herself up onto the stool and resting her elbows on the pocked wood of the bar. Alex was talking to a waitress at the other end, lifting a pitcher of beer from the tap, and placing it next to the woman's tray, where she'd already stacked half a dozen glasses.

Alex wore a slim-fitting black top with short cap sleeves, tucked into dark, snug jeans. Her hair was pulled back into a low ponytail, and it hung to the middle of her back. She turned, and her gaze went straight to Elly. Her smile widened and she sauntered over.

"Hey, gorgeous," she purred, leaning over the bar to stroke a finger down Elly's arm.

"Hey." Elly felt her cheeks heat and her gaze flitted down to Alex's hand where it rested on the bar, then back up. She licked her lips. "Thought I should come on a non-karaoke night too."

"It's a little less crazy," Alex agreed. "What can I get you to drink? A vodka cran?"

"How about a screwdriver?" Elly suggested.

"That drink's almost healthy," Alex teased, tweaking one of Elly's curls.

"Almost." Elly returned Alex's smile, watching as she grabbed a shot glass and measured the vodka over a glass half-full of ice. Though she reached the top, she kept pouring, letting an extra quarter ounce trickle into the glass before she dumped the shot glass's contents. She poured orange juice over the top, filling the glass to the brim, then stuck a straw in it and set it in front of Elly.

"That one's on me," she said.

Elly hooked her fingers around the stem of the glass and pulled it toward her, bending to sip from the straw. "Are you sure?"

"Of course I am," Alex replied.

"Oy, Alex, where's that Caesar I needed?" A dark-haired waiter, his white shirt rumpled, leaned over the pass-through from the restaurant side.

"Coming," Alex called, taking a pint glass from the rack and dipping it in the celery salt, adding ice, vodka, and several dashes of Tabasco and Worcestershire sauce before adding Clamato and a stalk of celery. She took it over and the waiter set it on his tray.

"Thanks, love," he said, much mollified, before he hurried away.

Alex came back to the bar, but before she could say anything more to Elly, her chit machine printed up two new orders. She gave Elly an apologetic smile and went to work. Elly watched her move behind the bar, reaching for glasses, popping the caps off bottles of beer, pouring drinks. She made it seem easy, moving with precision, without wasting time or movement. The lounge filled, and a second bartender came behind the bar. Elly recognized him from the night before.

"Hey there," Eric said as he spotted her. "You're back." He gave her a friendly grin.

"I'm back," Elly echoed.

"Busy night, Alex?" Eric asked her.

"It has been," Alex replied as she stopped long enough to hold a small pitcher under the tap. "Looking to be a busy Saturday, as always."

"Good. I need the money," Eric quipped.

With the pair of them behind the bar, the orders went more smoothly and the plates of food passed through from the kitchen found their intended recipients more quickly. Elly was entertained watching them, though her gaze occasionally flicked up to the television hung behind the bar. It didn't hold her attention for long; she'd never been interested in Formula 1, or any kind of motor races. At the diner back home, it'd been football in the summer and hockey in the winter, with baseball thrown in and little else.

A woman plopped down on the seat next to her with a sigh, dropping her black apron on the bar, where it clattered on the wood. A few coins rolled from one of the pouches. "Sorry," she said, sliding the coins back toward her with her hand.

"No problem," Elly replied.

The woman wiped her forehead, pushing her curly dark hair back where it was coming loose from its ponytail. Her hands were slender, and her eyes were dark and almond shaped under finely plucked brows, which furrowed as she pulled out a thick handful of receipts.

"Charity, my favorite girl." Eric leaned on the bar. "What can I get you, darling?"

"Jack Daniel's, straight up," Charity said. "It's been a hell of a busy shift."

"Coming right up. Elly, don't mind Charity. She's happier once she's had a drink. She's more…charitable."

Charity glanced over, rolling her eyes. "He speaks the truth, even if he makes stupid jokes. Sometimes I wish my parents had stuck with an Asian name." She held out her hand. "Nice to meet you."

"You too. I'm Elly." Elly shook her hand.

"You going to work here?" Charity asked, pulling a roll of bills from her apron next and counting them out on the bar.

"Just here for a drink, to see Alex," Elly said.

"Oh. Cool." Charity kept counting, murmuring numbers under her breath. She took out a pen and made a notation on the top receipt. Then she stuffed the bills back in her apron and took out the handful of coins that had made the clatter. "Lucky you. She's the most popular bartender here. Except for Eric, of course, who is more my style, being a man and all."

"Have you worked here long?" Elly asked, though Charity's words had distracted her. Just how popular was Alex? She glanced over, spotting Alex at the other end of the bar, leaning against it as she chatted to a woman who had been there last night. They laughed, and the woman touched Alex on the arm, a casual, flirty touch. Alex leaned in, smiling.

Elly tore her gaze away, taking another sip of her drink instead.

"Been here longer than I'd like to admit," Charity said once she'd finished counting her change. She organized her receipts. "But it's fun sometimes. Just not today. Some tour bus of old people showed up, and I was run off my feet. None of them could manage to order refills at the same time. And then the tip…barely fifteen percent." Charity shook her head. "And I still have to tip out to the kitchen."

"That's awful," Elly said. She'd never had that happen to her, but she knew what it was like to not get a decent tip. "There isn't an enforced gratuity on those kind of groups?"

"Not here," Charity replied. "I wish. Hey, do you work in a restaurant too?"

"I did," she said, "back home. But I'm a graphic artist, and looking for work at the moment."

"Good luck. I wish I could work in my major," Charity said, writing down another number on her paper. She totted up her receipts and sighed. "The kitchen's going to love me tonight." She took out the bills again and counted out a small pile.

"What did you take?" Elly finished her drink, sucking the last bit of orange juice from the ice cubes. She pushed the glass back a bit.

"Kinesiology," Charity replied. "But I still have to do my teacher's degree if I want to get anywhere with it, or spend my life taping ankles." She rose to her feet. "Save my spot, I'll be back." She hurried off, back into the restaurant side, with her money.

"Another?" Eric asked, gesturing to Elly's empty glass.

"I suppose one more wouldn't hurt," Elly said. "It's a screwdriver."

"Sure thing." Eric dumped the ice into the sink and put the glass in the dishwasher. "You want to look at a menu too?"

At the mention of food, Elly's stomach growled. "I should. That way I can drive home later."

Eric handed her a laminated menu and then set to work making her drink. Elly scanned the list. It was pretty standard pub fare: fries, loaded potato skins, nachos, pizza, hamburgers.

He set the drink in front of her. "What do you think?"

"Potato skins?"

"Good choice." Eric took the menu. "Hard for the kitchen to mess that one up. Extra sour cream?"

"Sure. Does the kitchen always mess up orders?"

Eric winked. "Not too much." He went to key in her order and she took a sip of her new drink.

"Having fun?" A familiar husky voice spoke, warm breath brushing over her ear. Elly turned, coming face-to-face with Alex.

"I didn't think it'd be so busy," she replied. Alex slid an arm over the back of the stool, resting against Elly's shoulders, leaning in for a kiss.

"It's Saturday," Alex said. "But I'll be off in a few hours, if you want to wait." She winked.

"I'll wait," Elly said.

Alex grinned and leaned in for another kiss. This one was more, Alex's lips pressing insistently against hers, her tongue teasing the seam of Elly's lips until she parted them. The touch was a balm, taking away last night's sting.

"Mmm. I can't wait." Alex kissed her again quickly, then started away. She cleared glasses from a table nearby and carried them back behind the bar.

Elly watched Formula 1 while she waited, but auto racing bored her. Eric slid a plate of potato skins in front of her, and she was glad of something to keep her occupied. As she was biting into the first one, Charity returned, carrying a black PVC jacket. She'd changed out of her work clothes and wore a slinky black sleeveless dress that showed off the delicate flower tattoos that wrapped her upper arms.

Eric whistled. "Gorgeous, Char. Got a date?"

"A hot one," Charity confirmed, settling onto the chair next to Elly.

"Who's the lucky guy?"

"You don't know him." Charity blew him a raspberry, then tossed back her drink. "He's a babe."

"Where are you going on your date?" Elly asked.

"He's taking me to a club. Then back to his place for some party time." Charity grinned.

"Sounds fun."

"Be careful, Char," Eric chided. "Vicious was raided by the cops a couple of weeks ago."

"They've cleaned up the place since then," Charity said. "I'm sure we'll be fine." She pulled a bill from her purse and held it out. "See you tomorrow."

"Thanks, Char." Eric took the bill and tucked it into his pocket. "Have a good one."

"Have a good night," Elly said.

"Nice to meet you." Charity rested a hand on Elly's shoulder. "Enjoy yourself." She squeezed gently, then let go, sliding off the chair. In another moment, she was gone.

Elly ate her dinner and finished her drink, turning down a third from Eric, changing to water. She'd have to drive, after all. Though Alex occasionally smiled or winked at her, it was too busy for them to have a conversation, and Alex lingered at her tables. Formula 1 racing ended, and the sports highlights show began, and it held her attention even less than the cars did. She supposed she could try to talk to some of the others in the bar, but everyone seemed to be in their own little groups, and it wasn't like home, where she knew everyone. She felt uncomfortably alone. Maybe she should just go home. She looked for Eric, to pay her bill.

"I'll be another hour or so." Alex paused on her way to a table. "You're not leaving yet, are you?"

"Well…" Elly wavered.

"Wait for me?" Alex asked. "I'll beg Eric to let me go early."

"All right." Now that Alex was here beside her, things didn't seem so lonely.

"Good." Alex kissed her cheek, then hurried to the table.

"Getting impatient?" Eric teased, leaning over to grab her empty plate.

She willed herself not to blush. "Just a bit bored. Is there anything else on TV?"

Eric shrugged and picked up the remote. "What do you want to watch? We keep it mostly on sports, or people get fussy."

"There's MotoGP on that one satellite channel," a familiar voice said. "That's better than the crap you've got on now, by far."

Will plopped down into the chair next to Elly. "Hey, stranger," he said. "Back again?"

"Hey." Elly smiled. Finally, a familiar face. Sort of. "I thought I should see what Parry's is like without the karaoke."

"Less frightening?" Will quipped. He stood up on the rungs of his chair and waved at Alex. "Oy! Bellerose!"

Alex stood on the far side of the lounge, near the window, talking to a customer, but she turned and laughed as she saw Will. Elly saw her shake her head, and she moved back toward the bar.

"Don't have a home to go to, poor baby?" Alex teased when she got nearer.

"Where else would I go? Besides"—Will gestured at the television, now showing motorcycle racing—"the MotoGP's in Argentina. I couldn't miss it."

Alex turned to watch, and Elly sank back into her chair. Next to Will, and the apparent fascination of the racing, she felt nearly invisible.

"Rossi's going to beat the lot of them," Will said.

"You're just saying that because you're Rossi obsessed," Alex replied. "Marquez is still better."

Will snorted. "So you think." He turned to Elly. "Who do you think's better, Rossi or Marquez?"

Elly couldn't think of anything to say; she had no idea whatsoever about either racer. It'd be like asking her to choose whether Dom Pérignon or Veuve Clicquot was the best champagne; she'd never tried either. She shrugged, looking to Alex for help.

"She doesn't watch MotoGP," Alex told him. "We'll just agree to disagree."

"If Rossi wins this one, you pay for lunch next time we ride. Deal?"

Alex rolled her eyes. "Marquez will beat him, but if you want to bet on it, you're on. I can't wait for you to buy me lunch."

"And you," Will turned to Elly, and she tried not to squirm under his gaze, "will watch MotoGP with me and learn."

"I've never watched it, ever," Elly said.

"Then there's no better time to start." Will reeled off names and statistics and Elly's head swam. Alex went back to work, answering a wave from a customer, leaving her to Will's teaching. She tried to keep up, but none of the names meant anything to her. Instead of trying to keep track of Will's excess of information, she kept her eyes on the television, watching the riders speed around the track.

"Argentina's awesome," Will said, leaning closer, "but it's Laguna Seca that's the best track of the whole MotoGP, in my opinion." He continued talking, and by the time Alex had her jacket and had come around the bar to join them, Elly thought she might not do too badly at a pub quiz on motorcycle racing, as long as she didn't have to name any bike models.

"Ready to go?" she asked, slinging an arm over Elly's shoulder.

"Just let me pay my bill." Elly reached into her purse for her wallet, looking at the receipt Eric had set facedown on the bar. She pulled out a couple of bills and some change and set it on top of the receipt.

"Where you two headed?" Will asked.

Elly glanced at Alex, who shrugged and said, "Probably my place. Or maybe Elly's. Just us, though."

"Thought as much. Don't stay up too late, girls."

"Yes, Mommy," Alex retorted.

Elly put her wallet back in her purse and pushed back from the bar as Alex put her jacket on. Slipping her own jacket on, Elly followed Alex out of the lounge and into the cool night air.

"My place?" Alex asked.

"Or mine, if you'd like," Elly replied. Her bedsheets were clean, and she'd tidied up a bit before she'd come. The apartment, small as it was, would pass muster.

"I'd like to see yours. I'll follow you on the bike."

They parted and Elly slid into the driver's seat, starting the car and waiting as Alex put on her protective gear and got on the bike. When Alex was ready, she pulled out of the parking lot, heading back home, glancing at her rearview mirror, seeing the bike following her, the green panels occasionally glinting in the streetlights.

At the next red light, Alex pulled up beside her and revved the engine. Elly shook her head, giving a slight laugh. Alex couldn't possibly think she'd dare to race, did she? Crazy. The light turned green, and Alex sped ahead, slowing only once she was several car lengths in front. At the next light, she tucked back in behind the sedan. Elly led the way home, but by the time she found a parking spot near her place, Alex had already pulled in and put down the kickstand and was pulling off her helmet.

They met on the front sidewalk. "In a rush?" Elly asked, trying not to sound like a stick-in-the-mud.

"With you, always," Alex replied, leaning in for a kiss. "There's no time to waste."

Elly dug out her keys and let them in the front door, wincing as it slammed behind them. It was late and the building was quiet; she hoped they hadn't woken anyone. It was a short flight up to her door and she let Alex go in first, coming behind and easing the door closed with barely a click.

"Nice place." Alex set her helmet on the wobbly dining table and toed off her boots.

Elly wasn't sure if she was joking or being serious. The apartment was nearly bare; over the past month she'd managed to bring a few things from home, but it still didn't feel lived in. More like a way station. "It was the best I could find on short notice."

"They're hard to come by. Still job hunting?"

Alex turned back toward her and Elly grimaced. "Yeah." She set her purse by the door and hung her jacket off the knob. The failure of it stung, even though rationally she knew she hadn't been trying very long. "But I don't really want to talk about it."

Alex caught her hand. "Then let's not talk." She tugged and they came together in the tiny hallway, Elly catching the lapel of Alex's leather jacket to maintain her balance. Their first kiss was slow, almost luxuriously so, given Alex's earlier desire for speed, but it didn't stay that way. Alex pressed closer and Elly found herself stepping back, her shoulders hitting the wall as Alex deepened the kiss, cupping her cheek, Alex's thumb stroking over her jawline.

The touch sent a quiver through Elly's body and she was glad for the security of the wall when her knees weakened. She'd never felt this way with anyone, this consuming desire and need.

When they came up for air, Alex cocked her head to the left. "Bedroom there?"

"Yes," Elly managed breathlessly.

They half walked, half stumbled down the hallway and Alex pushed open the door. For a split second, Elly saw her room as Alex might: old-fashioned, the worn quilt and old bedstead nothing like Alex's own minimalist room. But then it didn't matter. Alex let her jacket drop to the floor, its zippers and buckles clanking on the hardwood, and Elly wanted her to lose the rest of her clothes, starting with the slim-fitting black uniform shirt with the Parry's logo in green on the left breast. She caught at the hem and lifted, and Alex obligingly raised her arms, letting Elly tug it up and off. Her skin was pale against the black lace of her bra and Elly undid the hook at the back and pushed it down her arms. Reddened half-moons marked where the underwire had pressed against her skin and Elly bent, gently kissing the spot between Alex's breasts, caressing the undersides of her breasts as she did.

"More." Alex shivered as Elly cupped her breasts, thumbs brushing her hardening nipples, tongue trailing up over her sternum to the pulse point in her neck, where Elly gave her a brief nibble. Alex's skin tasted a tiny bit salty, and there was a touch of perfume too. Elly lifted her head and Alex kissed her, wrapping her arms around Elly's neck, her warmth seeping through Elly's thin shirt.

Elly fumbled with the buttons on her own shirt, finally managing to get it undone. Alex pushed it off her shoulders and made short work of her bra, undoing the front clasp and helping it to join the shirt. She didn't stop there, going straight for the button of Elly's jeans. Between the two of them, both sets of jeans and Alex's chaps fell to the floor and they moved to the bed, becoming a tangle of limbs as they embraced.

Elly found herself on her back, her head half on a pillow. Alex bent over her, dropping kisses over the swell of her breasts. "I love your freckles here," she said between kisses. "So cute, so you." Her fingers traced over Elly's ribs and down to her hip. "And here."

"I've always wanted to be rid of them," Elly confessed.

"Really?" Alex lifted her head in surprise.

"Really. I'd rather be like you, with your English-rose complexion." Elly smoothed a hand down Alex's side, under the black cotton bikini panties she wore.

"English rose? I've never heard that before." Alex's breath caught as Elly pushed down the bikini panties and stroked Alex between her thighs, feeling the damp curls and the hot, wet center. Alex's hips tilted toward the touch and Elly crooked her fingers, pressing upward. Alex shivered, sliding back onto the bed. Elly slid with her, going lower, brushing over her stomach and then between her legs, tasting the flavor that was uniquely Alex, her tongue at first flicking delicately, then with more pressure.

"You're an English rose even here," Elly murmured, taking Alex into her mouth, using her free hand to hold down Alex's thigh as her legs tensed with the pleasure. She didn't let up even as Alex moaned and shuddered; she loved knowing she could bring Alex to this state. She stroked Alex's G-spot in time with her movements on her clit, and Alex whimpered and stiffened, giving a gasping cry as she came. Then her body went limp and Elly slowly withdrew, resting her head on Alex's thigh. She felt Alex's hand on her hair, a gentle caress.

"That was…" Alex began. Elly lifted her head. Alex's cheeks were flushed and her hair had partly come loose from its ponytail. "Incredible."

Elly moved up the bed to lie next to her. "Good."

Alex tugged at Elly's panties. "Take these off. I can't be naked if you're not."

Elly shifted on the bed, lifting her buttocks and bending her knees, sliding her plain cotton panties down and off. "Better?"

"Much. I'd hate for you not to come too."

"I don't think it'll take much tonight."

"Let's find out." Alex chuckled low in her throat. She rolled onto her side so they were facing each other and feathered a kiss over Elly's lips as she hooked her hand under Elly's knee, drawing her leg up, her fingertips skating up the back of her thigh. So close, and yet…

Elly let out a disappointed breath, only to have Alex chuckle again as her fingers began the torturous climb upward once more. Closer, this time, along the edge of her wetness, then away. Elly could hardly stand it and she flexed her leg, her heel behind Alex's knee, pushing her forward.

"Oh no, not yet," Alex said, giving her the gentlest of spankings.

"Do I have to beg?"

"Maybe."

This time Alex slid a finger into her, and Elly gasped at the welcome penetration.

"Please, Alex…"

Alex pressed her clit with her thumb and Elly closed her eyes, arching into her touch.

A loud thud on the ceiling startled her back into awareness, and she heard the couple upstairs moving around in their bedroom.

"Ignore them," Alex said. "Look at me."

Elly shifted her attention back to Alex, to the dark-lashed eyes and the reddened lips.

"That's better," Alex said. She moved forward and Elly met her halfway, eagerly anticipating the kiss. Alex's fingers thrust inside her and Elly moaned into Alex's mouth, but Alex didn't let up on the kiss, or on her thrusts, managing to stroke tiny circles on Elly's clit. Elly broke off the kiss to gasp in a breath, her head falling back, her eyes closed once more. A delicious quiver started in her belly and moved up her torso and down her legs until she couldn't stand it anymore. She spasmed around Alex's fingers, a guttural groan escaping her, the perspiration prickling along her spine.

There was a shuffling step above them, and a quiet laugh. Elly felt the flush growing, starting at her cheeks and spreading down onto her chest. She'd been so loud. She buried her head in Alex's shoulder.

"All right?" Alex asked, stroking her hair.

"They heard, didn't they?" Elly said, her words muffled.

"And you're worried? I'd bet money they're jealous. Don't worry about them, El." Alex wrapped her in a hug, and Elly loved being skin to skin with her.

"But still…what if I see them?"

"So what? You think the woman that lives downstairs from me hasn't heard sex noises before? And so have the people above you. That's just the way of it. If they're polite, they won't say anything."

"I know, I do." Elly lifted her head and looked at Alex. "I'm just not used to it, with so many people around all the time."

"It's not so quiet as a farm," Alex agreed. "You could have a screaming orgasm and no one would hear you. Just the chickens."

"Yeah." Elly remembered the night they'd had there. She hadn't worried about being overheard, knew there hadn't been anyone nearby. "Maybe we could go, next weekend?"

"To the farm? Well…" Alex paused. "What about Thursday night? We could take the bike, stay overnight, and then come back Friday in time for me to work."

"If I don't have any interviews those days, that'd be perfect. But on the bike?" Elly felt the familiar nervousness creep in.

"Unless the weather's bad, then we can take your car," Alex said. "It's a beautiful ride. I think you'd like it. City riding sucks, anyway. Riding on the secondary highways is the best."

"I'll think about it," Elly said. She relaxed into Alex's embrace.

"Let me know by Wednesday," Alex said, "and I'll make sure the bike's ready for the ride." She stroked Elly's back, then shifted away, sitting up in bed. She swung her legs over the side. When she began to pull on her clothes, Elly sat up in surprise.

"You're going?"

"I have an early morning tomorrow," Alex said. "I want to get in a few hours of riding before my shift."

Elly's heart sank. It had been so cozy just then, and they'd been so intimate, yet here Alex was leaving. Again. "Stay anyway?" After last night, she knew it was unlikely, but she had to ask. She'd hoped it had been an anomaly.

Alex had her jeans on and buttoned, and was fastening her bra. "Not tonight." She paused, her shirt in her hands, her stance softening. "I just don't stay. I haven't changed since yesterday."

"Oh." But wasn't that what lovers did? She'd been hoping for something more, thought that there'd been more to them than just the physical spark of lust. "I understand." She didn't, but it had been a long while since her last relationship, and maybe she hadn't read the signals right.

"I'll call you when I get back into town," Alex said, resting her hand on Elly's knee. "We can have a bite to eat before my shift."

Elly looked up. Alex seemed apologetic but not about to change her mind. "Sure, let's. I'll be spending tomorrow sending out resumes again."

"And you'll need the break." Alex bent to kiss her, and Elly accepted the kiss, though it stirred a painful longing in her. When they broke apart, she rose from the bed and pulled on her robe that hung on a hook on the back of her bedroom door.

Alex preceded her from the bedroom, heading straight to put on her boots and shrug on her jacket. She scooped up her helmet as Elly waited, leaning against the wall. "See you later?"

"Call me when you're back."

Alex opened the door, resting her hand on the knob. She leaned over and they kissed once more, briefly. "Good night, El."

Then Alex was gone.

Elly shut the door and locked it, and paced back to her room, her arms wrapped around herself. Her bed seemed lonely, the sheets skewed and rumpled, taunting her with what had just happened. She lay down on the bed and Alex's scent rose from the sheets. How had she misread Alex? If she wasn't interested, then why had she come over?

She curled into a ball, the robe dragging around her, though she tried to tug it down to cover her legs. Their first time, at the farm, had been so incredible, and even the last time had been great, aside from having to go home. She knew she shouldn't take it so personally, but she couldn't help it. Three times they'd made love, but Alex wouldn't stay.

An image of Alex flirting at the bar floated in front of her closed eyes and Elly pressed her lips together. It was silly to cry, but that didn't stop her eyes from burning with tears. She swallowed hard, and turned her face into the pillow.

CHAPTER FIVE

Monday morning was crisp and chill when Alex left, heading south out of Calgary, darting through the early morning traffic, leaving the city on Highway 2A toward De Winton. The sun was low in the sky yet, and though she hadn't slept overly long the night before, the energy surged through her the farther she went from the city. She kept the chin vent open on her helmet, and left the visor cracked so she could breathe the fresh morning air. On such a day, she was tempted to head as far south as Pincher Creek and take the number 22 back all the way north to Bragg Creek. She might make it all that way. It was early.

Alex slowed as she reached the outskirts of Okotoks, a town growing thanks to its proximity to the city. Sometimes she used to stop there, but now, she wanted to avoid cities and traffic as much as possible. The bike purred under her, urging her on. Usually Will would be with her, but he'd scored some hours at a construction site for the next few days, and he needed the money too much. But she was fine on her own. She'd been riding for years, and it was as natural to her as breathing.

She kept heading south. Green farmland stretched as far as the eye could see, dotted by high power lines. The road ahead was empty and she shifted gears, opening the throttle and letting the bike fly over the pavement. The speedometer climbed—100 kilometers an hour…110…120…but still she pushed it, the speedometer clocking 150 kilometers an hour before she had to slow down, seeing the outskirts of Nanton.

When she hit the town, she slowed, cruising down Main Street and looking for a place to stop for a coffee. She'd left so quickly this morning she hadn't wanted to waste time. She pulled into a parking space near the Tumbleweed coffee shop. The open sign flickered in the window and she dismounted, removing her helmet and pushing the hair off her forehead. When she walked in, all eyes turned to her.

"Good morning," she said to the waitress as she took a seat at a free table, placing her helmet on the chair beside her. The woman came over.

"What can I get you?" She was on the plump side, an almost-grandmotherly type, her graying hair pulled back in a bun.

"Coffee, and some bacon and eggs," Alex said after glancing at the menu.

"Sure thing. Over easy?" When Alex nodded, the woman made a notation on her pad and headed back behind the counter. "Earl, eggs and bacon, over easy!" She came back with the coffeepot and filled Alex's cup, placing a bowl of creamers next to the sugar.

"You headed farther south? You were in here a few weeks ago with your boyfriend, weren't you? You look familiar."

"Yeah, I probably was. Will and I come out here a lot. I'm not going much farther, maybe to the Chain Lakes. Why?" Alex leaned back in her chair. Will wasn't her boyfriend, not exactly, but she wasn't about to explain the particulars.

"Heard there was a wind warning down Lethbridge way. Probably not that good on a bike."

"Thanks for letting me know." Alex smiled. "Did they say anything about Pincher Creek?"

"Not sure."

"Pincher has the warning too." A man nearby leaned over, his face tanned from years working outdoors, a grizzled beard gracing his cheeks. "You'd be better off heading west from here, if you're going to the Chain Lakes. No sense going farther south than you need to, girlie."

"Thanks." Alex unzipped her jacket and hung it over the back of her chair.

"You got a nice bike there," the man said, nodding to where the Ninja sat, green and black and small amongst the pickup trucks.

"A 2013 Kawasaki," Alex said automatically. "Lots of power in it."

"Maybe a little much for you?" the man asked. "My son's got a Harley, you see, but those sport bikes are too zippy for his taste."

"I love it," Alex said honestly.

"Long as you can handle it," the man added. "Surprised you're not riding with your boyfriend or something."

Alex laughed. "He can't keep up with me."

The man chuckled. "I bet he can't."

The waitress brought out the bacon and eggs. "Enjoy."

Alex dug in, her empty stomach happy to get food and coffee. The meal would keep her going for the rest of the ride. She didn't linger once she'd finished, just got up and went to the till to pay.

"Have a good day," the waitress said.

"You too." Alex headed out, giving a wave to the man, who nodded his head and lifted his coffee cup.

She went west as he'd suggested, heading through Nanton and on to the Chain Lakes, the rough foothills rising in front of her. The sun was high overhead when she got there, and when she pulled into the parking lot in the day-use area, she peeled off her leather jacket, letting the light breeze slide its fingers through her cotton shirt.

She walked along the lakeside a short distance after hanging her helmet off the handlebar and found a spot to sit, leaning back against a picnic table, resting her elbows behind her. She tilted her face up toward the sun and closed her eyes. The gentle sound of waves lapping at the shore combined with the occasional squawk of gulls and other birds, and though she could hear the occasional vehicle, the place was peaceful, calm. If she could spend hours here, she would. Far better than hours in the bar, though she loved her job.

Would Elly want to come out here? It wasn't a farm, but it might be close.

Alex opened her eyes. Where had that come from? She'd never taken girls out on her bike, not that many of them ever asked. The bike was her time, hers alone. Even if Will came with her, he understood her desires and held the same himself, the need for the adrenaline rush. But she had promised Elly she'd call.

Alex dug her phone from the inner pocket of her jacket, checking the time. Mentally calculating the distance home, she realized she had better get moving. Breakfast in Nanton, quick though it had been, had set her back, and Highway 22 was slower than some of the others, thanks to traffic. But she loved the ride, loved the view, the rolling foothills, the copses of dark trees dotting the landscape. If she could, she'd live out here, at least in the summertime. She glanced at her phone once more. No calls.

She rose and made her way back to her bike, shrugging on her jacket and zipping it up. She pulled her helmet off the handlebar and put it back on, threading the chin strap through the loops and snapping it closed. When she pulled out onto the highway once more, she found herself behind a slow-moving RV, and she itched to pass it, swerving out to check the lane, wishing for a broken yellow. She kept her feet still on the footpegs, though she wanted to tap her toes impatiently. Finally the double yellow broke on her side and she checked the lane, swerving out and accelerating, blowing past the RV like it had been standing still.

She slowed back to the posted speed limit once she'd passed; the cops were known to watch this section of highway for speeders, and she had no intention of getting her bike impounded. Plus, the scenery along the road was breathtaking, one of her favorite parts of the province. She had enough time to enjoy it.

At Longview, she pulled over and walked across the road to the café to get a cup of coffee and use their bathroom. The open metal snaps on the bottom of her leather chaps jingled and the thump of her boots sounded hollowly against the creaky wooden steps she ascended to the door.

Alex didn't linger, buying only a small coffee and drinking it on the porch. She pulled out her phone again. One missed call. From Elly. She frowned and dialed her voice mail, listening to Elly's quiet voice.

"Hi Alex, it's Elly. I won't be able to meet you later. Got a call just now from one of the places I'd put in a resume, and I have an interview late this afternoon. Give me a call back, maybe we can do it another time."

Alex deleted the message and sent Elly a quick text instead of calling. *No problem, just let me know when.*

There wasn't even a slight pang of disappointment; now she could take her time heading back to the city, instead of rushing. She finished the last of her coffee, then tossed the cup in the garbage and walked back to her bike.

❖

Elly dressed in her most professional suit, black and crisply pressed. She straightened the collar of the white shirt underneath, checking carefully in the mirror before she left the apartment. Her hair had curled in multiple directions after her shower, and she'd smoothed it back the best she could with a clip, wishing she'd had more notice. But a job interview wasn't to be sniffed at, even if an entry-level job at an oil company wasn't exactly what she'd been looking for. Okay, it wasn't what she was looking for at all, but she'd placed resumes for numerous jobs not entirely suited to her background, desperate for anything decent to pay the bills.

The elevator at the bottom of the fifty-floor skyscraper opened, and she stepped on board, pushing the button for the twenty-fifth floor. A television prattled business news in the top corner, and she glanced up, then away again. The elevator dinged and the doors slid open. Elly checked her reflection in the mirrored glass and took a deep breath.

At the reception desk, she gave her name and the receptionist indicated a chair. "I'll let Melanie know you're here."

After a short wait, an older woman with bobbed bottle-blond hair came clacking down the corridor, stopping in front of Elly. "Eleanor Cole?"

Elly rose and held out her hand. "Ms. Miller? Nice to meet you."

"Please, come this way." Ms. Miller led her back down the corridor and into an office. Another woman sat at a table with several chairs, and Elly could see her own resume at the top of a pile of papers. "Thank you for coming with such short notice. We had a cancellation in our schedule today."

"It's no trouble at all," Elly said. She took a seat, when Ms. Miller indicated a chair, and unbuttoned her suit jacket, then smoothed the wrinkles in her trousers. She hoped her nerves didn't show.

The other woman looked up. "Good afternoon, Ms. Cole. I'm Ms. Terry. We've reviewed your resume, and we decided to have you come in." She fixed Elly with a firm, hazel-eyed gaze.

"I appreciate the consideration." Elly tried to keep her voice from sounding stiff, but the formality of the situation intimidated her. She was used to super-friendly HR staff, and Ms. Terry had a cool demeanor that seemed unbending.

"You're not the usual sort we get in for this position," Ms. Miller said. "We like our applicants to have previous experience in reception, and with oil companies, but given your education…"

"I am a fast learner," Elly replied, "and I've worked with many different sorts of people, so I'm sure I could adapt easily."

"That's good to hear," Ms. Terry said. She made a note on Elly's resume. "Why is it that you left your previous employment?"

"The diner?"

"The graphic design job," Ms. Terry clarified.

"I was made redundant, unfortunately, as the firm restructured because of the recession." She didn't know how to put a positive spin on it.

"And then you went to work at a…diner?"

"My parents passed away and I had to deal with their estate, their farm. I needed something to tide me over."

Ms. Terry frowned. Ms. Miller's expression became a bit strained. "Do you have much knowledge of the oil and gas business?" she asked.

"As much as anyone who has lived in Calgary," Elly said.

Ms. Miller smiled. "You're willing to start at the bottom? As you don't have specific oil and gas experience, you'd quite possibly start in the mailroom. Isn't that right, Ms. Terry?"

"Quite likely," Ms. Terry replied. She made another notation on Elly's resume.

Their next questions were conversational, easy, and she began to relax. By the end of the interview, Ms. Terry seemed to have lost some of her coolness and Elly took that for a good sign.

"Thank you for coming in," Ms. Miller said, rising from her chair. "I'll show you out to the elevator."

"Thank you," Ms. Terry said, glancing up only briefly from her stack of papers. "We'll be in touch."

Elly rose from her chair. "I appreciate the opportunity."

Elly stepped into the elevator and, when the doors closed, let out a breath. This could be her chance. Getting a foot in the door here could mean promotions, raises…She'd put in the hard work to move up. The sky would be the limit.

❖

At home, Elly took off her suit and flopped onto the sofa in her yoga pants and T-shirt with a sigh. She glanced at her watch. Alex would be at work by now. A tingle started in her belly at the thought of Alex, of her in her riding leathers. She'd love to see Alex, but the thought of going to the bar for another evening, so soon after the last, made her feel more tired than she had after her interview.

She pulled out her phone, read Alex's text again. They could do a meal on Thursday before they went out to the farm, if Alex still wanted to. Elly smiled at the thought, remembering their delicious evening the night they'd met. Would Alex want to recreate that?

Thursday for something to eat, then to the farm? she texted.

Alex was surprisingly quick to reply. *How about the diner in the town near your place?*

The diner? Elly debated it. If she took Alex to the diner, tongues would wag. Or at least, would wag more than they usually did. An intended romantic evening would turn into having to introduce Alex to the entire town, or whoever stopped by their table just for a chat. She rubbed her eyes.

How about dinner on the way there?

Sounds perfect. Gotta get back to work.

Thursday, 3pm?

Will be there. Wear jeans.

Jeans. Elly swallowed. She knew what that meant. Alex wouldn't want to take her car out. Maybe she should hope for rain. The idea of speeding down a highway had her stomach churning with anxiety. She shuddered. It just wasn't safe. But yet…she had a feeling Alex might not come at all if she didn't get on the bike.

Chapter Six

On Thursday afternoon, Elly heard Alex before she saw her, the growl of the motorcycle apparent from a couple of blocks away. She watched the green and black bike pull up to the curb, Alex dressed in all black leathers and black jeans. She pulled off her helmet as she walked up to the door. When the buzz came, Elly let her in, and heard her clump up the stairs. She opened the door.

"Hey, babe," Alex said, leaning in for a kiss.

"Hey."

"You ready to go?"

"Almost." Elly frowned. "I was thinking we could take my car."

"But I brought the bike."

"I know, but what if it rains?"

"The forecast is clear, and even if it does rain, I brought rain gear for you."

"Oh." Elly couldn't think of another excuse, though she wanted to.

Alex paced into the living room. "What are you bringing with you? We're only staying a night, aren't we? I have to work tomorrow."

"I just have a small bag," Elly said, indicating the soft-sided gym bag laying by the door.

Alex eyed it. "That should fit in my saddlebag. Or you can wear it cross-body if it doesn't, though that'd be a bit awkward." Alex shrugged. "You're going to love this, El. The wind in your hair, the open road…" She grinned.

"You won't go too fast, will you?"

"But that's the whole point! C'mon, El, let's go." Alex scooped up the bag and waited by the door while Elly grabbed her leather jacket and a pair of gloves. "We'll have to get you a proper jacket soon too."

"Proper?"

"One with better protection, though that'll do." Alex held the door open. "After you."

Protection? Elly's stomach churned, and all she could think of was falling off the bike. She took a deep breath. She wouldn't fall. She'd hold on so tightly that she'd never fall.

Beside the bike, Alex opened the saddlebag on one side, pulling out a mass of folded black leather. Alex handed it to her, and she held it uncertainly as Alex shoved her gear into the space left by the leather and pushed down on the lid of the saddlebag until it clicked and closed.

"You need to put those on," Alex said, indicating the leather. "Can't go riding on the highway without them. You'd freeze. And this." She handed Elly a light wool buff for her neck.

Elly shook out the leather and found herself holding a pair of leather chaps like the ones Alex wore. They were heavier than they looked, and she couldn't quite figure out how to put them on. She unbuckled the belt, then paused in confusion.

"Unzip them first," Alex said, bending to undo one leg. Elly bent and unzipped the other, pulling apart the snaps at the bottoms. She buckled the belt and Alex helped her to zip the leather around her legs, starting from the top down. She was dimly aware being dressed in leather would be sexy if she'd relax. She wondered if her nerves were as much about Alex, about her refusal to stay the night, about the niggling sense that they were after very different things, as about riding a motorcycle. Too late to back out now.

The chaps sagged around her waist, though she'd buckled the belt as tight as it could go. "Is there any way to make it smaller?" Elly asked, tugging the chaps up so they'd sit where they were supposed to.

Alex frowned. "Might be able to tighten the laces in back. Hold on." She moved around and Elly felt her fumbling at the small of her back. "Dammit. No. It's as snug as it's going to get." She came back around, taking the buckle in her hand. "If I had an awl, I could punch another hole in the leather, but I don't. They're not too loose, are they? I guess I'm a lot bigger than you are."

Elly hitched up the chaps again. "I'll be sitting most of the time," she reasoned, "so it won't be too bad, I guess." She pulled the scarf over her head, pushing her now static-charged hair off her forehead.

"That's the spirit." Alex chuckled. "I should have thought about this ahead of time, but chaps aren't cheap."

"How much are they?" Elly took the helmet Alex handed her and held on to the chin straps, ready to put it on.

"A couple hundred bucks for the cheaper ones."

A month's groceries, easily. "That's a lot of money."

"It's not too bad. Better to spend that money than to not have anything between you and the road." Alex put her helmet back on. "Let's go. It's an almost three-hour ride, and it's two thirty."

Elly put on her helmet; it took her two tries to get it on and sitting right. She buckled the chin strap and pushed up the visor. Alex held the handlebar of the bike and Elly paused, trying to figure out the best way to get up on the bike without slipping.

"Foot on the peg and swing your leg over," Alex said, pointing to the footpeg.

Elly stepped up onto the footpeg, swinging her leg over as Alex had said, then shifting back onto the pillion seat. She felt high up and exposed, and she suppressed a shiver. She zipped her leather jacket right up to her chin and checked that her pockets had been zipped after she put on her gloves.

Alex started the engine and Elly gripped the bars at the sides of her seat. They rolled out into the road and Alex let out the clutch and turned the throttle. The bike zipped forward and Elly's heart pounded as she slid forward, then back, on the seat. They pulled to a stop at the corner while Alex waited for a space in the traffic. Elly took a deep breath, adjusting herself on the seat.

Just breathe. It was safe.

Alex looked back at her. "If you need me to stop for any reason, tap my shoulder. All right?"

"Got it."

"Enjoy the ride. Once we get clear of the city traffic, it'll be much better."

Alex turned into the free space and joined the line of cars going west. It took over half an hour to get out of town, stopping and starting through traffic lights, but once they hit the highway, their speed increased.

Elly gripped the bars tight as she could. The wind buffeted her torso and she tensed, trying to keep from moving too much. She hunched over a bit, tucking herself behind Alex, lessening the pressure. Alex patted her knee, holding it a moment before she put her hand back on the handlebar. Reassurance? Maybe. Elly felt warmth blossoming inside her and knew her cheeks had gone pink behind the visor. Then she let her gaze move away from the back of Alex's head to the stretches of grassland at the sides of the highway, the fences and power lines stretching to the horizon. And she forgot her nerves.

It was beautiful. She'd never quite appreciated it like this, driving to and from the farm in her car. Usually she was impatient to get where she needed to go. But the wind brought the scents of the grass and of the nearby farms through the vents in her helmet, and a sense of peace filled her. These scents were home, family. She closed her eyes for a moment.

The bike growled under her and jerked, speeding ahead. Elly's eyes snapped open and her heart skipped a beat. Alex veered out into the other lane, passing an older large sedan, the sort her father used to call a land yacht. An old man, probably the age her father would be if he were still alive, was driving, and he shook a finger at them as they passed, looking furious. Alex zipped back into place, and they left the land yacht behind.

They reached the outskirts of Okotoks, but instead of going straight through into town, Alex turned aside, much to Elly's relief. Alex was right—highway riding was better than being in the city. She could relax on the bike, let her legs rest loosely on the footpegs, her hands equally loose on the bars. The speed was constant, predictable. Elly smiled to herself. If she didn't know any better, she'd think she was getting used to this.

They went through the town of High River, Alex slowing to match the traffic, but doing it so gradually that Elly found herself naturally adjusting to the reduced speed. It would be Nanton next, and Claresholm, and then Fort Macleod. She knew this drive like the back of her hand. At a red light, Alex looked back, pushing up her visor. Elly pushed up hers.

"Okay so far?" Alex asked, grinning.

"Yeah." She grinned back.

"Great. We'll stop in Fort Macleod so I can fuel up, and we can stretch our legs. That okay?"

"Perfect." Elly shifted on the seat. Her butt was starting to get a bit numb, but it wasn't too bad yet.

The light changed and Alex faced forward again. Elly braced herself against the footpegs, her knees pressing Alex's hips as the bike accelerated. She could get used to this.

❖

Alex stopped in Cardston as well, having felt Elly shifting uncomfortably behind her since they'd left Fort Macleod. She pulled into the parking lot at the grocery store and parked the bike.

Elly leaned forward, pushing up her visor. "Why are we stopping here?"

"I needed another break," Alex said, a slight lie. She could have gone for another hour or more, but having Elly shift around on the back was throwing off the balance of the bike and becoming irritating. "And I figured we should pick up something to eat, unless you still have food at the farm, or if you want to stop at one of these little restaurants. You don't, do you?"

"I hadn't thought of that," Elly replied. "I don't know what there'll be at the farm."

Alex dismounted and held the bike as Elly slid off. "We have space for a few groceries, though not too much. A bag's worth…ish."

"What do you like for breakfast?" Elly asked.

"A beautiful woman," she replied, patting Elly's ass. Even though the chaps were loose on her, they still made her look delectable. She couldn't wait to get them off her once they reached the farm. Elly pulled off her helmet and Alex saw the blush on her cheeks.

"For breakfast. Food," she emphasized, laughing a little.

Alex shrugged. "Cereal, toast, whatever. I'm easy." She hooked her helmet in one hand and put her arm around Elly's waist. "Get what you want."

They strolled into the store and Elly moved away to grab a basket and put it over her arm, awkwardly juggling it and her helmet.

"I'll take that," Alex said, taking the helmet from her. "You shop."

The store must have been familiar to Elly, because she moved purposefully down the aisles, plucking out a box of healthy cereal, a loaf of bread, some pastrami, lettuce, cheese, and a two-liter jug of milk.

"Sandwiches for dinner okay?" Elly asked, glancing at her.

"Works for me." Food was food, she wasn't picky. Her stomach growled. "As long as we can eat when we get there."

"I'm hungry too." Elly grabbed a chocolate bar from the rack near the cash register. "Grab one, Alex, it's your dessert."

Alex perused the selection and finally chose the peanut butter cups.

"My favorite," Elly said.

"Then why didn't you get them?" Alex asked, tossing the cups into the basket.

"Because I decided to be adventurous."

"Riding the bike isn't enough?" Alex teased. She hadn't expected that from Elly, the quiet farm girl. Maybe it'd be worth keeping her around.

"Well…" Elly smiled, and it lit up her face, her blue eyes twinkling. "I suppose that is more adventurous than chocolate." She began placing the groceries onto the small conveyor belt.

Alex dug into her pocket for her wallet, placing her helmet on the conveyor belt momentarily. "I'll get those."

"No, I will," Elly said, covering Alex's hand with her own, her fingers warm and soft. "You paid for the gas, after all. It's only fair."

Alex decided not to press. She had paid for the gas, but it wasn't all that expensive, not in comparison to what it would have cost to fill the tank on Elly's old car.

They headed back to the bike, Elly carrying the groceries. Alex followed a step behind, purposely slower, watching Elly in the chaps, smiling to herself when Elly had to hitch them up again. They'd have to get her a proper pair that fit, if she came riding a few more times. At least the helmet seemed to fit her, though. Replacing that would be more expensive than chaps, and Alex didn't have much use for her spare helmet. Her Shark helmet suited her just fine.

She set the helmets carefully on the bike's seats, propping them so they wouldn't slide, and stowed the groceries in the hard-case saddlebag at the back of the bike. The groceries fit, though she had to lay the jug of milk on its side. Elly grabbed her helmet and put it on, and Alex noticed how she'd done it the first time and was now buckling it with the ease of a pro. Almost, anyway. She fumbled a bit with the snap, but that was minor.

"You look good in that, like a biker chick," Alex said, coming back to the side of the bike and putting on her own helmet. "Hot, even." She winked and smiled when Elly blushed. Again.

"I don't feel like a biker chick," she replied, hitching up the chaps once more. Alex patted the seat and Elly mounted the bike, swinging her leg over.

"You definitely look like one now," Alex insisted, resting a hand on Elly's knee and squeezing gently. Elly sat straight, her shoulders back, confident as anything, or at least pretending to be, and Alex wished they were at the farm already, near a bed, or at least had some privacy.

"If you say so," Elly said.

"I do." Alex took her seat and started the engine. Not long now, though the road from Cardston would be slow, bumpy, and scattered with gravel. It would seem like forever, with Elly's knees pressing against her hips. She wanted to be between Elly's legs, but not like that.

She took the turn out of the parking lot faster than she'd intended, and Elly's knees squeezed her hips tight. It was torture of the best kind.

Chapter Seven

When Alex made the turn onto the one-lane road, the last short stretch to the farm, Elly could hardly sit still. The bike slowed and Alex pushed up her visor.

"Not far now," she said. "Sit still just a little longer. You're like a kid."

She was like a kid, Elly knew, a kid waiting for the promised treat.

Once Alex pulled into the drive and killed the engine, she could barely stay still while Alex made sure the bike was steady and put down the kickstand, dismounting. As soon as it was clear, Elly slid off the bike, landing on the grass and gravel with both feet and taking off her helmet.

She was home.

The farm looked much the same, though the grass had grown a little longer, and the clover was in full bloom. Elly inhaled deeply. It was perfect.

Alex unlocked the saddlebags and took out Elly's gym bag from one, her own bag from another, and then the grocery bag from the back. "Lead the way, El."

Elly skipped up the steps to the front porch, hitching up the chaps as she went. She unzipped her jacket pocket and took out her keys, opening the front screen door—which didn't sag or screech anymore—and then unlocked the front door, pushing it open. She stepped inside, the rag mat muting her footsteps, and moved aside to let Alex enter with all their gear. She set her helmet on the bottom step, then shed her jacket and hung it over the knob at the bottom of the banister.

"Let me take that," she said, grabbing her bag and the groceries from Alex. She set her bag down by the steps, then went through to the kitchen. The floor squeaked under her steps, but she hardly noticed. All she could think was that she was home.

"This place looks like it did back then," Alex said, coming through the door, combing her fingers through her dark hair. "You haven't changed a thing, have you?"

Elly shut the fridge after putting the perishables inside and straightened. "I haven't changed anything," she said. "It doesn't need changing."

"It's cozy." Alex flopped down onto the sofa that faced into the kitchen, on the other side of the large Formica kitchen table.

"It's home." Elly took a glass down from the shelf and went to the sink, running the water for a minute before she put the glass under the tap, filling it. She drank deeply, quenching the thirst from the ride. "Want a glass?"

"Sure." Alex came over, took the glass that Elly handed her, and stood beside her at the sink. She filled it half-full, then drank it down as fast as Elly had.

"More?" Elly asked.

"Sure, but not water," Alex replied. "You've been driving me nuts all day, El. All that squirming. I'm impatient." She hooked her fingers in Elly's belt loops and Elly found herself snugly against Alex, their hips resting against each other. Alex bent her head and Elly lifted hers, meeting her halfway for the kiss.

Alex's scent surrounded her, a heady combination of leather and her light, surprisingly flowery perfume that she couldn't name. She wanted this moment to last, and it did, stretching out into minutes, until they finally broke apart, both breathing heavily. Resting her head on Alex's leather-clad shoulder, she closed her eyes. "I wish I hadn't waited so long," she said, her voice barely a whisper. She felt Alex cup the back of her neck, stroking in gentle circles.

"You had my number all that time?"

Elly nodded, not lifting her head.

"And you never called." Alex sounded disappointed, and her hand on Elly's neck stilled.

Elly didn't know what to say.

The clomp of heavy boots on the porch kept her from having to say anything at all.

"Elly? You here?" Jack called, giving a perfunctory knock on the screen door.

Elly lifted her head and she and Alex broke apart.

"I'm here," she called back. She heard the screen slam shut as Jack stepped inside, and she met him in the hall.

"I wondered whose bike that—" Jack took in her jeans and leather chaps, his brows rising. "Oh."

She heard Alex behind her, felt the edges of her jacket brush her back and her hand at her waist. When she glanced back, she saw that Alex had locked gazes with Jack, a challenging look in her eyes and in the set of her jaw.

"You staying for long?" Jack asked, his gaze moving back to Elly. He didn't acknowledge Alex.

"Just overnight."

"I'm working the fields on your section to the north today," he continued, "so if it's all right, I might pop in a little later for a glass of water and such."

"That's fine." Elly heard Alex's indrawn breath but ignored it. Jack was welcome, as always. "Just knock."

"Of course." At the door, he glanced back once more. "See you later. Nice leathers, by the way. Didn't think I'd ever see you wearing any."

Alex's exhalation warmed the back of Elly's neck. "Does he always just show up like that?"

"He's leasing the land from me—he's allowed to be here," she replied. "He probably wondered if someone had broken in."

"That's a bit scary, that someone can just walk in."

Elly followed Alex back into the kitchen. "It's just Jack, and anyway, it's different out here. I hardly ever even lock the doors."

"Really?" Alex shrugged off her jacket and dropped it on the sofa. "That's risky."

"It's not Calgary," Elly replied. "I know almost everyone in the whole district." She looked out the window over the sink, saw the fields stretching out to the horizon, freshly plowed and ready for planting.

"It sure isn't."

"So what brought you out here last year then?" She hadn't asked at the time—they'd been otherwise occupied and by the time her brain had cleared enough for questions, Alex was gone. She knew Alex was a city girl, but her suspicion of the country—there really was no other word for it—was a surprise.

"My grandmother's birthday. I was looking for a gift, something she might like. Something vintage. A friend told me a lot of the smaller towns had good antique shops."

"There are quite a few. I'm pretty sure every town between Calgary and the US border has at least one." Elly's stomach grumbled, and though it wasn't quite dinnertime, she wanted something to eat. "Sandwiches for dinner, or cereal?"

"Either sounds good to me, unless you're hiding some other food."

"I wish I'd bought something more. I'm in the mood for a feast."

"A feast would be fantastic. But if there's still a bit of your father's whisky left, we could have a glass for dessert."

"Might be." Elly opened the cupboard above the fridge. A bottle of whisky sat there, looking dusty and forlorn. A couple of inches of amber liquor sat in the bottle.

"Oh, good"—Alex came up behind her—"we're in luck." She reached over Elly and took down the bottle, setting it on the kitchen table. Elly took the sandwich ingredients from the fridge and set out four pieces of bread. She made the sandwiches up quickly, and put them each onto a plate while Alex observed.

"Want a glass of milk with it?" Elly asked, taking the plates to the table.

"Just water's fine. Milk and whisky don't go so well together." Alex made a face and Elly chuckled.

"I hadn't thought of that." She hardly ever drank whisky. She poured two glasses of water and brought them to the table. They settled across from each other, and little was said while they scarfed down their meals.

Alex finished first, while Elly still worked on the second half of her sandwich. "You eat too slow," she teased, taking a sip of her water.

"You eat too fast," Elly countered. "You should be savoring your food."

Alex shrugged. "Habit. Comes from working in the bar too long."

She rose and took her plate to the sink, then went into the hallway, coming back with her phone in hand. She fiddled with it, then frowned.

"No service here," Elly said apologetically. "If you need to make a call you'll have to use the house phone."

"Thought I'd check my texts," Alex said, sitting back down and placing her phone on the table. She grimaced. "Guess not. I didn't think we were that far in the middle of nowhere."

"It's the hill," Elly said. "It interferes with the signal. I'd turn your roaming off if I were you. Sometimes we'll get a signal but it'll be from a tower across the border, and that gets expensive."

Alex frowned. "Right." She fiddled with her phone some more, then set it back down, tapping her fingers on the tabletop in an uneven tempo.

Elly finished her sandwich and rose to place her plate in the sink. "But we have lots to do aside from texting."

"I don't know how you could manage out here without your phone," Alex replied. "I'd go nuts. I'm going nuts already."

"You get used to it. And if someone really wanted to get in touch with me here, they could call. My number's in the book."

"People use phonebooks, still?" Alex laughed. "How weird. What else do you do out here?"

"I did work at the diner in town," Elly said, trying to keep the defensiveness from her voice, "but when I wasn't there, I used to go walking in the fields, down to the river. Or I'd read."

"Not cleaning?" Alex's gaze moved to the hallway, beyond which lay the entryway and its attached mudroom with its clutter.

Elly hardly saw that now; she was so used to it. Her dad had kept a collection of odds and ends, just in case he needed something for a repair. She hated that Alex didn't understand the reasons behind keeping such things. They were on a farm, not in the middle of the city next to a big-box store. Alex's words had turned her father's foresight into a mess to be thrown away.

"I meant to, but—"

"I'm teasing. It's no big deal," Alex said, interrupting her explanation. "What's a farmhouse without clutter? It's like an antique store without price tags and a sales clerk."

Elly smiled, though it was tentative. "I will clean it, one day soon."

"Will you sell?"

Elly's heart stuttered and her breath caught in her throat. "I'd never sell. It's family."

"A farmhouse is family?" Alex sounded puzzled.

"The land, the farmhouse, it's been in the family for generations," Elly clarified. "I could never give it up."

"Must be nice to have something from family," Alex mused. She picked up her phone, then put it down again when she seemed to realize that it was useless out here, her hand clenching into a momentary fist.

"Don't you?" Elly asked.

Alex looked down at the table, her finger tracing a crack in the Formica. "Not really. But it's not something I want to get into, to be honest."

"Oh." Trying not to fidget with discomfort, Elly rose from the table again, going to the stove and lifting the kettle from the burner. She filled it with water from the tap and put it on to boil. Her grandmother had always said that tea was the best thing for solving problems. *And if it doesn't work to solve them, then at least you have a cup of tea,* Elly remembered her saying. She heard Alex sigh, and the click of the cell phone on the Formica once more.

"Making tea?" Alex asked, her voice sounding more cheery.

"Tea is best for what ails you," Elly said, quoting another saying of her grandmother's.

"It is," Alex agreed, "but even better if it has a touch of whisky in it, for fortification."

"We can arrange that."

"But before we do," Alex said, coming nearer, "we should be reliving last year." She drew Elly into her arms, bending her head to kiss her. Elly parted her lips, allowing her access, remembering back to that other evening and Alex kissing her while the pasta boiled on the stove.

A crunch of gravel and the sound of an engine broke them apart.

"Whose car is that?" Alex asked, looking out the kitchen window. An old navy-blue Buick rumbled along the road, slowing to a stop before turning into the driveway. Elly sighed. She wanted just a few hours alone with Alex. Jack must have told his grandmother that she was back.

"That's Mrs. Calderwood. She's Jack's granny, and a bit of a gossip. I'm sure she's come out to see you for herself."

"People actually do that? That's a bit *Little House on the Prairie,* isn't it?"

"She does." It wasn't the 1800s, and Elly resented the implication.

"They don't call before coming over?" Alex was incredulous.

"You've never lived in the country, have you?" Alex was such a city girl, and her comments, though not meant to hurt, stung in their excess. "People just drop by for a visit, unannounced. They're usually on their way and just thought they'd stop in, as Mrs. Calderwood always tells me. It's a small-town thing, I think."

"It would drive me nuts," Alex replied.

Elly went to the front door, opening it just as Mrs. Calderwood made her way up the porch steps.

"Oh, there you are, dear," she said, carefully navigating each step, her cane in one hand, the other clutching the rail. "Jack said you had come back for a visit, so I thought I'd stop by and say hello. It's just not the same since you left. The diner's not so pleasant without your smiling face."

Mrs. Calderwood gave her a hug, and Elly returned it, gently, being careful of Mrs. Calderwood's fragile form. The widow was getting close to eighty years old, and she wasn't as hale as she used to be, though she'd never admit it.

"Would you like a cup of tea?" Elly asked as Mrs. Calderwood stepped over the threshold. "I've just put the kettle on."

"That would be lovely, dear." She followed Elly through to the kitchen, her lavender-water perfume scenting the air. When she saw Alex, she stopped.

"Mrs. Calderwood, this is my friend Alex Bellerose," Elly said by way of introduction, watching Alex carefully, hoping she wouldn't make a snide remark.

"How do you do?" Mrs. Calderwood said, quite formally, holding out her hand to Alex, who rose and came around the table.

"It's nice to meet you," Alex replied, taking the woman's hand. Elly relaxed a fraction.

"I don't know if Elly's told you about me, but I've known her since she was a babe in arms," Mrs. Calderwood said.

"She hadn't mentioned it. I'd bet you have a lot of stories to tell, ma'am."

"Don't stand on ceremony with me, my dear. I'm not old enough to be called ma'am. Just Doris will do, or Mrs. Calderwood, if you must. I do have many stories." She chuckled. "When Elly and Jack were little, they used to race around on the lawn, running through the sprinkler Elly's pa would set up for them. Of course, Jack's always been sweet on our Elly."

Elly stifled a wince, watching as Mrs. Calderwood took a seat at the table. The kettle began to whistle and she went to the stove, turning off the heat and moving the kettle to a cool burner. She grabbed a couple of tea bags from the tin in the cupboard and plopped them into the old Brown Betty teapot of her grandmother's, pouring the hot water over them.

"I can see why Jack would be sweet on her," she heard Alex say. "I mean, who wouldn't?"

"But Elly's never been sweet on him," Mrs. Calderwood replied. "I just don't understand it."

Elly turned and caught Alex's glance. Since Mrs. Calderwood had her back to her, she shrugged and made a face. Alex tried to hold back her smile.

"I suppose perhaps Jack isn't Elly's type," Alex said diplomatically.

"I suppose not."

Elly brought the teapot to the table and went back for three cups and the sugar bowl and the milk from the fridge.

"Thank you, dear." Mrs. Calderwood pushed her cup over closer to Elly. "Would you pour me a cup now? I don't like for it to get too strong anymore. It keeps me awake nights."

Elly poured her tea and then set the teapot down. She needed it to steep longer, and when Alex nodded, she sat back down in her chair.

"So, is that machine out there yours?" Mrs. Calderwood asked, looking at Alex.

"The bike? It sure is."

"A bit much for a lady, isn't it?"

Elly bit her lip and tried not to smile. Alex shook her head

"Not too much at all. Have you ever been on one?"

"Goodness me, no. I'd be too worried about falling off." Mrs. Calderwood looked scandalized, yet amused.

"You really should try it," Alex said, and Elly couldn't decide if she was being serious or not.

"If I were a few years younger, I might just," Mrs. Calderwood replied. "Elly, are you becoming a biker now? Should I be worried?"

Elly felt her cheeks flush. "Only just the once," she said. "I don't think I'd ever buy a bike or anything."

"Sensible." Mrs. Calderwood nodded to herself.

"Never?" Alex's question was directed at Elly. "Really?"

Elly shrugged. "I don't think so. It's just so…I don't know… dangerous."

Alex sighed and took up the bottle of whisky, pouring a dollop into the bottom of her teacup before she poured in the tea.

"You take tea the way my husband did," Mrs. Calderwood observed.

"It's the best way." Alex took a sip. "Especially after a long ride." Her gaze flicked up to Elly's, and she winked.

"You came all the way from Calgary today?"

"We did stop a couple of times," Elly said. "But it was a long ride. Not nearly as comfortable as a car." She poured her own cup of tea to cover her embarrassment, hoping that Mrs. Calderwood wouldn't recognize Alex's double entendre.

"You don't speed, do you?" Mrs. Calderwood looked at Alex.

"No, I don't," she replied. "Not with a passenger."

"So you do, then, sometimes?" Elly couldn't resist asking. It had been a blatant lie, but to Mrs. Calderwood, the truth would have been a bad thing.

"On occasion. But it's perfectly safe."

Mrs. Calderwood tsked. "Not much to protect you from the road, or other cars. Or"—she shuddered—"trucks."

"I'm a skilled rider," Alex said, sounding defensive. "I've taken all the courses, and I pay attention to the road." She looked at Elly, but Elly didn't know what to say. Did Alex expect her to back her up? Several times that afternoon, she'd thought Alex had been going way over the speed limit, but she couldn't be sure. Being on the bike made almost every speed seem too fast.

"You'd be better off without the bike," Mrs. Calderwood proclaimed. Elly cringed, seeing Alex stiffen. It was just Mrs. Calderwood's way, but she had no way of explaining it to Alex, not while the widow was still there.

Alex rose. "If you'll excuse me," she said, "I need to make sure the bike is tucked out of the weather, in case it rains tonight." She left the kitchen, her tea only half-drunk.

"I hope you're not riding with her all the time," Mrs. Calderwood said, turning to Elly and sipping her tea. "It's just so dangerous. What would your parents think?"

"I don't know what they'd think," Elly said, her throat tight. "It was never a subject that came up."

"I'm sorry to mention them, dear," Mrs. Calderwood said, patting her hand. "I know you must miss them desperately. A year isn't very long at all."

Elly nodded, looking down into her teacup, pressing her lips together. A year wasn't very long, hardly any time at all. And being away from the farm made it worse, especially now that she was back. Her apartment in the city had no reminders of them, and it wasn't home.

"Oh, Elly." Mrs. Calderwood's voice was soft, and Elly looked up. The widow was teary-eyed, and at the sight, Elly had to swallow and blink hard in order to keep her own tears at bay. Mrs. Calderwood patted her hand again. "I should go. You need a bit of time, I'm sure."

She rose from the table and Elly rose with her, walking her to the door. "I'm glad you came over," she said. "Don't mind Alex, though. She doesn't mean to be standoffish."

"Not a worry. That one's used to having her own way, I can tell. Reminds me of me, back then. Now, if you need anything, you call me, you hear?"

"I will."

Elly walked Mrs. Calderwood to her car. Alex and the bike were nowhere to be seen, but Elly knew she hadn't gone far. She'd have heard the engine, after all.

Mrs. Calderwood pulled out of the driveway and drove slowly down the road, giving Elly a wave as she went. Only once the car had disappeared over the hill did Alex reappear, coming around the side of the house.

"So she's gone?" Alex asked, coming to stand beside her.

"She is," Elly confirmed. "I wish you'd stayed. She's actually quite nice, you know."

Alex shrugged. "That type is never really nice. My own grandmother is like that, a busybody, nosy sort. You couldn't do a damn thing without her finding out and scolding you for it."

"Still, Mrs. Calderwood is a friend."

"Some friend." Alex turned toward the house.

Elly trailed her back inside, frowning. "I know she's not always the nicest of people, but she means well." She tried to explain, but her words felt hollow.

"Don't worry about me, El. I'll be fine." Alex pulled off her boots and headed back into the kitchen. "Are you sure we should stay overnight? If we left now, we could be back not too late."

"That's a long ride for an evening," Elly said. "And we just got here. I don't want to go back yet."

Alex sat down at the table and took a sip of her tea. She rose again and took her cup to the sink, dumping the cold tea and whisky. She filled her cup from the pot and retraced her steps. "Just a thought," she said, adding a dollop of whisky to her cup.

Elly took up her own cup and refilled it. "You don't like it here much, do you?" She had to ask.

"It's all right," Alex said. "I'm just not used to it. I like the city. Love it. And being without my phone is driving me nuts." She touched her phone where it lay on the table, spinning it on the faded gray surface. "I keep wanting to check for messages, then remember I can't."

"We can do other things," Elly said. "Do you like board games? Or we could talk, or read, or…" She couldn't think of anything else. Well, besides *that*.

"Board games?" Alex's doubtful tone startled her.

"Yeah. They can be fun, you know. Didn't you ever play Monopoly? It can get pretty cutthroat."

"I figured there wasn't much else to do in the evenings but shag," Alex remarked. "I bet that's why farmers always had lots of kids."

Elly coughed, sputtering on her tea. "Not in my house. I was an only child."

"Birth control," Alex said wisely. "But before then, lots of kids."

Once she'd regained her control, Elly asked, "Do you have any siblings?"

"Yeah, but I haven't seen her in ages. I'm not even sure where she's living."

"You don't even know where your sister lives?" Elly couldn't hide her surprise. If she had a family still, she'd know where all of them were and would see them as often as she could. She couldn't imagine not knowing.

"She was in Vancouver a while back, but she moves around a lot." Alex shrugged. "It's always been that way."

"Oh." Elly stifled the feelings of pity. Not everyone's family was close like her own had been.

"I don't mind," Alex said. "She's five years older, so we never really played together much as kids, and she left home as soon as she could. But I don't really want to talk about family, there's not much to say, and what there is sucks."

Elly turned her teacup back and forth, not sure what to say to that.

Alex rose again and paced to the kitchen window. "Looks like it might rain," she said conversationally, filling the silence.

"I like it when it rains," Elly said. "In my bedroom, you can hear it on the roof. I used to fall asleep to it. I miss that, in the apartment. I can't hear a thing."

"Too bad you didn't get a top-floor apartment," Alex said, turning back to her.

"I could have, but it was too expensive." Elly finished her tea and brought the cup to the sink. She glanced out the window at the sky. The clouds hung dark on the horizon, quickly getting closer.

"I put the bike in the barn out back," Alex said, "in case you're wondering. It was empty in there so I figured it would be all right."

"It'll stay dry there," Elly replied.

"You know, for a farm, there sure aren't any animals around."

"We had a few, but not many. Once my father passed away, my mother couldn't keep up with all the work, so we sold most of them."

"I suppose you had to muck out stalls as a kid."

"All the time."

"Gross. I don't know how you could stand it." Alex shuddered.

"It wasn't too bad." It had been life, and she hadn't minded it most of the time.

"At least you don't need to now."

Elly wanted to be able to. That would mean she'd be able to afford the place, instead of being in a tiny apartment hearing sirens every night. She looked out the window again. No sirens here, no ambulances speeding by. Just fields.

Alex brought her cup to the sink and rinsed it out. "What shall we do now?"

"Want to see the house? The rest of it, I mean?"

"Sure. How much of it is there?"

Elly smiled to herself. "More than you might think."

Chapter Eight

Alex followed Elly from the kitchen and back into the hall. She opened a door Alex hadn't noticed, just below the stairs, and pulled the chain on a light. A set of wooden steps was illuminated, leading to a cement floor.

"It's mostly storage down here," Elly said. "But we used to play down here too, in the summertime when it was too hot to do anything else. There were lots of great hiding spots among the boxes. One time Jack climbed up into the ceiling, hiding on top of the ventilation. We wouldn't have found him except for the noise."

"Did he fall off?"

"Collapsed part of the tin. It made an awful racket, and my dad wasn't pleased. Jack was too heavy to be up there." Elly shook her head. "I'll need to go through all the boxes, eventually."

"Your parents kept a lot of stuff." Alex had never seen such a collection of clutter in her life. She'd certainly never had it in her own place, or when she still lived at home.

"They didn't want to throw anything out if it could be used again." Elly shrugged. "Their families lived through a lot of hardship, so they learned those habits." She peeked into a box and pulled out a photo album.

"Makes sense, but it'll be hell to clean when you sell."

Elly opened the album, and Alex peered over her shoulder, trying not to block the light. The pictures were old, starting to yellow, but from the looks of the clothes worn by their subjects, they were perhaps thirty or forty years old.

“Who are they?” Alex pointed to a young couple mugging for the camera. The guy had shoulder-length curly hair, and the girl was short and slim, with a pixie cut.

“Mom and Dad,” Elly said, touching the edge of the photo with a fingertip. “That was high school, 1971, I think. Maybe a bit earlier.”

“You look like her.”

“A bit.”

Alex looked more closely at the photo, and several others around it. “I can see the resemblance with both of them.”

“I got my dad’s curls,” Elly replied, her voice shaky. She closed the album and put it back in the box, sliding the lid closed. “Sorry, it hurts to look at them.”

“They weren’t very old when they died.” The gentle statement came out more like a question, though Alex hadn’t meant it to sound that way.

“Car crash, and cancer.” Elly sighed. She turned away, heading back upstairs. Alex followed, shutting the basement door.

“I’m sorry.” She knew it wasn’t much, but she had to say something.

“It’s all right,” Elly said, resting her hand on the banister. “It’s still hard sometimes, though.”

Alex rested her hand over Elly’s, wanting to do more, but not sure what to do. Her family hadn’t really been affectionate, and any funerals she’d been to had been straitlaced, stiff-upper-lip type affairs.

Elly stepped forward, and Alex found herself embracing her, the movement surprisingly natural and easy. Alex stroked slowly down Elly’s back, up and down, and she felt Elly relax against her, taking a deep breath. They stayed that way for several minutes, until Elly straightened and eased herself away.

“Thanks.” Elly paused at the front door, seeming more herself. “If you want, we can go out to the shed. That’s my favorite place. If it does start to rain, we can always run back. It’s not far.”

“Sure.” Alex sat down on the stair to pull on her boots, and Elly laced up a pair of battered old sneakers that sat next to the door. Once outside, they headed around the side of the house. Alex had seen the shed when she went to move the bike, but it had several steps up and she hadn’t wanted to shift the bike that far. Elly took a set of keys from her pocket and unlocked the door. It didn't look like much from the outside, just a weathered gray wood building, past its prime.

"So, why do you like the shed?" Alex asked.

Elly turned on the light. There was a worktable, and tools hung along one wall, scraps of wood piled in a bin near the door, but then there were shelves—shelves filled with bric-a-brac, an antique hunter's dream. Tons more clutter. Alex could picture at least two Dumpsters filled with the stuff Elly's parents had accumulated.

Alex stepped around Elly and went to one of the shelves, lifting a box of washing powder that sat unopened. The label was old-fashioned, a simple typeface and basic color scheme that she'd never seen on that brand, not ever. Next to it were two sets of salt and pepper shakers, one a set of smiling tomatoes, and the other a fancier, though tarnished, silver. She picked up each of these in turn.

"See what I mean about the shed?" Elly stepped up beside her.

"What is all this stuff?"

"Family stuff, some from my grandparents, or great-grandparents, that sort of thing. My dad didn't know what to do with it, so it ended up out here." Elly lifted one of the tomatoes. "These were my great-grandmother's. She bought them at the store in town, way back when. The silver ones are from her grandmother, but she never liked them as much, as she thought they were too fancy for everyday. She told my mother that she wouldn't have anyone thinking they were too good."

"Do you know stories like that for everything here?" Alex swept an arm toward the shelves, piled as they were with various odds and ends.

"Pretty much." Elly moved to a shelf on the other wall, rising up on her toes to grab a box from a higher shelf. A wave of dust covered her when the box tilted down, and she sneezed, twice, then again. She turned and set the box on the worktable and lifted the lid. Alex peered in, but all she could see was plastic.

"What is it?"

Elly sneezed again and rubbed her nose. "Teacups." She lifted the plastic carefully and revealed a mass of crumpled paper inside the bag. Setting it on the worktable, she drew out one of the lumps of paper, unwrapping it slowly to reveal a delicate china cup with a gold rim and painted with tiny pink roses. "My mother always worried that they'd be broken if we used them or kept them in the kitchen, so she wrapped them up and stuck them out here. A shame, really. They're so pretty."

Alex didn't quite see the fascination. A teacup was a teacup; she was sure she'd seen many similar ones at thrift shops and the like, but she didn't want to say as much to Elly, who handled the cup with the care one might give to a Ming vase.

"My great-great-grandmother brought these with her from Germany," Elly explained, carefully wrapping up the teacup once more.

"You should bring them into the house," Alex said. "Use them."

"I don't know." Elly bit her lip, putting the wrapped cup back into the bag and placing the bag carefully in the box.

"Good Lord, El. No one will scold you," Alex said, giving her a gentle nudge. "And we can have tea in them in the morning, like old-fashioned ladies."

Elly chuckled. "You, old-fashioned?" she teased.

"I can pretend. If you can look past the jeans."

"I'm sure I can." Elly put the lid back on the box. She glanced around the shed. "I don't think there's anything new since I was last in here."

"You should take the salt and pepper shakers with you back to Calgary," Alex suggested. "They're small enough to fit in the saddlebag."

"I should." Elly went to the shelf and picked up the two tomatoes. She handed them to Alex. "Let's go back to the house." She picked up the box and went to the door, peering out.

"Raining yet?" Alex came up behind her. She held a tomato in each hand and felt rather silly.

"Not yet, but it will be. Can you get the light?"

Alex pulled the chain, plunging the shed into darkness. They stepped outside and Elly locked the door. Alex felt a spatter of rain hit her cheek.

"Hurry," she urged, nudging Elly in the back. They scrambled across the grass, now damp, and toward the house. As they reached the covered porch, the sky broke open and rain spilled down, pattering heavily on the gravel drive, pinging off the eaves troughs.

"That was close," Elly said. Alex pushed the door open

The rain struck the kitchen window as they brought their finds into the kitchen, placing them on the table. The tomato salt and pepper shakers were bright against the dull gray of the Formica, but they looked as if they belonged. Alex pushed them to the center of the table, bracketing the napkin holder that sat there.

Elly opened the box again and lifted out the bag. She slowly unwrapped the teacups, all six of them, and placed them carefully in their saucers. Three were patterned with the roses they'd seen earlier, and the other three were patterned with delicate purple violets. "I think there were four of each, originally," Elly said, fingering the gilt rim of one cup. "Do you think we could fit these in the saddlebags too?"

Alex calculated their size. "We should be able to, but not in the box. Wrapped in paper and plastic they should be safe enough. I think."

"Good." Elly's smile, absent since the conclusion of Mrs. Calderwood's visit, returned.

Elly did seem in her element here, relaxed and moving about, puttering in the kitchen, and finally sitting on the worn sofa in the living room. Far different from the tension that seemed to fill her when they'd been at the bar, or even anywhere in the city. Maybe that was what home was like, and security, the certainty of family. Alex didn't know, but a flicker of envy and worry shot through her.

This wasn't her place.

She picked up her phone, glancing at it before she slid it into her pocket. Still no signal. Once they hit Cardston tomorrow, she'd check for messages.

"Come sit down, relax," Elly said. Alex glanced up. Elly held out her hand, wiggling her fingers. Alex moved to the sofa and sank down next to Elly, resting her arm over Elly's shoulders. Elly snuggled in, happily, and Alex started to relax, allowing herself to sink back into the soft cushions. She put her feet up on the edge of the coffee table. The rain rattled the eaves troughs.

"This is nice," Alex said, her voice low. Nice, but not her place.

"It's just about perfect," Elly replied. She rested her head on Alex's shoulder and Alex looked down at her, stiffening.

Too much, too close. This wasn't friends and occasional lovers but had veered into girlfriend territory, and the thought of being shackled made her stiffen further and pull away, easing Elly's head from her shoulder.

Elly shifted away, looking puzzled and a bit hurt, her expression bewildered.

"Bathroom," Alex said, rising. She headed toward the kitchen, pausing.

"Turn left," Elly said, "and just under the stairs."

"Right."

Alex locked the door behind her and stared into the mirror above the sink, a slight crack running partway down its side. She breathed deeply, but the tension wouldn't leave her. She didn't want to stay here in the middle of nowhere with Elly, who obviously wanted them to be more than what they were. It was a bad idea to come out here, and she didn't know what she'd been thinking. By the time she exited, she was determined to convince Elly to go back to Calgary.

Elly still sat on the sofa where Alex had left her, but she had picked up an old *Reader's Digest* magazine and was flipping through it, pausing now and then to read a page.

"I think we should head back," Alex said, stopping at the edge of the living room where it met the kitchen. Purposely out of reach.

"What for?" Elly frowned, putting down the magazine on a stack of others sitting on the coffee table. "We've hardly been here."

"It's too quiet here," Alex said, not wanting to bluntly say what was on her mind. "It's driving me nuts, and I really need to check my messages."

"Parry's hasn't burned down," Elly said, her voice sounding sharp for the first time, "and it's not like being out of reach for one night will hurt."

"Maybe not to you," Alex retorted, crossing her arms, and shifting from foot to foot.

"If you need a phone, there's one in the kitchen," Elly said. "But I don't want to go anywhere until tomorrow. Being on a motorcycle on the highway in the middle of the night is not my idea of fun."

"It's perfectly safe."

"No, it isn't," Elly said. "Alex, just relax. Come sit down, and we'll watch a movie or something."

Alex bit back her next words, knowing that even if she threatened it, she'd never knowingly strand someone without a vehicle, and Elly had no way of getting back to the city without her. "What movies do you have?" she asked reluctantly.

"There's a shelf there by the TV," Elly said, gesturing. "Pick whichever one you want. I like them all."

Pushing down her frustration, Alex scanned the shelf. All VHS tapes, and all dating from the 80s and 90s. Not really her thing. She took a closer look and finally, for a lack of better choices, settled on *Mrs. Doubtfire*. If nothing else, the comedy would keep her distracted.

"How's this?" She held up the tape in its worn cardboard case.

Elly brightened. "It was one of my favorites growing up."

Alex bent and put the tape into the dusty VCR and Elly turned on the TV. Alex watched the static give way to the film studio intros and then the opening credits. She turned, but instead of going to sit back down next to Elly, she chose the recliner. It creaked as she sat down and rocked back slightly, catching her by surprise. She heard Elly sigh but ignored it, focusing on the film.

❖

The evening darkened into night, and Alex was glad that the film had kept her attention, though she occasionally would glance over at Elly, who watched the screen, smiling and laughing at all the important bits.

When the film ended, Elly clicked off the TV and stretched, looking over at her. "I haven't seen that in ages. Good pick."

"It was good." Alex stifled a yawn. Elly rose to her feet, stretching again.

"Come to bed?" Elly asked.

Alex swallowed. Bed meant sleeping together, actually sleeping. Which meant that she wouldn't sleep at all, and Elly would get the wrong idea.

"Do you have a guest room?" Alex asked.

"What? Yeah, we do, but you slept with me before. Why not now?"

"I just don't," Alex said. She knew it was a cop-out, but the decision had been made.

"Then why did you come here?" Elly asked, her voice becoming sharp again, strident. "Why did you even bother?"

"I just don't," Alex repeated herself. "I can't sleep with anyone else overnight. I don't ever stay."

Elly crossed her arms over her chest. "Did you even want to come out here with me?"

Alex wanted to answer yes, but she didn't know why she'd

suggested the trip. To get out on the bike, she supposed. Nothing drew her more than the open road.

"It was a good ride," she said, shrugging. "And I figured you might like the bike, but obviously you didn't, from what you said to Mrs. Calderwood."

"So that's what this is about? Some sort of stupid punishment?" Elly shook her head. "Fine. I'll get out some clean sheets and you can make up the bed in the guest room. It's down here." She stalked off into the hall, and Alex heard the linoleum squeaking under her feet. Damn. That wasn't what she'd meant to do, but there was no helping it now.

❖

Elly woke when the sun filtered in through the windowpane, falling across the bed. She wanted to stay in bed, luxuriate in the warmth, in being at home, but then last night filtered back into her waking mind. She sighed and pushed the quilts off her, rising. She grabbed her robe from the end of the bed and put it on over her cotton nightdress. The stairs creaked as she went down to the kitchen and put the kettle on for tea. She drew her robe around her, peeking in on Alex, who still slept heavily, her dark hair a mess around her head, and moved out onto the front porch, breathing in the crisp morning air, seeing the light mist that hung over the fields. It would burn off soon enough, as the sun rose higher and the day grew warmer, but for now it seemed almost mystical, turning the freshly plowed field into a place where fairies might creep.

She heard the whistle of the kettle and retreated indoors, hurrying to lift it from the burner. By the time she had the tea steeping and a piece of toast in the toaster, Alex had stumbled out of the bedroom, her hair still askew. It looked as if she'd pulled on last night's clothes. She rubbed her eyes and pulled out a chair, settling in at the kitchen table.

"Sleep well?" Elly asked, taking down two mugs from the cupboard.

"Mostly. I woke up once, wasn't sure where I was. I think it's too quiet here for me."

Elly poured her a cup of tea and brought it over. She wanted to tell Alex to get out, but her mother's hostessing rules kept her from saying anything. Never be rude to a guest. And maybe Alex would explain what had happened last night, really explain. "I love the quiet here," she said, purposefully ignoring the elephant in the room. "I'm still not used to all the noise in the city." Her toast popped and she went to butter it and smother it in raspberry jam.

"You seem really at home here," Alex said. "I'm surprised you left it."

Elly took a deep breath, focusing on smoothing the jam over her toast. She didn't want to leave today, either. "I couldn't make enough money to live out here," she said finally.

"Will you sell it once you find a job in town?"

Sell. She couldn't bear the thought, but Alex kept bringing it up.

"I don't know. I don't want to. It's home."

"Did you hear from that company you interviewed with?"

Elly shook her head, bringing her toast and tea to the table. She sat down. "I hope I will soon. There's toast, and cereal. I hadn't thought to buy much else for breakfast since we weren't staying longer."

"Toast is fine," Alex said, but she didn't move. She drank more of her tea. "When did you want to leave? I have to work at four o'clock, so we really should be out of here by ten. It'll give us a bit of extra time, and then I can have an hour to relax before I have to work."

"Do you have a long shift?" Elly couldn't imagine working after a day's ride on the motorcycle.

"Four until two. Or until whenever they let me go. Karaoke night is always busy. You going to come?"

"Probably not," Elly replied, apologetic.

"Had enough singing for one lifetime?"

Alex's voice was teasing, but Elly still felt a flush rise.

"I didn't mind it that much, but I don't think I could do it every week. Once a month, maybe, if that." More, if Alex hadn't been so cold. She bit into her toast, savoring the sweetness of the jam, the pop of the tiny seeds between her teeth.

"I'll get you back up onstage again," Alex said.

Elly didn't answer; she finished eating her toast and took a gulp of her cooling tea.

"Or not," Alex added. "Unless you want to."

"Not this week."

Alex drank the last of her tea and rose, seeming awkward. "I'll shower before we leave, if that's all right. Do you have a hair dryer?"

"In the cupboard," Elly said. "And there should be towels in the closet next to the bathroom. Help yourself."

Alex put her cup in the sink and left, heading to grab her things, then to commandeer the bathroom. Elly leaned back in her chair, looking over the kitchen and into the living room. The quilt that rested over the back of the sofa was rumpled from when she'd sat there last night, and she rose to straighten it, smoothing out the wrinkles. Her mother had made that quilt, after her father had decided against the expense of new furniture. It hid some of the worn spots on the sofa's upholstery.

She was tempted to take the quilt with her as well, but her mother would have cringed to have the sofa looking old and ugly, so she left it where it was. The pipes rattled as Alex turned on the water, and Elly hurried upstairs to get changed and pack up her things. If Alex lingered in the shower, she'd have a bit of time to herself, to soak in the atmosphere, to sit out on the porch and watch the mist dissipate. She pulled on her clean underwear, bra, and shirt, and yesterday's jeans, and stuffed the dirty ones into her bag. She made the bed and then headed back downstairs, dropping her bag at the foot. She moved out onto the porch and sat on the step, the boards cool under her stockinged feet. Birds chirped and rustled about in the nearby bushes, and when she looked across the fields, she could see a tractor the size of a thimble moving across the horizon. That must be Jack, already hard at work. Her father had done the same for years, getting up with the dawn and working until lunch. He'd eat a hearty meal, then be back at it for the afternoon.

Elly leaned forward, resting her elbows on her knees. Her parents had always hoped she'd have kids, and stay and work the land, but she never had. If she could, she'd stay, but she couldn't work the land by herself. It was too much for one person, and she'd never known how her father did it all those years. She had helped with chores, and her mother had done a lot, but most of it had been her father's blood, sweat, and tears keeping the food on the table.

The screen door clattered behind her, but she didn't turn.

"You going to shower?" Alex asked, coming to sit next to her on the step. Her cheeks were flushed, and her hair was still damp in parts, though she'd blown it mostly dry. "There should be enough water left."

"I'll shower when I get home," Elly said. Alex nodded.

"It's nice out here with the mist," she observed. "Is that Jack out there?" She gestured to the tractor, which had come closer since she'd first seen it.

"Should be," Elly answered. "He's leasing all the land, planting wheat. I figured it'd be better than just letting it sit unused. Plus his land abuts mine, so it's easy for him to take care of."

"Would Jack buy the land if you wanted to sell it?"

"He might, but I think he's still hoping he'll get it in other ways." Elly rolled her eyes.

"The old-fashioned way, huh? He does know that you don't like men, right?" Alex chuckled.

"He knows, but I think he considers it a phase or something, like he could convince me to change my mind."

Alex snorted. "Totally clueless."

They sat quietly for a while, until Elly began to feel stiff. She rose, and Alex rose with her.

"Ready to go?" Alex asked. "It's getting close to time."

"I guess so." Elly knew she wasn't really ready, but she didn't have much other choice, not now.

"We need to pack up those teacups," Alex said. "Do you want to do that while I go get the bike ready?" She seemed to be kinder today, perhaps making amends for last night.

"Sure." Elly went back inside and Alex headed down the steps and around the side of the house. She found the cups where she'd left them on the table and began to rewrap them in the crumpled paper. By the time she'd finished, Alex had come back in and had put on her chaps and her leather jacket. Elly found a bit of newspaper and wrapped up the tomato salt and pepper shakers, placing them in the bag with the teacups.

"Ready?" Alex asked, standing in the doorway of the kitchen.

"Ready." Elly picked up the bag, and Alex took it from her.

"I'll get these put away, along with your overnight bag."

Elly followed her out to the front door, taking her borrowed leather chaps from the rail. She put them on, and then put on her jacket, scooping up her helmet from where it rested on the stairs. She glanced about, but they seemed to have gotten everything they needed. She'd call Jack later and let him know there was food in the fridge he could have.

Exiting the house and turning the key in the lock, she felt a pang of sadness. Leaving again. She took a deep breath.

The rumble of the motorcycle's engine interrupted her thoughts. It was time to go.

CHAPTER NINE

A cardboard drink coaster ricocheted off the side of her forehead, the rounded corner digging in. Alex turned to bawl out the customer who dared to have such nerve and saw Will sitting at the bar. He made a face, and she made one back.

"You jerk," she said fondly, coming over to punch him in the arm, leaning over the bar.

"You know it," he replied. "Busy tonight?"

"Always." Fridays were the busiest, thanks to the karaoke. She didn't normally mind, but the trip down south to Elly's parents' farm had been a long one, in more ways than one. She regretted the trip now. She should have stayed home, or gone riding on her own.

"You were quiet the past few days—I thought for sure you'd want to go riding yesterday. I had the day off."

"I didn't get your text till late," Alex said. "I was out of town."

"Out of town? Since when?"

"Thursday, until just a few hours ago. Elly and I went down to the farm."

Will started laughing.

"What?"

"You on a farm? I'd pay to see that, city girl, kicking cow shit off your boots. You missed a great ride out to the Minnewanka loop. We stopped for lunch at the Rose and Crown in Banff."

"We?"

"Me and Reg. I called him when I hadn't heard back from you."

"I couldn't get any signal on my phone down there. It was pretty much the middle of nowhere, just south of Cardston."

"Cardston? Mormon country, huh? Is Elly a Mormon?"

"Don't think so. But she never said one way or another. Do you want a drink? I need to catch those chits." The machine behind the bar had spit out half a dozen drink orders in the time they'd been talking.

"Bottle of Keith's. And a plate of nachos, loaded."

Alex rang in his order and popped the cap on the bottle of beer, setting it in front of him. Then she grabbed the chits and got to work, pouring a screwdriver, a vodka soda, and four beers, then filling a pitcher. The karaoke wouldn't start for another hour, but already things were picking up.

Eric brought three cases of beer from the back, strong-arming them through the door and setting them down with a groan.

"You don't have to act all manly around me," Alex teased, taking the top case from the stack and ripping open the cardboard. She knelt to stock the cooler.

"I know I don't have a chance with you," Eric replied, wiping his forehead. "You and Will are tight as always, even though you keep cheating on him with those girls."

"It's not cheating," Alex retorted. She didn't care to explain it to Eric, but it wasn't like that. She and Will had an understanding. That had always been the way.

"Whatever you say." Eric shrugged. "I was hoping to impress Charity, actually, but just my luck, she wasn't close enough to see."

"It'll take a bit more than hefting some beer to impress her, I think," Alex replied, "but it's worth a try."

"If you can talk me up to her…"

Alex snorted. "Do that yourself, lover boy." She pulled the next chit from the machine and put it in front of her on the mat, grabbing a pint glass from the rack. She mixed up the Caesar and handed it to the waitress who waited.

Bruce and his assistant Ron finished setting up their karaoke gear and he came over to the bar, plopping himself down on a stool. "Bourbon and cola, Alex, if you would." She poured the drink and set it in front of him. "Thank you. You're a lifesaver." He took a deep draft. "You going to sing tonight?"

"Not while I'm working."

"Sure you are," Will interjected. "You can't not sing on karaoke night. It's just plain wrong."

"Get Eric to sing," Alex replied.

"Oh no, not me." Eric shook his head. "Don't you even start."

"Coward," Will taunted. Eric flipped him the bird, and they both laughed.

"Alex, your nachos!" Charity stood at the pass-through, holding the plate.

"Right here, gorgeous," Will said, waving. Charity rolled her eyes.

"Doesn't he ever give up?" she said as Alex came to take the plate from her.

"Never. Sometimes it's part of his charm," Alex replied.

"Not today. My boyfriend's supposed to be here in a while and he'd lay into Will if he heard that." Charity turned and went back to the restaurant side before Alex could tell her about Eric.

"Thanks, darling," Will said when she brought him his nachos. "You're the best."

"Should I believe you?"

"Of course. You're my number one girl." Will rose on his stool and leaned over the bar, making a kissy sound and puckering his lips. Alex laughed, but she kissed him anyway.

"Sit down, you fool."

When there was a lull between orders, Alex confided in Eric, "I think you're out of luck."

"What do you mean?"

"Charity said her boyfriend's coming tonight. You should have made a move sooner."

"Damn. Well, she never seems to hold on to them long. I can be patient."

"And you think she'll hold on to you?"

"I'll sweep her off her feet," Eric vowed.

"For your sake, I hope it works." Alex felt a bit of pity for Eric, always pining after a girl he couldn't have. He hadn't learned better yet.

"Alex Bellerose, you're up!" Bruce bellowed. Still at the bar, Will laughed.

"Good luck, Bellerose. You'll like this one." He grinned.

Alex sighed, trying to hide her amusement. "You jerk. If I get in trouble, it's all your fault," she said, shaking a finger at him as she came around the bar.

"You won't. It's only one song. But what a song."

She stepped up onstage and Bruce leaned over to her. “Will chose ‘Toy Soldiers’ by Martika. That okay? If not, I can put something else on.”

“He’s really in an eighties mood tonight, isn’t he?” Alex quipped. Earlier, Will had sung a decent cover of a Genesis song.

“Must be. You’re good?”

“Yeah, I’m good.” She hadn’t sung it in a long while, but she remembered it, at least. It would be easy. There were a few hoots and whistles as she began, but the crowd settled in to listen, and she threw herself into the song. Afterward, she went back up to the bar.

“Nice one, Bellerose,” Will said, lifting his beer.

“Not very hard. You’re slipping.”

“I wasn’t trying to piss you off,” Will replied. “I figured you’d like that one.”

“Pulling your punches? Since when?” It was unlike him.

“Since I wanted to invite you home.”

“Smart move.” She hesitated, then brushed off the twinge of doubt.

“What time are you off?” Will took a swig of his beer.

“Two, or thereabouts, unless I sweet-talk Eric.” Alex pulled the chits off the machine and put them in front of her, pouring drinks as she talked. “But it’ll have to slow way down. And I could use the money anyway. I hope you’re patient.”

“Always,” Will said. “You know that.”

She did know, and she loved him for it.

❖

Elly had spent her weekend applying for more jobs, though she kept hoping for a callback from her interview the week before. She’d even taken the step of walking the neighborhood, looking for Help Wanted signs, but the only places advertising were the fast-food restaurants a few blocks over, and she wasn’t quite that desperate yet. But still, if she didn’t find a job soon, she’d run out of money. Everyone had said that jobs were easier to get if you lived in the city, despite the recession, and she had qualifications, albeit a Fine Arts degree and design experience. If only she could find a job at a design firm, but she hadn’t come across any listings for those, and she’d exhausted her local contacts in the industry.

She wondered if she should have stayed at the farm and found some way to make things work. The ache of homesickness had barely subsided, and with last week's visit it was back in full force. She set her laptop on the coffee table and rose from the sofa, going into the kitchen for a cup of tea, trying to distract her thoughts. From the cupboard she took one of the antique rose-blossom covered cups and a saucer. Alex had been right. She should use them, enjoy them, instead of having them hidden away in the shed.

Sensible Alex.

She'd thought the trip would have been too much for her, being alone with Alex that long, and being on the motorcycle especially, but she'd been surprised. She could see why Alex loved it, the speed, the feel of the wind, the expanse of the environment around them, far nicer than driving in a car, shut off from everything. The chances of an accident, though…

Elly shivered. There was no way she could do that often. Her knees had been jelly when they'd dismounted in the driveway at the farm, and she'd been thankful to have made it there in one piece. Mrs. Calderwood had a point.

The teakettle reached its boiling point and clicked off, and Elly poured the hot water into her cup with the tea bag. Her phone vibrated on the coffee table, a startlingly loud rattle, and her hand slipped on the handle of the kettle, which hit the gilded rim of the teacup. It cracked, and she stared in horror at the damage. Her grandmother's teacup.

She set the kettle down and rushed out into the living room, scooping up her phone.

"Hello?" Her heart pounded and she laid a hand on her chest.

"May I speak with Ms. Cole?" the voice asked.

"Speaking."

"Ms. Cole, it's Ms. Terry. You interviewed with us last week."

"Yes, I remember. How are you?"

"Good, thank you. I just wanted to call and update you, but I'm sorry to say it isn't good news. Unfortunately the position has been filled."

Elly could hardly speak, but she forced out a faint, "Thank you for letting me know."

"I hope you'll apply again if we have another position available," Ms. Terry said, sounding a tiny bit contrite.

"I may do that. Thanks."

Elly hung up the phone and sagged down onto the sofa. What now? It had been the most promising of her interviews thus far, yet she still hadn't gotten the job. The phone hung loosely in her hand and she thought about calling Jack and telling him that she'd come back to the farm, back to her real life. But she didn't want to give up so easily.

She checked her bank balance and sucked in a breath. She needed a job. But where, and on short notice? She went back to the kitchen, wincing as she saw the cracked cup. Maybe she should have left them at the farm after all. She took down a mug from the cupboard and filled it with tea, topping it up with cream from the fridge. If she wanted a job quickly, she knew she'd have to go into the service industry, or retail. It would be just like working at the diner.

Back in the living room, she dug out a few copies of her resume. There were lots of restaurants around. Maybe some of them were looking to hire servers. She wasn't sure she could work behind the bar, but she could serve tables easily enough.

She dropped resumes at all the restaurants she could along 17th Avenue, but her efforts were met with tepid enthusiasm. She kept one copy and took it into the lounge at Parry's. Alex grinned at her when she slid into a seat at the bar.

"Hey, you. I wasn't expecting to see you tonight. What do you want to drink?"

"Something strong," Elly replied, surprised at Alex's friendliness after their fight the other day. "It's been a rough day."

"Whisky and cola, then?"

"Sounds perfect."

Alex poured the drink and set it in front of her, then went to help some other customers.

"Hey there!"

Elly looked over. Charity stood in the pass-through to the restaurant. "Hey, Charity. How's business? Busy today?"

"Not so much, not yet, anyway." She came into the bar. "What's this?" She picked up Elly's resume, flipping through it.

"I didn't get the job I interviewed for last week. They called this afternoon. So I'm going to my last option, but I was hoping I wouldn't have to."

"What's that?"

"Back home, I used to work in the diner, and it looks like I'll have to do the same again here. I can't afford not to work."

"Where'd you apply?"

"Where didn't I?" Elly reeled off the names of a dozen restaurants.

"All those?" Charity looked impressed.

"But I don't know if I'll get much response. Most of the managers didn't seem too keen."

"They never are." Charity rolled her eyes. "But when one of their staff up and quits with no notice, they'll be happy to have people they can call. And you have experience."

"I can't wait around. But I don't want to work at McDonald's, either."

Charity grinned. "Give me a few minutes," she said, "and if anyone comes to the pass-through looking for me, tell them I'm restocking the pop."

"All right." Elly sipped her drink. "Where are you really going?"

"You'll see." Charity left, pushing through the swinging door into the back of the restaurant. Elly sat patiently, watching the football game on the TV over the bar, though she didn't know much about the teams playing. But it was something to do.

Charity came back, followed by an older man with thinning gray hair, wearing a slightly rumpled white shirt and a gaudy red striped tie. "Elly, this is Derek. He's the general manager here. And just the other day, he was saying to me how we needed another server, and how it was so busy. Weren't you, Derek?"

Derek smoothed his hand down his tie and grinned amiably at her. "I always need staff," he replied. "And Charity says you have experience. You could start tomorrow evening, and if it works out, then we could hire you on full-time."

"What's the pay?" Elly asked.

"Minimum wage plus tips. And you'd tip out four percent to the back-of-house staff."

"Done." Elly rose from her chair and held out her hand. Derek shook it.

"Wear black pants, comfortable black shoes, and a white shirt. I'll lend you a monogrammed shirt to wear. Your shift will start at five and end at eleven, unless it's slow."

A server called his name, and he frowned, turning. "See you then, and make sure to bring a float," he said over his shoulder as he headed back to the restaurant side. Elly sank down into her chair.

"That was fast."

"Told you." Charity said. "Gotta get back to work, but I'll see you tomorrow." She darted back into the restaurant.

Alex came back to the bar and poured two drinks that had been waiting on her chit machine.

"What was all that about?" she asked as she poured.

"I have a job," Elly said, feeling a giddy sense of relief.

"Do you? That's awesome. Where?"

"Here, in the restaurant."

"What? Since when?" Alex looked startled.

"Since now," Elly said. "Thanks to Charity."

"So we'll see each other all the time," Alex said, and Elly wasn't quite sure if she was happy about it or not.

"I think we will—I start tomorrow evening."

"You going to stick around?" Alex asked, putting the drinks on the pass-through. "We could celebrate after I'm off. Eric's coming in for the closing shift in about half an hour."

"I'll stay," Elly replied.

"You can sleep in tomorrow," Alex promised. "A new job deserves a few drinks. Or more. You're just lucky it isn't karaoke night."

CHAPTER TEN

From the moment she reached Parry's, Elly was on her feet, working hard. Derek had given her a uniform shirt, a short black apron with pockets for her cash and notebook, and a swipe card. He'd run her through a breathless recitation of the functions of their ordering system, then retreated to his office.

"You're in section two," he said. "It's the smallest. Any problems, ask Charity."

Feeling a bit shell-shocked, Elly stared after him. Where was section two? She took a deep breath. She could, and would, do this. It was just like the diner back home, except…bigger.

"Hey!" Charity came around the corner by the kitchen and waved. "Derek said you'd be starting. That's awesome."

"Is it just us working?" Elly asked, looking out over the mostly empty restaurant.

"A couple of others, Amie and Jesse, will be coming in at six. Did Derek give you the rundown?"

"He gave me the basics."

Charity snorted. "So not much of anything then, huh? Well, take a few minutes while it's slow to look at our menu, and try to remember as much as you can. Shay's our hostess tonight and I'll tell her not to seat you with too many tables right away."

"Thanks, Charity." Elly pulled a menu from the stack and opened it, the plastic laminate sticky on her fingers. It might not be as hard to remember as she'd thought. She'd read through the appetizers, salads, soups, and onto the sandwiches before Shay nudged her elbow.

"A table for you," she said, flipping her blond hair over her shoulder. She was a small and slender girl, but heavily made up, her hair obviously dyed. "I sat them at two-four." She pointed to a map of the restaurant tacked up near the computer, and Elly quickly located the table. She set down the menu.

"Thanks, Shay."

"No problem." Shay hustled back out to the hostess stand.

Elly squared her shoulders and took out her notebook and pen. She made her way over to the table, where an older couple sat, looking idly through the menu.

"Good evening, and welcome to Parry's. Can I get you two something to drink to start off with?"

"Beer," the man said, abruptly. "Pint of Molson's." He didn't look up from his menu.

"Oh, you're new, aren't you, dear?" the woman, her dark hair pulled back in a ponytail, said.

"I am," Elly replied as she wrote down the man's drink order. "Just started."

"We come here a lot," the woman said. "I'm Sharron and this is my husband, Tony."

"Nice to meet you." Elly smiled. Maybe this wouldn't be too bad. "Would you like something to drink, Sharron?"

"White wine, dear. Just the house brand is fine with me. We'll probably eat what we always do, but we'll give Tony some time to look at the menu anyway." She winked and Elly tried not to chuckle.

"Yes, ma'am."

She retreated to the computer to ring in her order, then went to the pass-through between the bar and the restaurant. Alex pulled the chit from the machine and Elly watched as she poured the drinks, starting with the pint of Molson's, the pale lager foaming as it hit the side of the glass. Once that was done, she poured the wine from a bottle she kept stashed in the cooler.

"First table already?" she asked as she brought the drinks over. "Must be Sharron and Tony. It's about that time of day."

"They are here a lot, aren't they?" Elly replied, grabbing a tray from the stack and placing the drinks on it.

"Every Thursday," Alex said, "like clockwork. But they're nice. Sometimes they sit in the bar, just to change it up a bit. Tony will have the vegetarian pizza, and she'll have a Caesar salad with a skewer of prawns."

"They don't ever change?"

"Not often." The chit machine began printing out another order. "I'll talk to you later." Alex blew her a kiss as she retreated, and Elly pretended to catch it. Then she took the drinks out to Sharron and Tony.

Derek let her go at ten o'clock, saying that the restaurant was too slow to merit keeping her on longer. He handed her a zipped pouch. "Do your cash-out and bring it to me in the office when you're done. I'll check it over and make sure you did it right."

Elly took the pouch from him and found herself a quiet spot in the back, away from the organized chaos of the kitchen and the movement of the back-end staff. On a clean page in her notebook, she calculated all her receipts and counted out her cash and credit card and debit slips. She balanced, and there was fifty dollars left over after she calculated the four percent tip-out. Using a couple of paperclips she found in the pouch, she bundled the money with the receipts, and the tip-out separately, and left the fifty dollars in tips aside. Zipping up the pouch, she went up the flight of stairs to Derek's office.

He glanced up when she knocked on the open door, then held out his hand. "That was fast." He unzipped the pouch, pulling out the receipts and money. "Take a seat, this won't take long."

Elly sat on the extra chair, its cushion worn and somewhat stained. It looked like it had once had life in the restaurant but had been taken out when it became too run-down. She watched Derek count, his lips moving, though he made no noise. It took him longer to check her work than it had for her to do it in the first place. But eventually, he finished and nodded.

"It all works out. Fifty dollars and change in tips, right?"

"Yes."

"Good." Derek tucked the pouch into the safe under his desk, then held out a form. "Fill this out for me before you go, and we'll get you all official. Charity said you did really well tonight, and Sharron talked to me on her way out. She likes you. That's always a good sign."

Elly bent to study the form, taking out her pen. She filled it in quickly, though it took her a moment to remember the full address for her apartment. When she'd finished and signed the bottom, she pushed it back across the desk to him.

"I'll put you on the new schedule when I do it up on Saturday night, but come in tomorrow for five o'clock."

"Five until when?"

"Midnight, or thereabouts," Derek said. "We have a split shift tomorrow so I probably won't need you for midnight until two."

"I'll see you then." Elly headed back downstairs. Instead of going straight home, she went into the bar. Alex was still busy, wiping tables and pouring drinks.

"Hey. How'd it go?" she asked once she noticed Elly sitting at the bar.

"Good. Decent tips." She'd never had so much in tips in one night working at the diner. If she could keep this up, it'd help her pay all her bills.

"The city's way better for that," Alex said, rinsing out her rag in the bar's small sink. "People have more money to spend."

"I'll still keep looking for other work, but this will definitely help in the meantime."

"What is it that you did, before? I can't remember."

"I was in graphic design, with a firm downtown. But they closed up just over a year ago, and I couldn't find any other work."

"That sucks. Hopefully you'll find something now. But until then, we're coworkers. Want a drink to celebrate?"

"Just water. I'll have to drive home, after all."

Alex set a pint glass of ice and water in front of her. "A bunch of us are going out after our shifts. Want to come? We usually go hit up one of the other restaurants nearby, have a bite to eat."

"Sure. What time is everyone off?"

"I'm off as soon as Eric gets here to close, and Charity should be off soon too, since she's the midnight shift. Amie and Jesse cover the closing."

❖

Alex hugged one of the regulars as they headed out the door. "See you next week, Peggy," she said warmly. Elly tried not to look as though she'd noticed, and she tried to ignore the jealousy, but the feeling was insidious.

Eric came in, shedding his leather jacket and hanging it on the hook behind the bar. "Elly! How are you? You going to become another of our regulars?"

Before she could reply, Alex hooked an arm over her shoulders. "She's one of us now, Eric," she said. "Just hired on today."

"Well done." Eric grinned. "Welcome to the team. Restaurant side?"

"Yes. I'll be in tomorrow too."

"Always nice to see another pretty face."

"You charmer," Alex quipped, and Eric laughed.

"Off to eat at Brewsters?" he asked.

"Probably. Depends on what Charity wants to do too," Alex replied.

"Now it's your descent into hedonism," Eric said to Elly.

"That bad?" Elly asked, trying to stifle her giggles.

"Worse." He chuckled again.

Charity came through the door, still pulling off her apron. "Let's get out of here. I'm starving."

Alex grabbed her jacket and she and Elly followed Charity from the lounge, out into the cool night air.

"We driving?" Elly asked.

"It's just a couple of blocks away," Charity said. "We can walk."

Elly followed a step behind all the way to the restaurant, listening as Alex and Charity talked shop. She had little to add, given that most of the people they spoke about she didn't even know.

"I heard Vanessa broke up with that girl," Charity said. Elly's ears perked up. She at least knew that name.

"Already?" Alex replied. "They'd only just begun seeing each other. But mind you, Vanessa's picky."

"I'm glad my boyfriend's not like that," Charity remarked.

Elly found a moment to break in with a question. "Have you been dating him long?"

"A few months. He works out of town, though, on the rigs up north, so I don't see him as often as I'd like. It's three weeks on, one week off. And he hates talking on the phone, so all I really get from him while he's away are texts."

"Is he cute?"

"Gorgeous," Charity confirmed. "Tall, dark, and handsome. Even in ratty jeans."

They reached Brewsters and Alex pulled open the door. "After you, ladies."

The hostess was perky and young, much like Shay was at Parry's. She seated them in a booth, and Alex slid in next to Elly, leaving a side all to Charity.

"Hey there, my favorite customers." A blond server approached the table, bending to exchange a kiss with Alex, and a hug with Charity. Her long hair hung in careful ringlets down her back, and she was beautifully made-up. Elly felt rough around the edges in comparison, sloppy in her work clothes. And the girl had kissed Alex. Elly resolved not to let it bother her, though it was hard to ignore the feeling of jealousy. Again. She knew she had no right to be jealous. Alex had been very clear about her lack of commitment. But still. "And who's the new girl?"

"Elly, this is Laura." Alex introduced them easily. "She comes and spends money at Parry's, and we come and spend money here."

"We really should just keep all our money," Charity quipped, "but that would be no fun at all."

"And I'd be bored out of my mind here," Laura added. "You're saving me from insanity."

"Glad to do what we can." Alex winked at her.

"The usual?" Laura asked. "Keith's, bourbon and cola, and…?" She looked at Elly.

"Vodka cran, please, and some water," Elly said.

"Vodka cran, and a water. Done. You girls eating too?" Alex nodded. "Then I'll grab you menus."

She brought them menus, then disappeared to ring in their drink order. Alex didn't even bother to open hers, but Charity did, and so did Elly. She scanned the menu, but she didn't know what to order. She wasn't very hungry and hardly ever ate this late in the evening. She settled on a side salad, spinach with almonds and bacon bits.

"What are you having?" Charity asked when they'd set their menus aside.

"Salad," Elly said.

"Butter chicken," Alex said, "as always. I love it here, even though it's not real butter chicken."

"It's real enough," Charity said.

"But this isn't an Indian restaurant."

"Still."

Alex shrugged. "I suppose so. What kind of salad are you having, El? Sure you don't want more than that?"

"It's late," Elly said. "I don't think I could eat much more than that now."

Under the table, Alex's hand landed on her thigh. "You might be hungry later."

Elly felt her face flame. "Maybe," she said in a quiet voice.

"Alex, you're embarrassing her," Charity chided.

"Elly's used to me, aren't you, El?"

"I am," she replied. "Mostly. Sort of."

Laura returned with their drinks, saving her from having to say anything more. "And for dinner? Alex, the butter chicken, I assume, and Charity…?"

"I can't decide. Who's working in the kitchen tonight?"

"Paul's in charge."

Charity perked up. "Ooh. I'll take the Thai pasta then. He's good at that."

"And Elly?"

"The side spinach salad, please."

"Anything on that?" Laura rattled off the list of add-ons.

"No, just the salad's fine." Elly gave her an apologetic smile.

"No problem." Laura scribbled on her notepad. "I'll be back with those in a bit."

Once she'd left, Alex squeezed Elly's thigh, though she looked at Charity. "You still have a thing for Paul, do you?"

Charity shrugged. "Not really. But he does make great pasta." She looked at Elly. "Sorry we're talking about people you don't know. That must be boring."

"It isn't too bad," Elly said, though in truth she did find it a bit dull.

"Well, me and Paul know each other from way back," Charity said. "When we were eighteen, I convinced him to get his first tattoo."

"And look where that led," Alex interjected. "He has a dozen."

"Not my fault," Charity replied. "And anyway, he looks good in them."

They continued in this vein and Elly felt like she was beginning to know their entire circle of friends, even though she'd never met them.

Paul came out to say hello, bringing Charity's pasta personally. "Hey, babe," he said to Charity, sliding the bowl of pasta in front of her. "Long time no see."

"Only a couple of weeks." Charity batted her eyelashes up at him. He was tall and burly, what Elly's dad would have called built like a brick shithouse. Tattoos covered his arms to his wrists, and he had a dark beard, though it was trimmed short. Charity laid her hand on his. "It's so sweet of you to bring it out yourself."

"We should go see a movie," he said. "Catch up."

"Call me."

Paul grinned. "I will. Enjoy your food." He headed back to the kitchen, and Laura placed the other dishes on the table.

"The manager has me doing all sorts of cleaning." She rolled her eyes. "Else I'd stay and chat. Enjoy."

Elly placed her napkin in her lap and dug in. Beside her, Alex mixed the butter chicken sauce with the basmati rice before breaking a chunk off the naan.

"Here, El, try some." She dipped the bread in the sauce and rice and held it out, but when Elly went to take it, she shook her head. "Open your mouth."

Elly let Alex feed her. It was good, and suddenly her salad didn't look very appetizing.

"Oh, how sweet," Charity crooned.

"Shut it, Char," Alex said, chuckling. "You're just jealous."

"Damn right," Charity replied. "My guy doesn't feed me anything."

"Nothing at all?" Alex raised a brow.

"Almost nothing," Charity amended, giving Alex a salacious grin. "You perv."

"Do you feed him?" Elly asked, swallowing the bite of butter chicken. It stuck in her throat and she coughed, then took a drink of her vodka cran, swallowing hard.

"If he'd allow it more often, I sure would. Men." Charity shook her head in disgust.

"You don't need a man, Char."

"You're the one who always gets away, Alex, my dear," Charity replied. She stuck out her tongue and Alex reached forward, trying to catch it between her fingers.

"Don't stick it out if you aren't going to use it."

"Be careful around her, Elly," Charity said. "She once licked Will's face because he said the same thing to her."

"Ew." Elly made a face, but she was laughing. It kept her from thinking too hard about what Charity had just said about Alex being the one who got away. Tongues had nothing to do with it.

"He deserved it," Alex replied. "And his face was clean."

"And he never did it again, did he?" Charity wiped tears of laughter from her eyes.

"Will's a fast learner."

❖

They walked back to the parking lot at Parry's, Charity giggling at a joke Alex had made, clinging to Alex's free arm. She'd given Elly her other arm as they'd left the restaurant and now the three of them made an awkward six-legged creature staggering along, their steps out of sync.

"Where you headed?" Charity asked.

"Home," Alex said, though she didn't know for sure. "You?"

"Home too, I suppose. See you tomorrow." Charity blew kisses at them and headed to her car, a battered little gray hatchback.

"So, home," Elly echoed.

"Mine or yours?" Alex asked. "It's early yet."

"I don't know. If this is just sex, I don't know that I'm that interested."

Alex nearly dropped her helmet in surprise. "What's wrong with sex?"

"Nothing, but when it's just sex, it's not enough."

Though she'd been single for almost longer than she could remember, no one had ever turned her down because it was just sex. Her surprise must have shown, because Elly stepped back, crossing her arms.

"Look, we do well together, and it's fun, but it's just not enough. We're totally different people, which became really obvious when we were at the farm. And since we'll have to work together now, I don't think it's a good idea."

"If that's the way you want it," Alex replied, the words coming easily, almost automatically. Usually she was the one initiating the talk and turning someone down. Elly had one-upped her.

"It is," Elly said. "Friends, I guess, but that's it."

"How about a movie, then?"

"My place?" Elly suggested. "My TV's not as big, but my place is closer. And I have popcorn."

"Done. Is it microwave?"

"Ew. No." Elly made a face, and Alex wanted to kiss her for looking so cute. "It's real popcorn, air popped. Or I could make it over the stove, if you want."

"I've never had that." It sounded delicious, and now that they'd established their boundaries, they could just relax around each other. Sort of. She still couldn't get her head around how often her gaze had been drawn to Elly, in the bar, while working, and while sitting at Brewsters.

"Then it's settled. I'll see you at mine. And do be careful."

"Always." Alex headed to her bike, going through her usual preparations. She heard Elly's car start up and turned to see it pull out of the parking lot. She swung a leg over the bike and started the engine, pulling out and following her.

❖

They sat near each other on the sofa, watching Elly's choice of movie this time, the old classic *Casablanca*. Now that she'd decided not to sleep with Alex, she felt far more relaxed, far more at ease with Alex being close. Friends was best.

"Damn, Bogart was incredible." Alex sighed, putting her empty bowl of popcorn on the coffee table. She tried to mimic Bogart's voice but failed miserably.

"What was that?" Elly laughed, then tried to stifle it behind a hand.

"What, you don't like my impressions?" Alex looked offended, then broke into a smile. "Look, if we're going to be friends, this is what you have to put up with."

"Someone should have warned me," Elly teased, rising to her feet. She picked up the popcorn bowls and stacked them, then took their empty glasses of pop and headed into the kitchen. Alex lingered in the doorway, leaning on the wall.

"I should head out," she said, and Elly noticed she did look sleepy. It was late, nearly two in the morning.

"And I should go to bed." She thought of how Alex had been in her bed once, at the farm, and overnight. What had changed between then and now? She still couldn't figure it out. Alex moved into the kitchen.

"See you tomorrow, gorgeous," Alex said, cupping Elly's cheek, leaning in for a kiss.

"Good night." Elly gave her a gentle peck on the lips, and there was that zing, the one she'd been determined to ignore once she'd made her decision earlier. Her statement had meant to end all that, but it hadn't worked. Alex turned and went to the door and Elly wondered if she'd felt anything, or if it had been all just her own attraction. She watched Alex flip the deadbolt and open the door, stepping forward into the entryway before Alex could slip out completely.

"'Bye." Alex leaned in for another kiss, and Elly gave in, allowing the gentle press of lips.

"See you." Her voice felt lifeless, barely a whisper, but Alex didn't seem to notice. She smiled and stepped into the hallway, then was gone. Elly shut the door and heard the heavy front door of the apartment building slam. She forced herself to stay where she was, instead of running to the window to see Alex walk down the sidewalk. The bike's engine rumbled to life, and a few moments later, she heard the bike shift into gear before it drove away.

Elly released the doorknob from her cold hand. Alex as a friend. She could do that.

She walked back into the bedroom and changed out of her clothes and into her robe. She turned on her heel and went out to the living room, plopping down on the sofa and grabbing her laptop from where it lay on the coffee table. She'd search for jobs instead of thinking too much about Alex.

Chapter Eleven

Two mornings later, Elly yawned as she drove up the block toward home. She had meant to get home earlier, but she'd fallen asleep on Alex's sofa after watching a movie, the second in almost as many days, because she didn't have much else to do after work aside from go home and be alone in her tiny apartment. Alex hadn't woken her. The sun was rising and she squinted into the dawn, her eyes sore from lack of rest. Once she'd found a place to park and walked in her front door, she tossed her coat over a chair and stumbled toward the bedroom, undressing as she went. She could sleep for several hours more.

Alex had been dead to the world, spread out like a starfish on her sheets, her dark hair tangled, when Elly had looked in on her. There was no room for her there, unless she wanted to curl up on the edge of the bed. If Alex had wanted her in bed, then she would have woken her earlier, and invited her in. But she hadn't, and it stung. Even though she knew Alex didn't like company, and knew that she herself had put up the ultimatum, it still stung.

She'd sleep better at home, as Alex seemed to profess. Except once she was in bed, she lay awake, watching the light brighten the blue curtains over her bedroom window, pushing away the darkness. She closed her eyes and forced her breathing to even out, counting breaths up to ten and back down, over and over.

She might have dozed, but the jangle of her phone jolted her awake. It was loud enough it couldn't be ignored, and Elly went into the kitchen and answered it without looking at the display.

"Hello?" She rubbed her eyes, feeling shaky on her feet, and slightly befuddled.

"Elly? I didn't wake you, did I?" Jack's low tenor came over the line and Elly wanted to hang up right then.

"You did, but it's all right."

"You always were an early bird," Jack said, sounding cheerful. "And I have news for you. Important news. It can't wait."

"What is it?" Elly yawned, turning to open the fridge and take out the carton of orange juice. She poured herself a glass, carefully balancing the phone between her shoulder and her ear.

"A fellow came by the farm yesterday," Jack said.

"Uh-huh." Elly wanted him to get to the point, but Jack seemed to be making an attempt at suspense.

"He wants to buy your farm."

The phone slipped from Elly's shoulder and crashed to the floor, the plastic case covering the battery skittering across the linoleum.

"Shit." Elly bent and scrambled to put the phone back together. She glanced at the screen. "You still there, Jack?"

"Still here," he confirmed. "What did you do?"

"Dropped the phone."

"I figured you'd be excited, but that's a bit much, don't you think?"

"A guy wants to buy the farm?" Elly repeated.

"Yeah. He's from that big conglomerate that's been buying up sections down near Medicine Hat. I have his card. Bernard Hamilton, of Hamilton Farms, Inc."

"Hamilton Farms? But they own so much already. What would they want with my farm?"

"I dunno. He didn't say exactly, just told me that they were interested and gave me his card to give to you. But you're not going to sell the farm, are you, El?" He sounded worried.

"I'd better talk to him first before I make any sort of decision," Elly replied. "Maybe he thinks he'll get it for peanuts because I'm not there. You know how these big-business types are."

"Yeah. Vultures all of them," Jack agreed. "Got a pen?" Elly found one and a slip of paper and he rattled off the information.

"I'll call him later," Elly said. "Thanks for letting me know, Jack. I appreciate it."

"Anything for you, El." He talked further, about how the planting was going, and how he hoped for a big crop this year, but Elly wasn't really listening. She traced over the phone number she'd written down. "Anyway, I should let you go. I have to get the barn mucked out before I head off to the store."

"Right. I'll talk to you later."

"And don't sell the farm, El. Not yet, anyway."

"I won't be doing anything today," she replied. "You don't need to worry."

She set the phone down and stared off into space. Selling the farm hadn't even entered into her plans. How could she possibly sell? Her family had worked the land since her great-great-grandparents' time. She'd grown up there, her father had grown up there. She felt the wetness before she realized she was crying.

She couldn't sell. She just couldn't. She'd make it work, even if she had to exile herself to the city permanently. To keep the farm, keep that hope and her family alive, she'd deal with the pollution, the noise, the sirens every night, anything she had to.

❖

"Hey there." Charity nudged Elly as she stood by the pass-through. Elly blinked.

"Sorry, what?"

"Did your mind go on vacation somewhere hot?"

Elly sighed. "If only." The thought of selling the farm had consumed her; she couldn't think of anything else. Bernard Hamilton's phone number sat on her kitchen counter, and for the last few days she'd fingered the piece of paper but hadn't gotten up the nerve to call. What if the offer was significant? That would make it harder to decide. It wasn't all about money, but yet it was.

"Snap out of it, babe," Charity said. "Derek will get on your ass if you don't pick up the pace. It's almost six and it's getting busy."

"Right. Sorry."

"I have a table for you." Shay came around the half wall. "Two-four."

Elly smoothed down her apron and went out to greet her

customers. A group of three women sat at the four-top and they hardly acknowledged her, continuing their conversation. She waited, her notebook out, pen poised.

"Good evening, ladies," she said, pitching her voice to try to cut through their chatter. "I'm Elly and I'll be your server tonight. Can I start you with some drinks?"

"We'll take a pitcher of margaritas," one woman said, breaking off her narrative to throw a glance Elly's way. "And when you get back, we'll be ready to order."

"No problem." Elly tried to smile, but she felt out of sorts. She hurried back to the computer to punch in her order. After she'd sent the order to the bar, she lingered by the pass through, watching Alex work.

Alex moved with efficiency, with little wasted movement as she poured drinks, cleared dishes, and helped the waitress. She stopped by the end of the bar to talk to Jan, who leaned in with a flirty smile, her earrings flashing in the light. Alex rested a hand on her shoulder and kissed her cheek. Elly had to look away. Jealousy shot through her and she focused on the white paper chit waiting on the machine, holding her drink order.

She grabbed a tray and waited.

Alex lingered with Jan, and Elly fidgeted, wanting to say something but not wanting to step into the bar. Derek had been clear the other night, only bartenders were to be in the bar, not restaurant servers. Cross the line at one's own peril.

"Those women at two-four are getting antsy," Charity said, coming up beside her.

"I know, but I need their drink order," Elly fretted.

"Oy, Alex!" Charity bellowed.

Alex turned, her expression turning sheepish. She patted Jan's arm, then headed toward them. "What's up?"

"Elly needs that drink order, stat. It's those three bitches again."

Alex snorted. "Oh, them." She grabbed the chit and put it on the bar, pulling out the ingredients she needed. She put the pitcher and three glasses on Elly's tray. "Sorry, babe. Knock 'em dead."

"Thanks." Elly walked as fast as she could without spilling her tray, bringing the drinks to the table.

"Took you a while," one of the women said sharply. "We've been ready to order for ages."

"Sorry." Elly served the drinks and then pulled out her notebook. "What would you like to eat?"

The three rattled off their selections and Elly struggled to keep up. When they were finished, she read back their orders.

"No, I ordered the sandwich without onions."

Elly scribbled down the correction. The women went back to their conversation and she picked up the menus, retreating to the back of the house. She let out a breath.

"It'll get better," Charity said, passing behind her with a tray full of pop glasses. "Those ladies don't give a good tip to anyone, so don't knock yourself out."

"Right." Elly rang in her food order.

Shay popped her head around the wall. "You have a two-top at two-one," she said.

"Thanks."

Elly reminded herself that she'd done this before. She wasn't green, but serving at the diner, where she knew everyone…it was different. It was home. She hustled out to her new table, greeting them with as much cheer as she could muster, getting nothing but disinterest in return. She retreated to the back, taking a deep breath.

"Doing all right?" Charity asked, coming out of the utility room. "Just had to change up the pop, the Coke was out." She wiped her hands on her apron.

"I'll be fine. Everyone has a bad night."

"You have tomorrow off, right?"

"I do. Thank goodness." Elly rubbed her already tired eyes.

"Sleep in, then come out for lunch with me," Charity said. "You're kind of new in town, and I bet you haven't done much of anything except work. Am I right?"

"You're right," Elly said, though she didn't feel like telling Charity about her evenings with Alex.

"I knew it." Charity squeezed her shoulder. "Just get through this night, and tomorrow I'll meet you on 17th Ave at the sushi place on the corner of 8th Street."

"Sushi?" Elly wasn't so sure about that, but Charity had already gone out to bring a food order to one of her tables.

❖

Alex leaned on the bar. "El, how was your shift?" Elly rubbed her eyes, and Alex thought she seemed a bit paler than usual, her skin wan.

"Never have I been so glad to have a day off tomorrow. I don't think I could take another night like this one."

"Tough time?"

"Those three bitches stayed for ages and kept me running, and then I was saddled with a kid's birthday party, and cranky parents. I think kids are great, but right now I don't want to see one, ever."

"Go home and rest tonight," Alex said. "Then tomorrow, we can head out to the mountains on the bike. I'll show you one of my favorite places."

"I can't, actually. I'm hanging out with Charity tomorrow."

"Oh." Alex hadn't expected that. She knew it was a bit silly, but she felt disappointed. "What are you up to?"

"Lunch, for sure. No idea what else."

"Sounds like fun. I'll have to go on my own then, I guess." It wouldn't be quite the same, but she'd gone on plenty of solo rides.

"Isn't Will around?" Elly asked.

"Working tomorrow, the jerk." Alex chuckled, gesturing at him where he played pool at the back of the bar. Lately their days off hadn't coincided; Will was getting too much contract work and couldn't say no.

"That's too bad," Elly said. "But I'm sure you'll have fun anyway. The weather's supposed to be hot." She slid off the stool and Alex wished suddenly that she would stay just a little longer. She checked herself. Since when did she care so much?

"Off already?"

"Too many late nights, and not enough sleep," Elly said. "And just stress."

"Like what?" Alex pulled a chit from the machine and placed it in front of her, but she didn't start making the Caesar. She looked at Elly, waiting. Elly did seem overly tired, not her usual friendly self.

"Just about the farm. It's nothing."

"Doesn't sound like nothing."

"I can't get into it right now," Elly said, putting the strap of her purse over her shoulder, plainly shutting down the conversation.

"No prob. Sleep well." Alex leaned forward, inviting a kiss, but

Elly stepped back. Slowly, Alex resumed her place, as if she hadn't tried.

"Good night," Elly murmured. She turned and gave a quick wave as she left the bar, heading across the parking lot to her car.

"Someone's in love," said a singsong male voice over her shoulder.

Alex turned. Will stood there with his pool cue. He'd been playing over at the single table in the back.

"I am not," she retorted, but Will raised an eyebrow.

"Oh, really? You sure? Looks like it to me."

"You're reading too much into it."

"Am I? Remember what happened with Heather? This looks like exactly the same thing to me."

At the mention of her ex, it was Alex's turn to flinch. He knew she hated talking about her. "I don't even want you to mention her name."

"Just be careful, Alex," Will said, wrapping an arm around her shoulders. "I remember you after Heather, and it wasn't pretty." He gave her a kiss on the temple and then tweaked a lock of her hair. She elbowed him in the ribs at that, and he retaliated by tickling her sides until she squirmed away, breathless with giggles.

"Will, leave my bartenders alone, will you?" Derek said. "Alex, don't you have work to do?"

Will lifted his pool cue and headed back to his game, and Alex slipped back behind the bar. Derek gave her a nod and retreated into the restaurant.

Alex grabbed a cloth and rinsed it in the sink, then wiped down the bar. No matter what Will had said, he was wrong. She wasn't in love. But maybe she'd stick around town instead. Lots to do, and she needed a few new shirts.

CHAPTER TWELVE

You look a little more alive today," Charity said as Elly met her on the corner of 8th Street and 17th Avenue. It was only a few blocks from her apartment, and she'd walked, finally taking in some of the sights. She'd been so busy and needing to husband her cash that she hadn't really gotten out to explore the neighborhood. And truth be told, being in the city again, this close to downtown, unnerved her a bit. There were so many people. And though she tried not to be a worrywart, being out after dark always concerned her.

"I slept fairly well," Elly replied. "So, where are we going for lunch?"

"Any preference?"

Elly shrugged. "I haven't been anywhere yet, so no. Not really."

"Excellent." Charity grabbed her hand and tugged her toward the side of an older brick building. "I know just the place."

They walked around the corner and Charity led her down a set of stairs, into a restaurant done in a minimalist white and silver. Elly sniffed, wrinkling her nose. "Fish?"

"Sushi," Charity corrected. "I woke up this morning with a total craving after thinking about it last night."

"Raw fish?" Elly knew she sounded like a little kid, but she couldn't stop from making a face. She'd hoped Charity hadn't actually wanted to go for sushi.

"You've never had sushi before?" Charity boggled, her eyes wide. "You've got to be kidding me. You're like the only person I know who hasn't."

“No sushi in Cardston,” Elly said. “People like their fish cooked there, preferably fried.”

“Ew.” It was Charity’s turn to wrinkle her nose. “That’s such a waste. Come on, El, I’ll make sure you only get the good stuff.”

The hostess led them to a table and left them with menus. Elly read down the list, but the names didn’t make much sense to her.

“Do you like tuna?” Charity asked. “Or salmon?”

“Yes to both,” Elly said. “Cooked.”

“What about crabmeat?”

“Had it once, it was all right,” Elly conceded.

“Then I know what we’ll start with.” Charity made a few notations on the list, and when the waiter came by, she handed it to him. “And we’ll have a small bottle of sake, and some water,” she added.

Elly scanned over the larger menu the waiter had left. “I can have this teriyaki chicken,” she said. “It’s cooked. And it sounds tasty.”

“Just try some sushi first,” Charity said, “and if you hate it, you can order that. And we can order some tempura too. It’s fried, but tastier than fish and chips.”

The waiter came back with two glasses of water, a small ceramic carafe, and two ceramic cups that looked about the size of thimbles. Charity took the carafe gingerly by the top, wincing. “It’s hot,” she said, “but it’s best to drink sake hot, especially if you’ve never had it before.” She poured some of the clear liquid into the two thimble-cups and pushed one across to Elly. “Cheers.”

Elly lifted the cup and sniffed. There was a faint scent of alcohol, but aside from the heat, it seemed quite harmless.

“Mmmm.” Charity sipped her sake, closing her eyes. “I knew this was a good idea.”

Elly lifted the cup to her lips and took a cautious, tiny sip. The sake burned on her tongue and down her throat as she swallowed, and she coughed. It was like drinking straight alcohol, vodka maybe, but with more burn. Her eyes watered, and she wanted to switch to water and not even look at the sake again.

“Try one more sip,” Charity urged. “It does get better, I promise.”

Charity looked so expectant, so hopeful, that Elly didn’t have the heart to refuse. She took a second sip, and it was easier. Her mouth and throat had already been shocked once, and this second sip went down smoothly. Her eyes watered again, and she dabbed at them with the sleeve of her shirt.

"Not bad," she said, her voice a bit croaky.

"Good." Charity took another, longer sip of hers, then refilled her cup. "Sushi without sake is just wrong, somehow."

The waiter came by with a long white dish, upon which were artfully arranged bits of raw fish and rice, a sort of roll with crab salad in the middle, and some green stuff Elly didn't know sandwiched between fake plastic grass and a slimy pile of pink slivers. She was sure her face went green just looking at it.

"So, there are salmon and tuna, and the rolls are California rolls. There's nothing uncooked about those—it's that already-cooked crab, with some mayo and seaweed." Charity gestured with her chopsticks before taking a small dish from the side and pouring soy sauce into it. She picked up some of the green stuff—"Wasabi," she said helpfully—and mixed it in.

Elly copied her, but when she went to put wasabi in, Charity put out a hand. "Best leave that for the first try," she said. "It's a bit on the hot side." She picked up a piece of salmon on rice and dipped it into her soy sauce. "Enjoy."

Elly tried a piece, dipping it in the sauce, then biting it in two. She chewed, and the fish was surprisingly tender, not slimy at all. The soy sauce was salty, and it went well with the fish, which seemed to melt in her mouth. She swallowed.

"Well?" Charity waited, her chopsticks poised over a piece of tuna.

"Not bad," Elly said. "Better than I expected, even."

"So you're not a country bumpkin," Charity teased. "Try the California rolls next—I think you'll like those."

Elly finished her salmon and reached out for a roll. In no time at all, it seemed they'd finished their order, and Elly couldn't remember ever finding fish so delicious, except for maybe the ones her father had caught in the river and fried in butter and pepper.

Charity sipped her sake and sat back in her chair. Elly took another sip of hers.

"Do you want more?" Charity asked.

"A few more." The rice had filled her more quickly than she'd expected. When the waiter passed by, Charity got his attention and ordered several more rolls.

"Now that we've sated some of our massive hunger—or maybe just mine, whatever—tell me about how you met Alex."

Elly felt her cheeks warm, and she hoped she could blame it on the sake. "Not much to tell, really." She didn't want to tell Charity about her one-night stand with Alex on the farm. It was her own special memory, even if right now Alex wasn't what she'd expected.

"Oh, come on," Charity urged. "Alex usually dates, or sleeps with, anyway, people who come to the bar. She's notorious. But none of us had ever met you before you came in that night. So, how'd it happen?" She leaned forward, resting her elbows on the table, looking eager.

"I met Alex down at the farm," Elly said, relenting. "She was riding, and there was a thunderstorm. She came knocking at my door for a place to rest while the storm passed."

"Oh…" Charity drew out the word, waggling her eyebrows. "And I'll bet she made an impression. I tell you, if I swung that way, I'd totally tap that."

"She did impress me." Elly cut her gaze down to the table and topped up her cup of sake to have something to do. "But I think it was the bike she was riding."

"Last year, that would have been her Harley, I think," Charity said. "I always liked that one better than her new one. But that's just me. So, did you stay in touch, then?"

Elly shook her head. "Just coincidence, we ran into each other when I moved here."

"Some coincidence," Charity remarked. "And now you're working together. How funny is that?"

It seemed like a rhetorical question, so Elly didn't answer. Funny? Maybe, but she hadn't realized what Alex was really like. She'd known so little of Alex, had built up all these fantasies about seeing her again, but she hadn't expected Alex to have a boyfriend, or whatever Will was, or so many girlfriends.

"I think she likes you," Charity said, interrupting Elly's thoughts.

"As a friend," Elly replied. A friend with benefits, she added silently.

"*F-T-F*," Charity said, and Elly frowned.

"What?"

"Friends that…well, you know." Charity grinned.

"That's not really my thing," Elly said, sure her face was beet-red by now.

"Not mine either," Charity confided, "but serial monogamy's not all it's cracked up to be, either."

"I thought you had a boyfriend."

"I do, but I get tired of them pretty easily. They always turn out to be jerks," Charity said. "This one's better than most, but…" She shrugged.

"What about Eric?" Elly asked, thinking about how the bartender had seemed sweet on Charity.

"Oh, Eric. He's a doll, but I don't date people I work with. Makes life a lot easier."

The waiter came by with the extra rolls, and this time Elly was first to the plate.

"Aha, I've created a monster," Charity crowed.

"It's good," Elly protested.

"Oh, I know. The best food in the world." Charity scooped up a tuna roll. She popped it into her mouth, making a sound that should have been in a bedroom. Between them, they inhaled the rest of the rolls and finished off the sake. With a groan, Charity sat back. "That's me done." She patted her stomach.

"Me too." Elly felt stuffed, but pleasantly so. "Why don't you ask Eric out anyway?"

"Don't want to ruin a good thing," Charity said. "Work things are tough. There's no rules against them, and if there were, it's a restaurant and not an office, but I just don't want to screw things up. He's cool, you know."

"Yeah," Elly said, thinking more of Alex than Eric. Alex was cool. Confident, poised, and tough. And totally not her type.

"And a total babe. Be still my heart." Charity mock swooned, and laughed.

"You should try that, next shift you have with him," Elly suggested. "See if he'll catch you. Then you'll know if he's a keeper."

"A lot of advice from a girl who looks at Alex like a starving woman looks at a meal, El," Charity teased.

"Two peas in a pod?" Elly offered.

"Maybe, but it's an awesome pod."

The waiter brought their check and they split it. Charity rose. "The day's still young, and now that I'm not hungry, I think it's time to shop."

"I'll just browse while you shop," Elly said, following Charity out of the restaurant.

"A bit tight for cash?" Charity asked. "No problem. We'll go to some consignment stores instead—they're way better anyway. You can pick up stuff that no one else owns, and look totally original."

Elly didn't think that Charity had any problem looking totally original, no matter what she wore. She envied Charity her sophisticated and sexy style, and her confidence.

❖

Alex strolled down 17th Avenue, enjoying the sun on her face and the slight breeze. She'd parked her bike on a nearby side street and packed her leathers into her saddlebag, and now she was enjoying the beautiful afternoon. She still wondered if she should have gone riding out to the mountains on her own, but with the sun shining, she didn't mind so much.

Feeling indulgent, she'd stopped for a small bowl of gelato, and she savored the last spoonful. She licked her lips, then brought her fingers up to her mouth, lightly rubbing at the corners to make sure she hadn't left any chocolate. Heading farther east, thinking of stopping to sit and enjoy the band playing music in the gazebo, she passed a consignment clothing store. On a whim, knowing she needed a couple of new shirts, she turned and went in, climbing the half flight of stairs up. The proprietor, a curvy blonde wearing a gray blouse and dark skinny jeans, gave her a wide smile and cheery greeting. Alex grinned back.

"Hey, Amanda."

"Long time no see," Amanda said as she attached price tags to a stack of new items.

"Too much work," Alex said, "and it's riding season."

"And no leathers to show off?"

"Next time."

"I hope so. Purple dots are twenty-five percent off, and black ones are fifty."

Alex nodded and continued on, heading first to the rack of jeans.

They were her weakness, and she flipped through the ones in her size, not really looking at color, but feeling for softness. Her hand hit one dark-wash pair that was nearly as soft as cashmere, and she pulled them out, putting them to her waist to check the length. Perfect. She slung them over her shoulder, two fingers hooked into the hanger. She looked for a second pair, but nothing caught her attention, so she moved on, heading to the rack of black shirts, with the row of white shirts beneath it. Amanda sorted by color instead of just size, and Alex appreciated it, given that her standard wear was jeans and a white or black T-shirt outside of work. Never bright colors if she could help it.

Once she'd picked out a few shirts, two black, one white, and one striped just to mix it up, she headed for the change room. Most likely everything would fit, but she liked to double-check. Money was better spent on her bike instead of ill-fitting clothes.

"Oh my God, that is *perfect* on you."

She heard the trilling, cheery voice before she saw the speaker. It was familiar. Then she came around a corner, and Charity stood there, her hands on her hips, looking at a woman who stood in front of the tri-paned mirror. She wore a dress in a lacy deep purple; it clung to her like it was made for her alone.

And then Alex saw who Charity was with.

Elly.

And Elly dressed up. Elly out of her trademark jeans and chambray shirt. Elly with her strawberry-blond curls mussed, her face flushed.

Alex felt a rush of attraction but shoved it back. Elly just wanted to be friends. She forced a smile, trying not to look like she was ogling Elly. However, she wasn't about to let this go, not entirely.

"Gorgeous dress," she said, stepping up to an empty change room.

In the mirror, Elly's cheeks went bright red, but she smiled back. "Thank you. I don't think I'm going to get it though. Just a bit too expensive, and not very practical. I didn't think you'd be here. You're not riding?"

Alex shrugged. "Change of plans."

"Oh, come on, El," Charity urged. "It's so worth it. That dress is brilliant."

"I don't know." Elly shifted her weight from foot to foot and Alex hung up her clothes before leaning against the wall, making a show of looking her over.

"It suits you, El," she said. "It'd be a waste not to get it."

"It's just..." Elly groped for the price tag that hung by the back of her neck, poking out of the back of the gown. Alex stepped forward and snagged it, her fingertips brushing against Elly's warm, bare upper back.

Her mouth went dry.

"How much is it, again?" Elly asked, trying to twist and see.

"Hold still," Alex managed to say, her voice a bit hoarse. She turned the price tag over in her hand: $120. But then she saw the black dot. "Regular price, one twenty. But this one's on sale. Half off."

"El, you have to get it," Charity urged again. "Half price, and it fits you like a glove."

Still Elly appeared to debate with herself, her eyes downcast, biting her lip. "I can't. It's too much right now. I can't afford it."

She looked up into the mirror, her smile gone, her shoulders slumped. She went back into the change room and pulled the curtain.

"But it was so perfect," Charity moaned, though quietly. "You thought so, didn't you, Alex?"

"Totally. But if it's too much, it's too much. Are you two hanging around long?"

"A little while longer, I think. I have stuff to buy." Charity indicated a pile folded on top of a shelf of shoes. "Just waiting now for Elly to change back out of that utterly fabulous dress."

"I have a few things to try on, so I guess I'll talk to you later," Alex said, indicating her change room.

Charity leaned over to peer in. "Jeans and boring shirts? Oh, Alex, surely you can do better than that."

"No dresses for me, Char."

Charity stuck out her tongue. "Lame, Alex. Totally lame."

Alex ducked into the change room and pulled the curtain. She stripped off her jeans and white T-shirt and pulled on the new pair. Perfect fit, and almost cozy in their softness. The shirts she tried on one after the other, and it was only the striped one that fit the way she liked. It was boat-necked and reminded her of Audrey Hepburn. She changed back into her clothes and pulled open the curtain, wondering if Elly and Charity had left yet.

At the counter, Charity scooped up her bulging silver plastic bag and smiled at Amanda. Elly stood nearby, looking at a flowery pair of Doc Martens.

"Those would be cute on you," Alex said, coming up beside her.

"You think?" Elly sounded doubtful.

"Not as fantastic as that dress, but they're cute. A bit rough and tumble, but girly." Alex moved over and placed her selections on the counter in front of Amanda.

"You're too predictable," she said. "But only one shirt this time?"

"The other ones didn't fit as well." Alex shrugged and pulled out her wallet from her back pocket.

"Stripes are a good choice," Amanda said. "Classic. Your total's forty-five."

Alex paid and accepted the bag Amanda handed her. "Thanks."

"Have a good one," Amanda trilled, then she waved, greeting a new customer. "Diane, how are you?"

Alex turned, not seeing Elly or Charity. She headed out and nearly bowled Charity over coming out the door. Charity was digging in her purse.

"There it is." She pulled out her phone. "I need a smaller purse."

"Hey," Alex said, "what are you two up to?"

"Char's going to meet her guy," Elly replied, watching Charity texting furiously.

"And you?"

"Home, I guess." Elly shrugged. "I'm not working tonight."

"Have you been down the strip yet?" Alex asked, "Or had a pint at The Ship?"

Elly shook her head. "What's The Ship?"

"Only the best pub in the city," Alex said. "It's nice out—we should find a spot on their patio and get a tan."

"Sounds fun."

"You two don't mind me," Charity said, not looking up from her phone. "I'll be meeting the boy shortly." She glanced up momentarily. "Have fun, and don't do anything I wouldn't do." She giggled.

Alex snorted. "That's an almost nonexistent list."

"I know." Charity waved them away. "Go on."

Elly put her hands in the pockets of her jeans and they began their walk down 17th.

"What do you think of living down near here?" Alex asked when Elly didn't start a conversation. She wondered why Elly was so quiet. It wasn't like they were strangers. Maybe Elly hadn't wanted to join her, but had felt she had to.

"I haven't been out much," Elly admitted.

"But you've been here a couple of months, haven't you?" Alex said, confused.

"I know." Elly's shoulders scrunched and she looked embarrassed.

"You've had a couple of months of nice spring weather and haven't been out to sit on a pub patio?" If she lived closer, she'd be on a patio every day off, soaking up the sun. Except when she was riding, of course.

"I don't like going out alone." Elly flushed and looked away, down the street ahead of them. Alex wondered at her statement, then considered. Downtown teemed with people; it was noisy and a bit dirty, and there were always a few panhandlers begging for change. It was a lively place, but it was a city thing. Main Street in Elly's town probably had tumbleweeds on it.

"It's safe here," Alex said, trying to keep her tone positive. "Not as quiet as the farm, but safe, nonetheless."

"It's a bit overwhelming," Elly admitted, though her shoulders straightened.

"It would be. Let me show you one of my favorite spots. To The Ship!"

CHAPTER THIRTEEN

Elly felt her phone vibrating in her pocket, and she pulled it out, frowning at the display. Across from her, Alex took a sip of her pint of beer, her sunglasses on, the light glinting off the dark plastic.

"Who is it?" she asked.

"I don't know." The number was unfamiliar, but it seemed local.

"Answer it anyway. Maybe you won the lottery."

Elly snorted. "Doubt it." But she did answer. "Hello?"

"Eleanor Cole?" a man's voice asked, confident with its deep baritone.

"Yes. Who am I speaking to?" She had to put a finger in her other ear in order to hear him over the chatter on the patio.

"This is Bernard Hamilton, Ms. Cole. Your neighbor gave me your number, since I hadn't heard from you. Do you have time to chat?"

"I do. I had meant to call you, but time got away from me."

Alex gave her a puzzled look. She mouthed *buyer for the farm* and Alex nodded.

"Perfectly all right. Now, I'd like to offer you half a million for the land, all the quarter-sections you own."

"Really?" Elly wasn't sure she'd heard him correctly.

"That's right."

"I'll have to think about it," Elly said. Her mind whirled, and the half a pint of beer she'd just drunk now churned in her stomach. With half a million dollars, she could buy a place in town, find a job better suited, and she wouldn't have to worry.

"Don't think too long," Hamilton warned. "We want to move fast on this deal. We have a few other ranchers nearby under consideration, but we'd prefer your property. It's much better situated."

"Situated for what?"

"Close to the highway, with access, good flat stretches, barring the farmhouse plot itself, of course. We'd likely use that as an office, if it's in good shape. What do you say?"

What would she say? Elly fiddled with her glass, turning it on its cardboard coaster.

"Ms. Cole? You still there?"

"Still here. Sorry, you've just caught me by surprise. Can I think about it and get back to you?"

"Call me whenever you've decided," he said graciously. "But the sooner the better. You can reach me at this number at any time."

Elly hung up the phone and set it shakily on the heavy varnished wood of the picnic table. Her beer sat before her, but her desire to enjoy her drink had fled. Selling the farm. It was for real now. She had to decide.

"You all right?" Alex asked, reaching across to pat her hand. "You look pale."

"That company offered me half a million dollars for the farm," Elly said, her voice barely a whisper.

"Holy shit." Alex gripped her hand instead. "That's a lot of money. You going to sell?"

"I don't know." Elly looked up at Alex, who gazed back at her with an excited expression.

"Hard to turn down half a million," Alex said. "Think of what you could do with that money, El. You could buy a place in Calgary, set yourself up good."

"I could. But it's home."

"It is, but you could get a better home. A newer one."

"I don't know." A newer home didn't have character like the farm did, and it wasn't where she'd grown up, where her family had lived. Nothing could replace that.

"Sleep on it," Alex advised. "There's no real rush, is there?"

"I can't wait too long on it, though. He said they're looking at other farms."

Alex squeezed her hand and let go. "Don't worry about it right now. Enjoy your beer, then we'll go wander along the avenue some more. You need to go to the candy store."

"What kind of candy?"

"All kinds. You'll see. Let's order another round."

❖

As they sat with their second drinks, Elly's phone rang again. "Damn, it's Jack." She answered the phone, though warily. "Jack?" Elly listened, and then her face flushed a dark pink, and her brow furrowed. Alex wished she could hear what he said, but the noise of the traffic on the road opposite them drowned out any sound from the phone's tiny speaker. What would a guy like Jack be calling for now? And how would he know she'd talked to the corporate guy? That seemed awfully quick. Elly really should sell, especially if she was having all this interest.

"I haven't decided yet, Jack. They did make a good offer, but I haven't said yes or no." She paused to listen again, chewing on her bottom lip. "I don't know, a ranch possibly." Alex heard a noise from the phone, and Elly winced, holding it away from her ear.

"Jack, it's my decision to make, not yours. You're not my dad."

Alex could see Elly getting angrier, something she hadn't realized was possible. Elly was usually so calm, so collected.

"I'll talk to you later…No, *later*. Good-bye, Jack."

Elly hung up the phone and turned it off before she slipped it back into her pocket. "Sorry about that."

"Jack doesn't want you to sell?"

"No. He wants me to keep it, or to sell it to him."

"Can he afford to buy it?"

"I don't think so. He's not that well-off. I don't think he could match Hamilton's offer. But he's furious anyway." Elly sighed. "He doesn't like that corporations keep buying up the land, pushing out the family farms, raising so many head of cattle."

Alex knew little about farming, and even less about cattle. What Elly had said might as well have been Greek. "You'll make the right decision. Just ignore him. He's probably just pissed you didn't offer to sell the land to him first." Elly didn't need the farm; she'd do just fine in the city with half a million bucks. They could work, play, and take the bike out on weekends. Elly could even afford to buy her own bike then, and she could come out with her and Will. She was starting to really like Elly, like hanging out with her.

"I'll try to ignore him, but it's hard. It's such a small community."

"Do what you want, not what they want," Alex advised. "It's what I'd do."

❖

It's what I'd do.

Elly mulled that line over as they walked back to her place. She envied Alex her easy confidence, her assurance that she knew what was best for herself. She should be more like that, but she didn't feel it inside. She wanted to.

"Do what I want to do," she murmured to herself, her words lost in the traffic and pedestrian noise. By the time they reached her apartment, she was determined not to let Jack bully her into a decision, but she still didn't know what to decide.

"Takeout for dinner later?" Alex suggested as they climbed the steps up to the apartment. "After a lazy afternoon like that, cooking seems like too much effort."

"Sure. Pizza?" Elly suggested the first thing that came to mind.

"You ever had pizza from Spiros? Best in the neighborhood, maybe even the whole city."

"Never."

Alex pulled up the restaurant on her phone and handed it over. "My favorite is the one with lamb. What don't you like on your pizza?"

Elly glanced at the menu. "No olives or onions. Or green peppers. Actually, no peppers of any kind."

"Not a pepper girl, huh?" Alex chuckled. "I'll remember that. Then how about a large lamb pizza, and maybe some calamari?"

"All right." Elly handed her back her phone, then went into the kitchen for a glass of water. Alex followed her in and Elly watched as she leaned on the counter, her legs stretched out before her, the jeans she wore snug over her hips, hugging tight to the curves. She remembered seeing Alex in those jeans, but with her chaps on, and there was something about her in leather that made Elly damp with desire. Yet she remembered what she'd said. No sex, just friends.

Alex made the call and ordered the pizza and calamari. "We can go pick it up," she said, "ready in about forty-five minutes. Then we can grab some pop and go back to my place."

"Where'd you leave your bike?" Elly asked, and then wondered where Alex had left all of her gear.

"A few blocks away. But it won't take me long to get ready."

Elly held her glass of water, frowning down into it. If she didn't sell the land to Jack, what would the town think? It had only just come to her, and the thought that she'd be ostracized or looked down on because she'd sold out to a corporation worried her. If she walked into the diner, there'd be disapproval instead of welcome; if she dropped by to see Mrs. Calderwood, the widow would be perfunctory instead of warm. She didn't think she could manage that.

"Hey, you." Alex nudged her gently, coming to lean on the counter by her, their hips just barely touching. "Earth to Elly."

"Sorry. Thinking."

"About the farm still? What's to think about? You walk away with a ton of money, and all's good."

Elly wanted to laugh. Of course, it seemed that simple on the surface.

"I grew up there," she said. "But it's more than that and doesn't even begin to cover everything that matters."

"I grew up in several houses," Alex replied. "More than several. But they're just houses."

"When I was five," Elly said, thinking back to a long-ago day, when the leaves on the tree in the yard had changed to a brilliant yellow, and the mornings were marked with low-lying fog, "my dad decided it was finally time to teach me to ride. I'd been bothering him for weeks about it, and he'd always said no, not until your birthday. So, my birthday morning, he got up early, and got Harriet, our oldest, gentlest mare, saddled up and brushed, and when Mom woke me up, she got me dressed in jeans and boots and a new little cowboy hat. It was red. She brought me out to the front porch, even before I'd had breakfast, and there was Harriet, red ribbons braided in her mane, and a birthday hat on her head, balanced carefully between her ears. And my dad stood there, grinning ear to ear, holding the reins."

She paused, taking a sip of her water to cover the emotion that welled in her chest. Alex was quiet.

"He hoisted me up, fit the stirrups up nice and short, and we did a turn around the yard. I'd ridden one of the pigs before, when it would let me, but being on Harriet was like being on top of a mountain by comparison." She smiled to herself. "Then he took me out of the yard and into the ditch by the road, and we walked all the way down to Jack's house. Mrs. Calderwood was there, and she waved at me from their porch. I waved back, feeling like…a queen, I guess. It was the best birthday ever."

Elly swiped at her eyes, blotting away the moisture with the hem of her shirt.

"I kind of envy you, growing up like that," Alex said. "Not the farm exactly, but growing up with both parents, and having those kinds of fun times."

Elly glanced over. Alex stared into the middle distance, looking unhappy.

"Do you want to talk about it?" Elly asked, keeping her tone quiet, gentle.

Alex shook her head. "No. Nothing will come of it. It's not like I can go back and change any of it, you know."

Elly took Alex's hand and led her out of the kitchen, into the living room, and onto the sofa. "I know you hate touchy-feely stuff," she began, and Alex snorted, "but give talking about it a try. If I promise not to judge you or pity you, would you at least attempt it?"

Alex let go of Elly's hand and rubbed her nose. She leaned forward, her elbows on her knees, not looking at anything in particular.

"Your life sounds like a fairy tale," she said. "I don't think you'd understand about my life. Most people can't, whenever I do mention something, so I just stopped talking about it. Or, like when I was a teen, you try to hide that you're in foster care, that you've been bounced from family to family because no one can commit to giving you a home for more than a year. Two if you're lucky."

That wasn't what Elly had expected. Alex was so together, so confident.

"There was my grandmother," Alex added, "but she wasn't around as much as she wanted to be. She's not in very good health, and even back then she couldn't have taken me in. I was too much for her to handle, but she did her best."

"At least you have some family," Elly said. "And someone who cares."

"She is that," Alex acknowledged. "It helped. And so did Will. I met him in junior high, and he's been through similar situations. The one real constant in my life. There's been no one else."

That explained a lot. But how could Alex be so committed to Will but not to anyone else? She liked women a lot, obviously enjoyed sex with women, but had she ever had a relationship with one?

Alex snagged the last of the calamari and popped it into her mouth. The squid had grown cool, but she still liked the crunch of the breading.

"Hey, that one was mine," Elly said, nudging Alex with her elbow, though gently.

"Didn't have your name on it," Alex replied cheekily. "Gotta be quick!"

"Last piece of pizza's mine, then."

"Deal."

Elly glanced back at the television and Alex turned her attention back to the screen. Hopefully Elly liked the film. She had suggested it without thinking, assuming as she did when she was with Will that a motorcycle film would be suitable. But even he'd once reminded her, *No one is as much of a gearhead as you are.* When Elly laughed at the sight of Anthony Hopkins trimming his nails with a grinder, Alex hoped that was a good sign. *The World's Fastest Indian* was one of her favorites.

Her phone vibrated on the side table and she picked it up, glancing at the number. "Hey, Will."

"What's up, gorgeous? You're not at work."

"Had the night off."

"Doing anything fun?"

"Watching a movie."

"I'll be over in a bit, then."

"With Elly," Alex added. At the mention of her name, Elly glanced over.

"Oh. I'll leave you to it, then." With a snort, Will hung up. Alex shrugged and put the phone down.

"That was quick," Elly said.

"Just Will. He wanted to hang out, but I'm busy." Alex laid an arm over Elly's shoulder and Elly cuddled in close. This was just about perfect. Maybe she could convince Elly to soften her friends-only stance.

"He doesn't mind, does he?" Elly asked.

"No, he won't mind." Alex leaned forward and grabbed a piece of pizza. Elly followed suit, taking a cautious bite and chewing slowly.

"This is good," she said, taking a second bite. In a matter of seconds, it seemed, the slice was gone.

"Told you," Alex said with satisfaction. She bit into her own piece, catching a bit of cheese on her finger and bringing it to her mouth. Elly set a paper napkin on her lap and Alex used it to dab her lips and wipe the grease from her finger.

"I've never seen a bike like that before," Elly said, her gaze fixed to the screen.

"I can't imagine riding that close to the ground," Alex said. Anthony Hopkins stretched out, almost horizontal, on the Indian.

Elly shivered. "I'd hope you wouldn't," she said. "That's just insane."

"You don't have to worry," Alex said. "I won't be going down to the salt flats to race." Not that she didn't want to; it was just too expensive.

❖

"What did you think of it?" Alex asked as they lay stretched out on the sofa, the credits rolling.

"Better than I expected," Elly conceded. She'd been having that reaction to a lot of new experiences lately. "Though I don't think I want all my movies from now on to be motorcycle-themed. Just so you know." She rested her head on Alex's shoulder, enjoying the cozy warmth from being sandwiched between Alex and the back of the sofa. She could almost fall asleep like this.

Alex's phone buzzed and she felt Alex sigh heavily as she reached for the phone and looked at the number. "It's work."

"Why would they call? It's your night off."

"I know, but I still have to see what's up." Alex answered the phone. "Eric, you know it's my night off, right?" she said after listening to the voice on the other end. "Dammit. Fine. I'll be there in a few. Keep him in the bar." Alex hung up. "Will's hammered and refuses to cab it home. Stupid idiot." She shifted on the sofa, sitting up slowly, inching out from under Elly's arm. "Sorry, babe."

Elly sat up. "Want me to come with you?"

Alex seemed to debate the idea. "I suppose you should. I only have the bike, and someone will need to drive Will's car home."

"You'd put drunk Will on the back of the bike?" Elly asked, surprised.

"I have done, but I don't like to. We'll shove him into the backseat of his car. He'll probably fall asleep before he's even home. Idiot," she muttered again. "He's usually not so stupid." She stood and stretched. "I'd hoped to have a night in. With you."

"We can come back here after." Elly swung her legs over the side of the sofa.

"Is that a promise of something more?" Alex teased.

Elly laughed. "I don't know yet." She stood. "Let's go, get Will home, then we can come back and talk about it."

Alex went to fetch their gear. Elly pulled on Alex's spare set of chaps and took up the spare helmet. There was a chill in the air as they headed outside, and Elly zipped her jacket right up to her chin, pulling her collar up as far as she was able.

"It'll be a quick ride," Alex said. "And it'll be warm in Will's car, assuming he got that thermostat issue fixed." She rolled her eyes. "Hop on."

They zipped through the dark neighborhood and out onto the busier roads, making it to Parry's as quick as Alex had said. She parked the bike beside a battered old Honda.

"Will's?" Elly asked, taking off her helmet.

"It's a piece of crap, isn't it? I keep telling him he needs to buy a better car. Come on, he'll be inside. Sooner we get him out here, sooner we can go home."

The bar inside was busy, but not overly so. Eric waved to them and indicated the end of the bar, where Will stood with a young woman, his arm flung casually over her shoulder. He held a pint of beer in his free hand and drank from it liberally.

"Babe, you made it!" Will caught sight of Alex and grinned, his face florid, his eyes bright.

"Time to go, Will," Alex said, walking up to him and taking the pint from his hand. "Give me your keys."

"I'm fine," Will said stubbornly.

"You're not fine," Eric retorted, coming up beside him. He gently disengaged Will's arm from around the young woman. "You've been cut off." The young woman smiled.

"Later, babe," she said, patting Will's arm and heading over to the pool table.

"That's my date," Will said, his words slurring slightly. "You jerk."

"Come on, Will." Alex hooked his arm, pulling it through hers. "We'll take you home."

"We?" Will blinked and Elly found herself in his sights. "Oh. Her." His mouth set in a frown, but he let Alex lead him out of the bar. Elly followed a couple of steps behind.

"Keys," Alex said, holding out her hand when they got to the Honda. Will pulled them from his pocket and put them into her palm. She handed them off to Elly, who flipped through the keychain until she found the right one. She unlocked the driver's side door.

"She can't drive my car," Will protested. He moved forward, but staggered.

"You're not getting on the back of my bike," Alex pointed out, "and Elly can't drive my bike, so she's driving you. Just be quiet and get in." Her voice was stern, almost sharp, like Elly had never heard it before.

"The things I do for you," she heard Will mutter as he climbed into the passenger seat. The smell of beer filled the car and Elly rolled down the window halfway. It might be a chilly night, but if she had to smell that, she'd tolerate the chill.

Alex shut the passenger door once Will had his feet inside, and came around to the driver's side window. "Just follow me, babe," she said, leaning down. "I'll take it slow. It's a bit of a drive—he lives out in the 'burbs."

Elly nodded and turned the key in the ignition. She waited until Alex was ready, then followed her out of the parking lot and down the road. Beside her, Will sagged in his seat, his eyes at half-mast.

It was a longer drive than she'd expected, out to one of the northwest suburbs she'd never been to. They turned into a community and she slowed her speed when Alex did.

Will struggled to sit up. "Pull over."

"What?"

"Pull over." He frantically rolled down the window and she pulled to the curb. He leaned his head out the window and she heard the sounds of vomiting. A sour smell wafted into the car and she grimaced. Up ahead, she saw Alex slow and stop.

Will sank back into his seat, wiping his mouth with the back of his hand. "Sorry," he muttered. Elly pulled back into the road and caught up to Alex, pulling up to the red light behind her. They turned onto a smaller street, and then made a second turn onto a cul-de-sac. Alex stopped in front of a town house and Elly pulled into a free spot.

Will pushed his door open and staggered out, vomiting again onto the lawn. Elly killed the engine and got out, locking the doors. Alex had dismounted and come over to Will.

"Jesus, Will, couldn't you have better aim?" Elly heard her say. She came around the front of the car and almost lost her dinner at the sight of the vomit-splattered passenger door.

"Oh, ugh." She wrinkled her nose.

Alex hooked her shoulder under Will's arm and shepherded him toward the door. He went with her willingly and Elly trailed behind, holding Will's keys. She unlocked the front door for them, and once inside, Will disentangled himself from Alex's hold, pulled the keys from the lock, and stuffed them in his pocket.

"*She* can stay out there," he said, holding on to the wall as he toed off his shoes, then staggered toward the bathroom.

"We're leaving," Alex said sharply, loud enough for Will to hear before he shut the bathroom door. She turned to Elly, who stood on the cement step. If Will didn't want her inside, she wasn't about to go. "Sorry about him. He's not usually such a jerk." She rolled her eyes. "Let's go. We need to carry on from where we were."

"Does he get like this often?" Elly asked as they went back to the bike. She'd had some pity for him when he puked, but after his obnoxious dismissal, the pity was fading.

"It's not common," Alex replied, "but I've had to come get him a few times. He's usually better at holding his liquor than that." They passed the Honda. "I think I'll leave that for him to deal with in the morning. Seems fair."

"More than fair," Elly agreed. Alex took Elly's helmet from the saddlebag and handed it to her.

"Hop up, gorgeous. We have a date with my bed, and we're late."

"Too late," Elly said, stifling a yawn. After that ride to Parry's and Will's cold shoulder and puking theatrics, all she wanted to do was go to bed. "Bedtime for me."

"My bed's warm," Alex said.

"No, my own bed," Elly replied. She thought Alex looked disappointed, but with the helmet on and obscuring her mouth, she couldn't be sure.

"If you insist."

Chapter Fourteen

Alex bit back a sigh, sitting at the kitchen table drinking her coffee. Yesterday had been just about perfect. Just about. She'd been so close to getting past Elly's edict of friends only.

Will. What the fuck was he thinking?

Alex grabbed her phone from where she had it charging on the kitchen counter and dialed Will's number. It rang and rang, and went to voice mail. She tried again, and finally he picked up.

"What?"

"No thanks for your late-night rescuers?" Alex said, trying for humor but not managing.

Will groaned. "Tell me it wasn't as bad as all that."

"Worse. Have you seen your car yet?"

There was a pause and she heard the shuffling of his feet. He cursed. "I don't remember that."

"That's how bad it was. Thankfully Elly doesn't have a sensitive stomach, or you could have been dealing with more mess."

"Elly?"

"She drove you. I rode my bike."

"Jesus." Will groaned again. "I need some painkillers. Want to go for a ride? We can zip out to that greasy spoon in Nanton and be back in time for your work."

Alex looked at the clock on the stove. It was just past ten, and she didn't have to work until five. She could use a ride. It'd get her out of this mood, if nothing else. "If I leave now, will you be ready when I get there?"

"Give me half an hour," he said. "I need to wash."

"Done. Breakfast's on you, though."

Will still looked green around the gills when she pulled up beside him in front of his place, but he was ready, straddling his R6 as it idled at the curb. His helmet hung from the handlebar.

"You ready?" she asked.

"Ready as I'll ever be." He put his helmet on and buckled it up.

"Did you wash your car?"

"Took the hose to it while I was waiting for you. It's been through worse."

"Ring road to the highway?" Alex asked.

"Yeah. Better than taking the Deerfoot, especially from here."

Alex eased out of the cul-de-sac and onto the road, retracing her route. She could hear the low whine of Will's bike behind her. When they reached the ring road, he cruised in the lane beside hers, edging up past her until she increased her speed, then dropping back.

Once they hit the highway, he blew past her, throwing her a jaunty wave. Typical Will. She shifted gears and sped after him, catching him after a short stretch. She passed him when the road was clear, and they leapfrogged each other all the way to Nanton.

At the town's outskirts, they slowed, and Alex let Will lead the way to the restaurant. Though she'd eaten a bit earlier, her stomach growled. Good thing Will was paying; she felt like she could eat a horse. Will pulled up in front of the coffee shop and she slipped in beside him.

"Welcome back," the waitress said, bringing over menus. "Can I get you some coffee?"

"Biggest mug you got," Will said, grinning. The woman laughed. "You got it."

"Sounds like you're feeling better," Alex said as she perused her menu. Maybe a hot roast beef sandwich, or the pancakes…

"Amazing what a ride'll do for you," Will replied.

"Been a while since you've been that shitfaced," Alex observed. "What's up?"

Will shrugged. "Nothing much. Just happens. I shouldn't have started with the rye." He looked over his menu.

"You do know better."

"But the hangovers never last, not for me, anyway. You, on the other hand, are a lightweight."

"At least I know it." Alex stuck her tongue out at him and he glanced up in time to catch a glimpse.

"Don't stick it out if you aren't going to use it," he warned, setting down his menu.

The tension between them snapped, and for the first time, Alex felt at a loss for words.

The waitress saved her. "What'll you have?" She filled their coffee cups.

"Hot beef sandwich with fries, please," Alex said.

"French toast, with the fruit, and the whipped cream, and bacon on the side. And thank you for this." Will drained half his cup of coffee in two deep swallows. The waitress topped it up.

"Sure thing."

The second cup went down slower, and Alex doctored hers with cream and sugar, sipping it slowly. The waitress came back again to top up Will's coffee. He gave her a winning smile and her cheeks went pink.

"Always the charmer," Alex said when she'd gone.

"If it gets me coffee, then hell, yes," Will replied. "But she's a sweetheart anyways."

"You were an ass last night to Elly," Alex said, "and she's a sweetheart. You should apologize."

"I don't remember what I said," Will replied, looking sheepish. Alex wondered. It had been a long time since Will had drunk himself into oblivion.

"Apologize anyway, even if you don't remember."

"That bad?"

"That bad."

"You like her a lot, don't you?"

The question surprised Alex. He'd never asked her that about any of the other people she'd been with.

"Yeah, I do. She's pretty damn awesome."

"And she's a babe."

"She is that." Alex grinned.

"Not like Heather at all, then?" Will noted, sipping his coffee.

Alex stiffened. “They’re all like Heather eventually.” Wanting more than she was willing to give, and then when she did, cheating on her. Heather had sworn up and down and sideways that Alex was the only one for her, and she was the one Alex could count on. Alex had believed her and had paid for it.

Their food came and Will dug in like a starving man. They ate in companionable silence. When their bill came, Alex pushed it to the side of Will’s plate. He glanced at it and pulled out his wallet, put down a twenty, then rose.

“Ready to race?”

Alex stood. “When am I not?” She scooped up her helmet and they headed back to the bikes.

“Up to Longview, or do you want to go east instead?”

“Let’s do Longview. It’s prettier. And closer to home.” Alex straddled her bike and pulled on her helmet.

“Last one to the café there buys coffee,” Will said, giving her a cheeky grin.

“You’re on.”

❖

Neither of them won.

An RCMP vehicle pulled out onto the highway behind them, curtailing any thoughts of racing, though both she and Will pushed the bikes right to the speed limit. She tapped her gloved fingers on the handlebars, watching the cop in her side mirrors. The car showed no inclination to pass them and she resigned herself to doing the limit. Will was just ahead of her, close to the center line, and they stayed in formation until they hit Longview and pulled off into the tiny parking lot of the café. The RCMP officer went right on by, though he turned to give them one last look as he passed.

“Stupid cop,” Will said, hooking his helmet over the handlebar and running his fingers through his flattened blond hair.

“I’ll buy you coffee anyway,” Alex said, “since you bought breakfast.”

“You’re the best, babe.” Will hooked his arm over her shoulders and leaned in for a kiss. He tasted of coffee and pancake syrup, his lips warm. She felt the light stubble brush her skin. It startled her into awareness and she felt a twinge of guilt. She broke off the kiss, but gently. She hadn't made any promises to Elly, had she? And it was Will, her Will.

"Pity there isn't a hotel here," Will said, giving her another brief kiss.

Alex snorted and ducked out from under his arm. "I'd be late for work then, knowing you." She mounted the wooden stairs and pulled open the door.

"It'd be worth it," Will said as he came up behind her, following her in.

"Derek would give me shit."

"We'll write you a doctor's note," Will quipped. "He'll take that, wouldn't he?" He mimed writing. "Dr. Will prescribed several hours of TLC for Alexandra Bellerose, necessitating her lateness to work."

"TLC? Is that what you're calling it now?" Alex went to the counter and ordered their coffees.

"Dr. Will always speaks in euphemisms," Will said, sliding around her to pick up his coffee cup. He took it over to the sugar and cream. "Derek wouldn't go for it if I said crazy shagging."

"That would give it away." Alex laughed, but inside she didn't feel the thrill Will's words used to inspire. She was tired today. Last night had been a late one and she hadn't slept as well as she usually did. Her brain just wouldn't shut off, bringing up memories of Heather, and of her childhood. She shouldn't have dredged that up, shouldn't have said anything to Elly about it.

Will headed out to the small patio, to a table in the sun, and she followed. She was reading too much into all this. Elly was a friend. A good one, like Will was.

❖

Elly's phone vibrated against the coffee table as she got ready for work and she hurried from the bathroom, letting her hair fall around her face, the clip still in her hand.

"Jack?"

"Did you say yes to Hamilton?" Jack asked, not even bothering to say hello.

"What?" She hadn't expected that question.

"Did you tell Hamilton you'd sell him the farm?"

"No. I told him I had to think about things and I'd get back to him." Elly puzzled over Jack's questions. "I wouldn't make that kind of decision on a whim. You know that."

"He's been in town, acting like his company's going to buy it," Jack said. "That it was a done deal."

"It's nowhere near done," Elly replied. "He's made an offer."

"What did he offer?"

Elly paused. It really was none of Jack's business. "Until I can get the place valued, I'll keep it to myself."

"How much?" Jack persisted.

"Enough."

"Right." Jack hung up.

Elly stared at her phone, then set it down on the coffee table. She turned on her computer and looked up Realtors online, finding one in Cardston. When she called the woman, Noreen Perrers, she explained what she needed.

"We'll get the valuation for you, and we can list the property almost immediately afterward."

"I always just thought the tax assessed value was the right one," Elly said.

"No, not at all. Market value, especially on farmland, is usually much higher. You can rely on me. I knew your parents, back when. We went to the same school."

"I'm still not sure I want to sell," Elly confided.

"It's family land," Noreen replied. She sounded sympathetic. "It's always a hard decision to make. Can you come down to our office next week? We can figure out then what you want to do for certain."

"I will. Maybe Wednesday?" Elly couldn't remember if she had that day off, but she thought she might.

"I'll pencil you in," Noreen said.

After ending their conversation, Elly sat back on the sofa. She had just under a week to make her decision, one way or another. The blank, off-white walls of the apartment stared back at her and a wave of homesickness overtook her. She wanted to be back at the farm, on the old couch there, curled up under her quilt, looking out the window and over the fields, hearing the birds in the hedge instead of traffic going by, or looking at the hodgepodge of pictures on the walls, the photos and notes stuck to the corkboard with little plastic pushpins. It wouldn't be the same anywhere else.

❖

Parry's was busy enough that Elly hardly had time to think, much less ruminate over her troubles. She was working with Charity and another server, but Charity was a mess, forgetting orders and, once, misbalancing an entire tray of pop glasses, sending them crashing to the red tile floor by the dish sink. At that, she covered her face with her hands and hurried into the back. Elly helped the dishwasher clean up the mess, then went out, taking care of Charity's few tables as well as her own.

Derek came to help almost half an hour later, swooping in and taking over Charity's section.

"Is she okay?" Elly asked when they had a quiet moment, waiting for orders to come up from the kitchen.

"She will be," Derek said. "She just needs a bit of time to pull herself together."

"But to cry over spilled pop?"

"She'll be fine," Derek said, snagging the two pasta dishes as they were set onto the counter. Elly took out the orders of hamburgers and fries, and a Caesar salad, to her table. As she headed back with dirty dishes, she heard a belligerent male voice.

"Where is she?"

Elly put down her dishes and followed the sound out to the hostess stand, where a tall, thickly built man stood. He might have been attractive, but he scowled at the hostess, his dark eyes narrowed, his thick hands resting on the top of the desk. Shay shrank back.

"Who are you looking for?" Elly asked, stepping up beside Shay. The girl was barely sixteen, a child compared to the guy glowering at her.

"Charity. Where is she?"

"Who are you?" Elly countered. She'd never seen him before.

"Her boyfriend," the man retorted.

Elly weighed her options. She could tell him Charity was here, but she was already upset enough, and an angry boyfriend would make things worse. He might be the reason they were worse in the first place.

"I'll go see if I can find her," Elly replied. "If you'll just sit there on the bench so we can seat the people behind you…"

The man turned and saw the couple who waited, looking concerned but patient. He grunted and shuffled over to the seat Elly had indicated.

"Shay, let me know if you need anything," Elly said in a low voice.

"I'll be okay." Shay's lips trembled, but she made a noticeable effort to contain her worry.

"You sure?"

At Shay's nod, Elly went back into the restaurant, into the back, following Charity's path. Upstairs, in the employees' area, she found Charity sitting in one of the old, rickety restaurant chairs, her knees pulled up to her chest.

"You all right?" she asked, dropping to a squat in front of Charity when she didn't look up. "What happened?"

Charity sniffled and wiped her eyes. "It's nothing."

"There's a guy here asking for you," Elly said gently.

Charity stiffened and her reddened eyes widened. "Big guy?"

"Yeah."

"I'm not here. Tell him I'm not here." Charity shivered.

"He said he's your boyfriend."

"Was," Charity corrected. "I broke up with him, but he wouldn't take no for an answer. He keeps calling me."

"Did you call the cops?" Elly asked.

"No. Don't know what they'd do, anyway."

"If he's threatening you—"

Charity shuddered. "He just won't leave me alone. He's never been violent, but he just can't seem to accept that it's over."

"I'll get Derek, we'll throw him out," Elly said. Charity wiped her eyes again, and Elly wanted to march her ex-boyfriend out of the restaurant herself, or throw him out physically.

Charity nodded. "Thank you."

"But you have to call the cops," Elly said. "What if he gets worse?"

"He'll go away eventually."

"That's not much of a guarantee. Call the cops, Char."

"I will." Charity pulled out her phone. "One of the guys over at the local precinct comes in here for lunch sometimes. I'll call him."

"Good." Elly rose and leaned over to give Charity a hug. "Stay up here as long as you need to, okay?"

At Charity's nod, Elly went back downstairs and found Derek. "He needs to leave," she said, indicating the burly man still waiting in the entryway.

"You think I can manage to throw him out if he doesn't want to go?" Derek looked incredulous.

"Derek, that's your job," Elly pointed out. "The well-being of your staff."

"Yeah, but he's freaking huge." Derek ran a hand through his gray hair, mussing it. "Maybe Eric can give me a hand."

Elly glanced back out into the entryway and saw a police car pull up.

"Or maybe that cop can help you," she said, nudging Derek.

The cop pulled open the door and strode up to the hostess stand. Elly went out to meet him.

"Hey, I'm Officer Fleming," he said.

"Charity's friend?" Elly asked, keeping her voice low so it wouldn't carry to the man waiting.

"Yeah. She here?"

"In the back, but she's scared of that guy there." Elly nodded to the man sitting. The officer frowned.

"Right." He went over to the man. "Sir, I'll have to ask you to leave."

"I'm waiting for my girl," the man said, crossing his arms.

"Well, she's not waiting for you." Officer Fleming waited a moment. "Come on, let's go. I don't want to have to ask again."

The man lunged up, sending Fleming back two paces, towering over him. "Piss off, you pig."

Fleming caught the man just above the elbow, turning him toward the door. The man shook free and shoved Fleming back. Elly stifled her gasp and hurried into the bar. Eric and Alex were working, and Alex looked at her in surprise.

"El?"

"Eric, Officer Fleming is dealing with Charity's ex. I'm worried something's going to happen."

"Dammit." Eric followed her into the restaurant side to the hostess stand. Officer Fleming was there with another cop now, and they'd subdued Charity's ex, who was sprawled on the floor, his hands cuffed behind his back.

"Are you all right?" Elly asked, moving into the entryway. She stayed carefully clear of the man on the floor.

"Just fine," Fleming said. "Tell Charity she should talk to a lawyer about getting a restraining order. I'll be happy to give my side if a judge has any issues."

"I'll tell her."

"Come on, upsy-daisy." The other cop helped Fleming hoist the man to his feet, and they took him out to their cruiser. Elly let out a breath.

"Where's Charity?" Eric asked, still staring after the strange threesome.

"Upstairs. I should go talk to her," Elly said, "let her know what happened."

"I have to get back to work, but if she needs a ride home later, I can take her."

"I'll tell her."

Upstairs, Charity listened as Elly related all that had happened. "I can't afford a lawyer." She rubbed her eyes. "I wish I'd never met that asshole. But he seemed so nice."

"The next guy will be," Elly said. "And by the way, Eric said he'd take you home later, if you needed a ride."

"That's sweet of him." Charity smiled as she pulled her dark hair back into a ponytail, smoothing it with her hands. "He's about as sweet as Alex. You're lucky to have her, you know."

Elly wasn't entirely sure that was the case. "I don't have her. We're just friends."

"Don't look like that," Charity said. "She has to flirt with customers for the job and tips, and she's always been a bit of a player, but so are we all. Just the way of the world in a restaurant, you know? She loves you. I've never seen her take any other girl for a ride on her bike. No one gets to ride. Except you."

"I didn't know that," Elly said. Her cheeks warmed and her heart did a little skip of joy.

"Trust me," Charity replied. She rose. "I know you have to get back to work, but come into the bar when you're done, and I'll buy you a drink."

❖

They stayed till closing, and Elly hadn't had such a good time in a long time. Her cheeks hurt from grinning, her sides ached from laughing at Charity and Eric's jokes. Alex came by to put in her two cents every spare moment she had, and each time she did, her hand would rest on Elly's shoulder, or tease a lock of her hair. Elly felt each touch like a brand.

When the doors were locked, she and Charity helped Eric and Alex tidy up, wiping tables and straightening chairs.

"I've never gotten out so early," Alex said as they walked across the parking lot to their vehicles.

"All those extra hands," Eric said. He put a hand on the small of Charity's back. "You're still up near the college, right?"

"Yeah, in that apartment."

"It's on my way home. See you guys tomorrow."

Elly paused at the driver's side door of her car. Alex leaned against it. "It'd be a shame to end tonight. It's still early."

Elly rested her hand on the door handle, debating. Spending the rest of the night with Alex would be fun, but that's all it would be. She thought of Charity's ex, and of what Charity had said about Alex, that she was a player. Maybe if she didn't expect anything more, then she and Alex could just have some fun. Tonight. Tonight only.

Alex leaned closer, giving her a nudge, seeming to realize she was teetering. "My place, or yours?"

Elly thought of the paper-thin walls at her place, the way she heard every movement of the tenants upstairs. She'd have to leave Alex's place later, but she could deal with that. Just tonight. "Yours. I'll follow you there."

"See you in a few." Alex pushed off the car, sliding her arm around Elly's waist. They kissed, and Elly slid her hands inside Alex's leather jacket. She could smell Alex's perfume and the leather, and she loved it.

"Get a room!" Eric called across the parking lot. They broke apart, and Alex laughed.

"You're just jealous," she called back.

"You bet."

Elly heard Charity's laugh.

"Come on, babe, let's go home." Alex headed to her bike, and Elly unlocked her car door and slid inside. She followed the bike's taillight out of the parking lot and, in what seemed no time at all, pulled up in front of Alex's place.

They barely made it inside before they were kissing again, dropping jackets, stumbling down the hallway toward the bedroom. When she nearly tripped over her trousers as they slid down to her ankles, Elly put a hand out and leaned against the wall to pull them off. She left them in a puddle on the floor and Alex tugged her forward again, into the bedroom.

"If I'd had a few minutes to spare, I'd have taken you into the storage room at work and locked the door," Alex confided, her voice husky.

"You wouldn't." Elly looked at her in surprise.

"I would have." Alex chuckled. "Don't look so surprised. You think that's never happened to anyone at Parry's?"

Elly thought of the diner back home, where something like that would have gotten out to the entire town if it had happened. "And no one notices?"

"If they do notice, they don't really care," Alex said, catching the hem of Elly's shirt and pulling it over her head. Elly shivered in the cool air, dressed only in her underwear. She sat on the bed and pulled the throw from the end of the bed around her as Alex undressed, tossing her clothes into the hamper.

"It wasn't this cold last time," Elly said as Alex turned back toward her.

"I turn the heat down to save money," Alex said. "We can crawl under the covers if you want."

Elly rose and Alex pulled back the coverlet and sheet. She slid under and Alex slid in beside her, flopping the blankets over them.

"Now, where were we?" Alex's cool fingers found Elly's bare stomach and moved lower, stroking the insides of her thighs. Elly found herself getting warmer, and she shifted onto her back, letting her legs relax and fall open.

Alex slipped a finger into Elly's wetness. "You're warm now," she said. "But you need to get warmer." She ducked under the covers and pulled them back up so Elly was covered to her neck. Elly could feel Alex's warm breath on her skin, and the large lump under the cover went lower and lower.

When Alex's tongue flicked her clit, Elly started in surprise, then relaxed. She tried not to giggle at the silliness of it all, seeing the lump that was Alex moving under the covers, the tickle of her fingers down Elly's thighs, but finally the ludicrousness of it all made her burst out laughing. Her breath caught in her throat as Alex took her clit into her mouth, sucking hard, her teeth rasping gently against the sensitive flesh. Elly gripped the coverlet in both hands and tilted her hips up, feeling the tremor in her belly, the need building.

She tried to keep her legs still, tried to keep from accidentally stifling Alex under the blankets, and she shook from the effort.

Alex's fingers curled up into Elly's G-spot, stroking in time with her movements on Elly's clit, and that was all it took. Elly gasped, and the gasp turned into a whimper as the orgasm swept through her. Perspiration prickled behind her knees, at the small of her back, between her shoulder blades.

Alex moved up, poking her head out from the covers, her black hair in static-charged disarray. "Warm now, aren't you?" she teased, and Elly started to laugh.

She reached out, stroking Alex's hair, trying to smooth out the errant strands, and failing miserably. She laughed, a deep belly laugh. "Down to my toes," she said between laughs. "You look a sight."

Alex came up beside her, resting on the pillow. "The curse of long hair," she said, tweaking one of Elly's curls.

"I guess." They looked at each other and Elly swore that the tension crackling between them wasn't just the remnants of Alex's static electricity.

Alex took her hand, and a spark arced between them. "Your hands are warm too," she said, bringing Elly's hand to her lips, her tongue darting out, lightly teasing the tips of her fingers. She moved Elly's hand down to her chest, and Elly took over from there, cupping Alex's left breast, her thumb stroking over the nipple until it puckered. She leaned forward, her lips tracing where her hand had been, her hand moving lower, under the covers.

Elly felt the curve of Alex's hip, the hollow of the inner hip bone, and then the soft curve of her belly, which tensed as she moved her hand over it, relaxing when she stopped and just rested it there. Ignoring Alex's indrawn breath, she teased both of her nipples, one after the other, bringing the pink peaks to attention. She pretended to have forgotten that her hand rested on Alex's belly, feeling Alex shift and squirm under her, tilting her hips, doing everything she could short of asking for Elly to move her hand lower. Kissing the spot between Alex's breasts, Elly smiled to herself and finally moved her hand.

Alex's relieved sigh was worth the wait.

She'd give Alex a mind-blowing orgasm, then leave her wanting more.

❖

Alex's bones felt like liquid, and she sank into the soft bed, Elly beside her. She could fall asleep like this, in the warmth, and the heady afterglow. Never had she felt so content, not with Will, not with Jan, or any of the others she'd taken home from the bar, and definitely not with Heather.

The realization came to her as she lay there under the duvet, Elly by her side.

This was more than just sex. Not just friends with benefits.

Alex's heart stuttered and skipped a beat, and her free hand, the one not resting on Elly's thigh, tensed and fisted in the sheet.

She heard Elly sigh, felt her shift and turn over. Then Elly threw back the cover and slid out, standing beside the bed.

Alex sat up. "You're leaving?"

Elly gave her a startled look, as if she thought Alex had lost it. And maybe she had. "I always go home to sleep."

"Stay?" Alex said, patting the bed.

"You sure?" Elly asked, sounding hesitant.

Was she? She wasn't entirely sure, but she'd come this far.

"I'm sure."

The smile on Elly's face was worth it.

"Right. I'll be back."

Alex flopped back on the bed after Elly had ducked out of the room, letting out a breath. She heard water running in the bathroom. When Elly came back, she turned out the light and slid back into bed, and they shifted and moved together until they were both comfortable.

Elly shifted one more time. "Sorry, my foot was tingly."

"No problem." Alex found herself shifting again so that their feet touched but there was a bit of space between their torsos. She heard Elly yawn.

"Good night, Alex."

Alex closed her eyes, listening to Elly's breathing. "Good night, El."

CHAPTER FIFTEEN

The road ahead stretched before her, and Elly put her foot on the gas, though she knew she would be over the limit. Maybe Alex's habits were rubbing off on her. She still couldn't quite get her head around Alex inviting her to stay the other night. As much as she wanted to call Alex and ask her outright, she couldn't. She wanted to get back to the farm and meet with Hamilton, go over the contract and see Noreen, and then start the business of packing. Her stomach twinged and she gripped the steering wheel. Selling the farm to Hamilton was the best she could do, and the money meant she could start over, settle into the city and take the time to get a real job, not just waitressing. Her parents might have been disappointed, but they weren't here now to tell her otherwise.

Noreen met her at the farm, a folder under her arm, and they settled at the kitchen table after Elly put the kettle on for tea.

"I'll be honest with you," Noreen said as she opened the manila folder, taking out several stapled documents, "word's gotten around about your selling to Hamilton Farms. I don't think it's going to go over well."

"I know Jack is not happy about it," Elly replied, "but that's his problem."

"I don't think it's just Jack," Noreen said tactfully. "I ran into Mrs. Calderwood in town earlier while I was grabbing a coffee, and she told me that she was disgusted you'd sell to a man like Hamilton." She handed Elly the first, thickest document. "This is the purchase agreement."

Elly looked down at it, the legalese in endless paragraphs on the page, blurring into a mass of incomprehension. She flipped through it slowly, but even though she read carefully, a lot of it was over her head. "What did Mrs. Calderwood mean, a man like Hamilton? Does she know him?" Her decision was hard enough, but to know that Mrs. Calderwood disapproved made it all the worse. A breeze blew in the open window, bringing with it the scent of the fields, that mix of loam and damp grass. The scent of home.

Noreen shrugged. "She probably does—she seems to know everyone. I suppose she's worried about a corporation taking over the land. They're not exactly good stewards most of the time, you must admit, even though they say they are. You're pretty close to town, and it'd affect them."

Elly frowned. "I figured he wants to use it for a cattle ranch."

"Cattle are all right, and a ranch is decent. I suppose the flat home quarter and the next one over are what he's eyeing. And you have river access too."

"We've never had cattle here," Elly said. "My father always grew crops." She paused on a page. "Can I specify what they can use the land for, if they buy it?"

"Afraid not," Noreen replied. "Aside from environmental issues, they'll use it for whatever they need it for."

"Have you read this?" Elly indicated the agreement. She rose from the table and went to pour their tea, then brought the cups back.

"I did. It's standard. And they've given me copies of the documents they'll register against the title until the sale goes through. You'll have to sign the agreement, then sign the documents to transfer title."

Elly looked up, her gaze going to the window and out over the expanse of fields, her hand cradling her cup. Could she?

"Take your time with it," Noreen urged. "There's no rush, at least, not quite yet. I don't think Hamilton will wait forever, but you have a few days at least."

"Is it a good price, do you think?"

"Half a million? It's nothing to sniff at. If the farmhouse was in better shape, you might have sold it to a family, since it's big enough to hold a whole crew of kids."

A family. Her heart ached, but she tried to ignore it. What if a family had offered for it? That was how the farm should be. But she was being an idealist, like her mother. "It does need work," Elly admitted, acknowledging the worn floors, the somewhat threadbare carpet on the stairs, and the general aged feeling of the place. But it was home. She swallowed. Soon it wouldn't be home at all.

Noreen rose. "I'll leave you for now. Read over the agreement, and then give me a call."

"I will." Elly walked Noreen to the door, then watched as she got into her truck and drove away. She was about to go back into the house when she saw Jack's truck rumbling up from the opposite direction. Would he ever leave her alone? He pulled into the driveway and got out, slamming his door with a bit more force than necessary.

"So you're going to sell," he said, not giving her a chance to say hello. "And to Hamilton, of all people."

"I can't stay here forever, Jack," she said, crossing her arms.

"But to Hamilton? Do you know what his farm corporation does?"

"Ranching mostly, isn't it? Cattle?"

Jack made a face. "If only that was all of it."

Elly had no idea what he meant. Her father had been the one who had kept abreast of other farms, not her. "Then, what?"

"Feedlots, El. Hamilton's been trying to buy up land since the slaughterhouse in Fort Macleod expanded."

"But they don't do cattle—"

"You really want your land to be used as a feedlot for horses? Where do you think the old horses go, or the unwanted ones, or those wild ones you see? It's barbaric. No one should be eating those animals, killing them."

Elly stepped back at the vehemence in his voice. "Hamilton didn't say anything about that to me," she said, knowing she sounded defensive. Her stomach churned. A smelly, cramped feedlot, with confused and panicking horses, on their way to slaughter.

"Of course he wouldn't." Jack's tone was scornful. "He probably painted some pretty picture, a small cattle ranch, all that nonsense."

"Well…"

"Thought so."

"I haven't had any other offers on it," Elly pointed out. "Do you have half a million dollars?"

"You know I don't. But I'd pay in installments," Jack offered. "And you know I'm good for it."

"Installments won't help me, though, Jack," she said. "How can I start a new life if I can't afford to live?"

"Your big fancy job in the big fancy city should take care of that."

"It isn't that easy, and it's not a big fancy job," she retorted. She felt behind her for the handle of the screen door. "I need to go back in, I have work to do."

Jack lingered at the foot of the porch steps, his hands in his pockets. "Don't sell to Hamilton, El," he said. "Hold on to the land longer. Someone else could want to buy it, and it wouldn't have to be a feedlot."

"You don't know that it would be," she replied, her voice shaky. "And he'd have to get approval, anyway."

Jack scoffed. "You think he doesn't have politicians and bureaucrats in his pocket? Approval will be the easiest part." He turned and headed for his truck, shaking his head. Elly watched him go, standing in the doorway of the farmhouse.

She returned to the kitchen and sat down with the agreement, determined to read it all the way through. It took several cups of tea and the use of a highlighter, but she eventually finished. It was true, it didn't say what they'd use the land for, but maybe she could finagle something before she sold.

Elly glanced at the clock. Almost five. Damn. She wanted to call Alex and tell her the news, but she'd be at work by now. Should she call Parry's? She was on her feet and at the phone before she could stop herself. Surely Derek wouldn't mind, if she kept it short. She dialed the number.

"Parry's, Charity speaking."

"Char, it's Elly. Is Alex around?"

"Hey, El, I thought you'd be working." Charity sounded cheerful as always, and Elly could hear the clatter of dishes in the background.

"Not for the next few days. I had to come home to take care of some stuff. Is Alex there?"

"Yeah, I'll grab her for you. She's just changing up a keg before Eric heads out. Gimme a sec." Charity put her on hold and Elly listened to a local radio station for several minutes. Her gaze went back to the agreement. Half a million dollars.

"El?" Alex's voice rang in her ear.

"Hey, Alex."

"So, what's happening with the farm? Are you planning on ways to spend all that cash?"

"I had a purchase agreement to read," Elly said. "I'm not quite there yet."

"So you've signed it? It's almost done?" Alex sounded eager.

"Almost. Haven't signed yet. I need to make sure I know what I'm doing."

"Of course you know. Half a million, El."

"I know." Elly frowned. Not once had Alex said anything about keeping the farm. She seemed fixated on the money.

"Get that done and come back, and we can race out on the bike to the mountains. I know a nice little hotel, we can have a night off together. What do you say?"

"I'm not sure when I'll be back," she hedged.

"Whenever. El, I gotta go. Eric's shift's done, so I have to get in there."

"I'll talk to you later, then."

"Don't call too early, if it's tomorrow," Alex reminded her. "I have the closing shift tonight."

"I'll remember that. Don't work too hard."

"I won't. Take care, babe." Alex hung up.

Elly set the phone back in its cradle. She eyed the paperwork on the kitchen table, then opened the fridge. It was bare but for a couple of cans of pop. She hadn't thought about what she was going to eat. Time to go into town.

❖

Alex wiped down the bar, her mind on Elly. She was so close to selling the farm, and when she did, she'd come to stay in the city full-time. Of course, she wouldn't work at Parry's forever, but that'd probably be a good thing. There was no one she needed to see on a daily basis, but she was starting to think she could make an exception for Elly. Elly wasn't clingy like Heather had been, not insistent and needy, bitching about how little they saw each other, or who else Alex was hanging around with. She rinsed the cloth in the sink and hung it over the faucet to dry, then glanced at her watch. Only a few more hours. If Elly were in town, she'd zip over to the apartment, surprise her with a late meal, and then make love to her.

Love? No, that wasn't right. Alex shook her head.

She straightened the bottles of booze on the shelf behind the bar, then organized the coolers. When she straightened and turned back to the bar, Will was there, leaning on his hand.

"Sorry, didn't hear you come in," she said. "Drink?"

"A Coke," Will said, sounding rueful.

"Still hurting after the other night?"

"The hangover's gone, but I think I'll just take it easy. Where's Elly? I didn't see her in the restaurant."

"She's at the farm for a couple of days."

"Derek didn't need her to work?"

Alex shrugged. "She took time off. She's trying to sell it, so she had to go see the Realtor and deal with the possible buyer."

"Ah." Will took a sip of the Coke she set in front of him. "That means we can go riding tomorrow. It's supposed to be a beautiful day. It'd be a shame to miss it."

"Where to?" It didn't really matter, as she'd ride anywhere, but she felt like at least making an attempt at negotiation of their trip destination.

"Out to the mountains, Lake Louise or something." Will slurped his pop. "Or farther, if you want to. You working tomorrow?"

"I close tonight. Let me check the schedule. Keep an eye on the bar, will you?"

"And do what? Pour drinks?" Will laughed.

Alex rolled her eyes. She zipped into the back and up the stairs to the office. The schedules hung outside Derek's door, and she skimmed down to her name. Not working tomorrow night, just as she'd thought. Nor the night after, surprisingly. She grinned and went back downstairs, taking the steps two at a time.

"Not tomorrow," she announced when she came back into the bar.

Will pumped his fist. "Brilliant. Let's go to Revelstoke, then, or farther. Maybe Nelson."

"There are some pretty rides around there."

"The stretch through Kaslo, for sure. And the ride out's good anyway."

"What time do you want to leave?" Alex hoped he wouldn't be too eager to get away early; she did need some sleep, after all.

"Nine?"

Alex grimaced.

"What? That's not the crack of dawn."

"It might as well be, when I'm closing. How about ten thirty?"

"You're getting to be an old lady," Will teased. "Make it ten, and you're on. I'll call that place in New Denver, see if they have a room going spare. They should, I'd hope."

"Two beds," Alex said, and Will gave her a strange look.

"Since when?"

"Since I said so," she retorted, surprised at her own vehemence. It had never mattered before.

"She has you whipped, eh?" Will asked, his tone light. The words rankled.

"Hardly."

"So did Heather, remember?"

"She's not like that. Christ, Will." Alex noticed a customer at the end of the bar and she left Will there, going to get their order. She pulled a pint of beer, and by the time she came back, her anger had mellowed somewhat.

"Sorry, Bellerose," Will said. "I just remember you after Heather, that's all, and you were gutted. I don't want to see that happen again."

"It won't," Alex said. "Elly's not like that." She hoped. Everything had gone all right so far, after all, even if Elly only rarely wanted to be intimate. She'd change that, hopefully. And Elly was reliable, sensible, on an even keel, as her grandmother used to say. Nothing at all like Heather.

"Good." Will finished his Coke and stood up. "What do I owe you?"

"On the house. It's just pop."

Will pulled a five-dollar bill from his pocket and smoothed it out on the bar. "For my favorite biker babe."

"Awww, you shouldn't have." Alex picked up the tip and folded it, tucking it into the pocket of her black trousers.

"For you, Bellerose, always." He blew her a kiss as he headed out the door, pausing to shout, "Ten o'clock, and don't forget to set your alarm."

❖

Elly walked into the diner, and all conversation stopped. Every head turned, and it was as if she was a stranger, an oddity to be stared at and gossiped about. She'd grown up here, among every one of the people sitting at the tables, but she'd never felt so out of place. What she'd feared, even though she hadn't even sold the farm yet, had happened. She swallowed hard and took a seat at the counter.

"Coffee?" Leigh, the diner's longtime waitress, asked.

"Please. And a BLT, please, with fries." Elly couldn't remember the last time she'd looked at a menu here. She knew it by heart.

"Sure thing." Leigh poured her a cup, leaning forward slightly as she did. "Don't mind them. They've all got their panties in a bunch. They never thought you'd sell, or move away."

Elly smiled at her, though it was a tight smile, an attempt at being jovial.

"Eleanor, how nice to see you."

Elly turned to see Mrs. Calderwood coming across the diner, moving steadily and carefully with her cane, her gnarled hand resting on the rubber grip. Elly's palms went damp, and she braced herself for the expected talking-to.

"It's nice to see you too," Elly replied, trying to keep her voice steady.

"I hear from my Jack that you're selling to Hamilton Farms," Mrs. Calderwood said, getting right to the point, as Elly knew she would. She always had been a straight shooter.

"I'm considering it," Elly replied truthfully. She hadn't signed the agreement yet, after all.

"Your father would be rolling in his grave to know that you'd sell it to an outfit like Hamilton's. He didn't maintain that land just so it could be turned into a feedlot." She shook her finger at Elly. "It'll wreck the property, having hundreds of head of cattle or horses there."

"Plus it's barbaric, feedlots," someone else chimed in, though Elly wasn't sure who had said it. The entire diner seemed riveted to their conversation.

"He didn't say anything about feedlots to me," Elly said, raising her voice a fraction so that it would travel to the entirety of the diner.

"Of course he wouldn't. That man knows what he's doing." Mrs. Calderwood's voice hadn't gotten any louder, but it felt like she was yelling. "You should keep the land, dear," Mrs. Calderwood said. "It's what your parents would have wanted."

"I can't afford to keep the land," Elly retorted, letting frustration get the better of her. Her mother would have tsked, hearing the tone she used.

"My Jack would help," Mrs. Calderwood replied, calm and collected, as if her statement were obvious.

"You mean he'd marry me, don't you?" Elly said, and Mrs. Calderwood's face brightened.

"It makes sense," she said. "Your farms adjoin, and he could work the land. It'd work out perfectly."

Elly wanted to laugh, but she didn't dare. She wasn't sure she could explain it. Mrs. Calderwood meant well, but it was impossible. No doubt she and Jack were meant to have a marriage of convenience, maybe turning to love. The widow read too many romance novels.

"It would never work," Elly said.

"Why not?"

Elly didn't want to explain it. Everyone should know by now; it wasn't like she'd kept to herself all these years, but she supposed some people just didn't want to see. Leigh saved her by bringing over her meal.

"Your BLT, hon," she said, setting it down on the counter. "Best eat while it's fresh."

"You should consider it," Mrs. Calderwood said, even as she turned to go back to her seat. "Jack likes you an awful lot."

"She's never gone with any of the boys round here," a voice said. Elly kept her focus on her meal.

"We'll just have to make a fuss if she sells," another said. "A big community protest might help convince Hamilton to stay away." The voices dissolved into an excited murmur, and Elly decided she didn't want to stick around.

She set down her BLT. "Leigh, could I get this to go?" she asked, quietly.

"Of course, hon," Leigh said, bringing over a Styrofoam container. "Lots to do, I bet."

"Lots of paperwork," Elly agreed. She took out her wallet and paid Leigh, leaving a good tip. "I should get back to it. I haven't made a decision yet, after all."

"Take care, and don't be a stranger," Leigh said, scooping up the money.

Elly picked up the takeout container. "I'll be around," she said. "Thanks."

❖

The phone jangled shrilly the next morning, startling Elly awake. She'd stayed up late, going through the rooms of the old farmhouse, making lists of what to pack and what to donate. There was so much clutter in the house, she knew it would take her ages to clear it all.

"Hello?"

"Ms. Cole? Bernard Hamilton." His voice was gruff, angry. "Seems someone went to the local member of the legislature, made a big stink. I've just heard that any development I have on your property won't be approved."

"What?" Elly rubbed her eyes, trying to make sense of it all.

"He told me he'd make certain that my applications failed," Hamilton said. "Bastard. He doesn't want any economic development in his riding, then fine. I won't create any jobs there."

"You never told me you were going to make this place a feedlot," Elly replied.

"It had always been a consideration," Hamilton said, "but I had an offer from a possible supplier and it all came together. So what? Feedlots are allowed."

"But they're awful," Elly retorted, coming fully awake.

"How do you think you get your meat at the supermarket? You should know better than most. You're a farm girl, aren't you?"

The venom in his voice shocked her, and she stood there with her mouth open.

"Bloody hippies, the lot of them," Hamilton muttered. "Ms. Cole, our deal's off. I've got a better place to buy, anyway. Where they're not so damn picky." He hung up, and the slam of the receiver made her wince. She hung up her phone far more gently.

In a daze, she wandered over to the stove, taking up the kettle and filling it with water, then putting it on to boil. Now what would she do?

She turned off the stove and left the kettle sitting there. Sitting around having another cup of tea wouldn't help her think. A walk, however, would. It had been a while since she'd been to the end of the property and back; she was curious to see how Jack's farming was doing, and her mother had always said that a walk was good for what ails you. Not that she likely would have expected a potential sale to a giant farm corporation to be the ailment.

After going back upstairs and pulling on a pair of jeans and a sweater, Elly shoved her feet into her old sneakers and left the farmhouse, heading west. There was part of a quarter section that bordered the river, and it had been left fallow for almost as long as she could remember. She walked along the shoulder of the road, mindful of cars, not that there were many, crossing over the intersecting road and heading for the gate in the fence. Unhooking the latch, she slid through and rehooked it, and started toward the river. The ground sloped gently downward, and she angled south, knowing that this part of the quarter section ended in a sharp cutoff and drop to the water.

She knew the property like the back of her hand, but she still kept flicking her gaze down to be sure she didn't stick her foot into a gopher hole and break her ankle. In spots the prairie grasses grew so long that she had to push through them, and she was glad to finally hit the old rutted road that ran down to the river.

Partway down, she paused and looked back. Though it wasn't visible from the gate, now she could see the sandstone cliff gaping from the hillside, a warren of holes and hollows. When she was a kid, she'd spotted a marmot living there, in one of the hollows, and she'd been fascinated.

"Do you think he has a family?" her mother had asked as they watched him pop in and out. She'd held Elly's hand.

"I bet there's a Mrs. Marmot," Elly remembered saying. "And baby marmots."

"What do you think they do all day?"

"Swim. Marmots swim, don't they?"

"They sure do."

Elly remembered her mother smiling down at her, the sun shining through her curly strawberry-blond hair.

"Then they'd have to have swimming lessons," she'd said.

Elly looked up at the cliff, but she didn't see any movement.

Maybe the marmots had moved on. She kept walking, reaching the riverside. She took off her sneakers and rolled up the legs of her jeans and found a log to sit on that jutted out into the water. The water was cold but refreshing, since the sun had risen farther and the day was becoming warm. As she looked out across the river at the opposite bank, heavy with grass and wildflowers, she was glad Hamilton Farms had decided to go elsewhere. To see this land ruined by a feedlot would have been awful, but the chance of finding a farming family to buy it would be slim to none.

A farming family.

Elly straightened in surprise. When had she started to think about selling, for real? She couldn't pinpoint when, but now that she thought about it, her thoughts had begun to change. As much as she wanted to stay, she knew it wasn't going to be realistic. She couldn't work the land herself, and leasing it wouldn't help the empty farmhouse from being neglected and unloved. It needed a family: determined parents, maybe a little girl who would love the room under the eaves with its slanted ceiling and the secret places in the barn that the cats would find to have their kittens, or a little boy who'd explore every nook and cranny of the property like she had.

When she got back to the house, she'd talk to Noreen, and tell her what she was thinking. Hopefully Noreen knew of a family looking for a home.

CHAPTER SIXTEEN

Alex opened the throttle and pushed the bike almost to its limit, racing down the highway. She could hear Will behind her on his R6 and knew he'd catch her soon. The bend up ahead drew nearer and she slowed, though she still took it faster than she ought to have done. She'd never admit it to Will, but her heart leapt into her throat, sliding back down when she made it through the bend and onto the next straightaway. She slowed further as the speed signs indicated a drop in the posted limit. A sign for the ferry flashed by and she sighed. Her speedometer dropped to fifty and Will cruised up beside her, his visor open. He stuck out his tongue. She cracked her own visor and did the same, waving him off.

They came to a stop behind a line of cars and Will craned his neck, looking over the dozen or so vehicles ahead of them. "We'll be able to get on this one," he said. "It's big enough and they'll find a spot for our bikes."

"I hope so. I don't want to wait another hour for the next one." Alex unzipped her jacket partway, letting the light breeze cool her off. The sun was hot on this exposed stretch of road, unlike the section they'd just been through, bracketed by pine trees.

"We won't," Will said confidently. "Two bikes will fit in between the cars, even if we don't get a full spot."

"Right. I hope they have coffee. I'm going to need it."

They inched forward as the cars tightened in the line, eager to get on board the ferry. Will inched ahead of her and thumbed his nose.

"Oh, please, you're only a few inches ahead. Save it for when we get off the ferry at the other end." Alex rolled her eyes.

"Don't you worry about that," Will shot back with a laugh. "I'll be first off the boat, and you'll be eating my dust."

Alex flashed him her middle finger in retort.

Her bike jerked forward, wobbling precariously, and she scrambled to get her hand back on the handlebar, but it was too late. She felt the bike falling, and she tried to keep it upright, but her balance was off.

She landed hard on her right hip, her helmet clipping the asphalt, rattling her head inside, the weight of the bike pinning her down.

"*Fuck.*" Her leg hurt, and the engine lay heavily on her boot as she tried to shimmy free. She heard Will shouting and saw him come up beside the bike, gesturing furiously at someone, or something. Alex turned to look over her shoulder. A half-ton pickup truck was behind them, and its owner stood in front, shouting back at Will.

"You fucking idiot," Will shouted. "Watch where you're going!"

"You bikers shouldn't be allowed on the road," the driver retorted.

"Will," Alex said, trying to get his attention. Her voice came out a pained croak, to her surprise. She tried to shove at the bike, but the angle was bad and she had no purchase. The bike shifted harder into her ankle and she winced.

"Babe, you okay?" Will lifted the bike, and she grabbed at the asphalt, pulling herself out from under the bike. He righted the bike and propped it on its kickstand. Alex rolled to her knees. She tried to stand. The pain shot through her leg and she saw stars, her vision narrowing.

"Fuck," she muttered, catching herself as she fell forward, taking the brunt of the short fall on her forearms. She'd never had an icepick jammed into her leg, but she would bet money it felt a lot like what she felt now.

She rolled to her back and sat up, gritting her teeth. Her chaps were dusty but not torn, and her boots looked the same, but for…oh God. Her right foot sat at an unnatural angle. Alex took a deep breath, then another, willing herself not to be sick. She was tough, she could take it. With shaking hands, she pulled off her gloves and fumbled with the strap of her helmet.

"Jesus fucking Christ," Will said, dropping down beside her.

A crowd had gathered by the time Alex got her helmet off, but she didn't look at them.

"It's bad, isn't it?" she asked Will, not willing to look at her foot again.

"Looks it, babe," he said, serious for a change.

A man stepped forward. "I saw what happened," he said, "I was in the line beside yours. That truck hit your back wheel solid, and you went down." He glanced at her foot. "You'll need a hospital. It looks like it's broken."

"Where's the nearest?" she heard Will ask.

"Take the ferry over and go to Nelson, I think," the man replied.

She heard other voices, a man's voice raised in anger and a cool baritone responding to him, but she couldn't make out the words.

The man crouched down on her other side, glancing at her, then at Will. "I'm Richard," he said. "We can lift you, take you to my truck. It's just a few feet that way." He pointed to a large black truck, with a quad in the back. "It's got a full cab, we can put you in the backseat and you can stretch out."

"But my bike…"

"We'll leave your bike here," Will said. "We can get it sent back somehow."

"There's space for the bike too," Richard said. "But we won't make this ferry before we can get it loaded."

"I'll wait," she said through gritted teeth. "We're not leaving the bike."

"Stubborn," Will muttered, but he smiled at her and made a face.

"Damn right."

Richard and Will worked together and scooped her up, carrying her carefully toward the truck. Will held her while Richard opened the door, and they set her up onto the seat.

"We'll get the bike now," Richard said. "You okay here for a few minutes?"

Alex nodded, but when that made her head swim, she stopped.

"Lie back," Will advised. "We'll get this sorted."

Alex let herself sink back stiffly onto the soft cushioned seat, and she closed her eyes. The pain was a dull throb now, not the sharpness that she'd felt when she'd first fallen. She tried to move her foot and the pain intensified. Not a good idea. Deep breaths. She counted her breaths until the pain returned to the dull throb. Thoughts zipped through her mind: she'd have to have the boot cut off, how would she get her bike home, what would she do about work. She shifted again and her vision narrowed and went black.

❖

Elly took her mother's spiral pad with her from room to room, taking notes on a massive to-do list. Though Hamilton had nixed their agreement, she knew she'd need to work hard to get the farmhouse ready for sale. Her parents weren't exactly hoarders, but her father had pack-rat tendencies and her mother had enabled him. She thought of Alex's place, the stark minimalism of her living room, and she wished that she could make a similar home for herself, albeit one with more of a homey feel. If she bought a condo in Calgary or found a small house in the suburbs, she could decorate to her heart's content.

On a new page, she started a list of items she wanted to take with her, those little sentimental things she knew she'd never be able to do without. The framed painting on the living room wall that her great-grandmother had painted; the collection of china, slightly mismatched, from both sides of the family; the quilts on the beds. And, if she was honest with herself, a few other things as well. If she wasn't careful, she would end up with a place that looked like a pack-rat's haven.

Elly paused at the foot of the stairs. The sun was low in the sky, and she hadn't realized how much time had passed. She headed into the kitchen and set the notepad on the kitchen table. She could take the table. The old Formica was her favorite, even with the chips and marks from decades of use.

She heard the rumble of a truck coming down the road and she leaned over the kitchen sink, craning her neck to look out the window. Jack pulled into the driveway, his truck jouncing over the ruts. He got out, and she could see his hard-set face, a frown marring his features.

Jack knocked but didn't wait for her approval before he came inside. "El? You here?"

"In the kitchen," she called back.

He came through, his steps heavy on the linoleum floor. "You can't sell your land to Hamilton," he said, not even letting her speak. She opened her mouth to explain, but he plowed forward. "The man's a crook, and he doesn't care about anything but money. He'll make it a feedlot, and it'll ruin the watershed on the quarter section. And it'll be horses for sure—I heard from a friend of mine whose brother was angling for a deal with Hamilton."

"Wait. Just wait," Elly said, holding up a hand.

"I won't wait. You can't say anything that will convince me," Jack said. "That fellow is bad news."

"Hamilton withdrew his offer." Elly raised her voice over his rambling, stopping Jack in his tracks.

"What?" Jack looked flabbergasted.

"Someone called the MLA, who told Hamilton that he would make sure approval never came through." Elly crossed her arms. "I don't know if I would have signed, but now I can't even make that decision." A sudden fury rose in her. She hadn't wanted the farm to be a feedlot, but the interference of the townspeople frustrated her. She used to like that small-town family feel, but lately it had been irritating her. Maybe she was getting used to being in the city, and being truly on her own.

"Thank God." Jack relaxed, the frown fading, his features shaping into the easygoing pleasantness they always had.

"*Not* thank God, not at all," Elly snapped. "I want to get on with my life, but if I can't sell the farm, I'm stuck. I could have sold it."

"Sell it to me."

"Jack, we've been over this." A million times, she thought.

"I know, but I can get a loan, I know I can. I've been talking to the bank, and they're considering it."

"Can you give me half a million?" Elly asked bluntly. There would be no beating around the bush. Hamilton had offered her exactly what it was worth, and no more. Noreen had confirmed that with the appraisal.

Jack's happy demeanor faded. "No," he admitted.

"Then I don't know that I can sell it to you."

The phone jangled.

"You don't even know how much I'd offer," Jack retorted. "It wouldn't be half a million, but it would still be worth your while."

"Is it close to that?" Elly moved to answer the phone, but Jack held out a hand.

"Don't take any other offers until I can get something together… please, El?"

"I don't know, Jack." She picked up the receiver. "Hello?"

"Elly?"

The voice was unfamiliar. "Yes? Who is this?"

"It's Will."

"Will? Why are you calling?" Elly's hand tightened on the faded white plastic receiver. Will had no reason to call her. A twinge of jealousy shot through her. Alex's best friend and FTF, as Charity put it.

"It's Alex," Will said. His voice sounded tired, the words coming across the line with reluctance.

"What's happened?"

"El, hang up. You need to promise me—" Jack stepped up beside her, but she held up a hand.

"She's hurt. We're in the hospital in Nelson. She fell off the bike."

"Oh my God." Elly sank against the counter, clinging to it as her knees trembled. "What happened? Will she be okay?" She thought of how fast they'd gone on the bike, how dangerous it would be to fall from a bike going at such speeds. Alex could be paralyzed, broken, bloody. Elly's stomach roiled. She'd only just started to think of a real possibility of being with Alex, and now it was over.

"Some asshole rear-ended her, and the bike fell over and fell on her. She broke her ankle. Probably two or three bones, the doc said."

Elly let out a breath. Not dead. "I wish she would be more careful."

"More careful?" Will sounded incredulous. "She was careful as could be. If she hadn't been wearing her boots it would have been way worse. Jesus, Elly."

"Sorry," Elly replied, taking another deep breath. "It's just…"

"Whatever," Will said. "She wanted me to call you so you wouldn't worry."

"How are you going to get home if she's broken her ankle?"

"She can't ride, and the doc is debating doing surgery, so we might be a couple of days. She'll have to stay overnight, he said."

"Should I come out? How far is it to Nelson?"

"Do you have a trailer on your farm?" Will asked.

"A trailer?" That wasn't what she'd expected him to ask.

"Yeah, for Alex's bike. We can't leave it here, and she can't ride it home."

"I—" Elly considered the outbuildings on the farm. It was possible, but she didn't know for sure. "I might. I don't know."

"Find out." She heard an announcement on the PA in the hospital, a garbled voice. "Look, I'll give you my number. Call me when you know. Otherwise I'll have to find another way for Alex to get home,

Chapter Seventeen

Alex eyed her foot in its brace when Will swept the sheet off her leg. Her head swam from the pain medication, but the foot seemed all in one piece now and not bent at an unnatural angle.

"How many plates?" she managed to ask.

"Just one, I think," Will said, sitting down on the side of the bed. His leather jacket lay on the chair nearby, along with hers, and he still wore his chaps.

"Where's all my gear?"

"Your helmet's with your bike, in the saddlebag, though it's done for. All your luggage and extra clothes are there too. I brought you a clean shirt and stuff." He pointed to a bag on the floor by the chair. "The nurse said you can wear a pair of scrubs home, since you won't be able to get any of the rest of your jeans over that brace."

"The rest of?"

"They cut your jeans off, babe," Will replied. "And"—he winced—"your chaps. But you can buy another pair."

"Dammit." Alex tried to control the fury, but she couldn't. "They could have unbuckled them. Idiots." Her fist hit the bed beside her.

"The docs say you can go home whenever you want. They'll forward your information to the Foothills in Calgary and you can get a follow-up there."

"How am I supposed to get home? Riding on the back of your bike?" She rubbed her eyes.

"Nope, no passengers on my bike," Will joked, though it sounded halfhearted to her.

"How, then?"

"I called Elly. She's got a trailer and she's going to bring it out, so we can take your bike back, and you."

"Oh, thank God." Alex closed her eyes and sighed in relief.

"She sounded freaked, just so you know."

"Did she?" Alex asked. Her mind felt foggy and her body was heavy, sinking into the bed. She heard Will chuckle.

"Sleep, babe. I'll wake you when Elly gets here."

❖

Elly found the roadside motel easily, her eyes burning with exhaustion. It had been a long drive to Nelson, longer than she'd expected. All she wanted was to crawl into bed and crash. She pulled into the parking lot, found a space usually reserved for RVs, and cut the engine. A motorcycle sat outside one of the rooms, an R6. Will's? She called his cell and he answered after two rings. "I'm here."

"Cool."

She saw a figure step out from the room. He waved, and she waved back. "I see you."

"Come on in, there's two beds," he said, then hung up.

Elly yawned, then wiped her watering eyes. She grabbed her overnight bag and headed across the parking lot to the room. Will had left the door open and she stepped inside. The TV was on, and he was watching racing, stretched out on the bed nearest the door, his head propped against the headboard.

"You must've been pedal to the metal most of the way," he said, glancing at her.

"I got lucky, not much traffic this time of night," she said.

"Help yourself to the other bed." Will gestured at the other queen-size bed with its ugly flower-print coverlet. "It's not much. And I snore, just so you know."

"As tired as I am now, I don't think it'll matter," Elly replied. She dropped her overnight bag on the bed and went into the bathroom, washing her hands and splashing her face with water.

She glanced up into the mirror and saw her reddened, sleep-deprived eyes. If it were earlier, she'd go see Alex before going to bed, but she could hardly think straight. She ducked back out to grab her bag, brushed her teeth, and changed into her pajamas. She'd brought her most modest ones: long cotton trousers in a light blue gingham, with a matching long-sleeved shirt. When she came out of the bathroom, Will gave her a once over.

"Nice pj's."

"Thanks," she said, bemused, not sure if he was joking or being serious. She pulled back the coverlet and crawled between the sheets. The pillow was lumpy, and she fluffed it a few times until it became somewhat comfortable.

"I know it's a shithole," Will remarked, "but I wasn't exactly planning on staying in Nelson tonight. Alex and I usually ride up to New Denver. There's a nicer hotel there."

"Do you ride out here often?" Elly asked, stifling a yawn. She turned over in bed to face Will.

"A few times every summer," Will replied. "As many times as we can manage between coordinating days off and having the money. Some of the best biking roads in Canada are around here. Not that you'd have really seen them in the dark."

"What I could see was really beautiful," Elly said. She yawned again.

Will lifted the remote and flicked off the TV. "What time do you want to get up? I'll set the alarm." He eyed the battered clock radio on the nightstand between the beds. "If I can."

"What time will they discharge Alex?" Elly asked.

"Nine?"

"Set it for eight, then. That should give us enough time."

"We'll have to pick up Alex's bike at Crawford Bay. The guy at the ferry was kind enough to store it overnight. But I think we should pick up Alex first. She'll want to see her bike."

"It's her baby, isn't it?" Elly said it jokingly, but Will nodded, serious.

"It is. Fortunately it fared pretty well, though she'll have to take it to the mechanic when we get back. Hard to know if the hit from that truck threw anything out of alignment. And there are a few scratches to get out of the engine case."

"Was the guy going fast?" Elly asked. "You didn't say much on the phone."

"Nah, not very fast, but he was changing lanes and didn't look, the idiot. Any faster and he'd have run her right over. As it was, the momentum was enough to knock the bike over, and Alex too."

"Did the cops say anything?"

"He'll get a ticket, I think, maybe a summons. I don't know. I was too busy making sure Alex got to a hospital, and that her bike was safe. That was probably the longest ferry ride ever." Will shook his head and rose. He scrubbed a hand through his already mussed hair. "I'm beat. Good night, Elly." He went into the bathroom and closed the door. Elly turned onto her back and stared at the stippled ceiling with its stained, watermarked circles. She thought she'd take a long time to fall asleep, but it only took seconds.

❖

The alarm buzzed shrilly and Elly turned over with a groan. Her back twinged from sleeping on the sagging mattress, and her eyes felt scratchy. In the next bed, she heard Will grumbling, and the creak of the old springs as he moved about.

"Fuck," Will muttered.

Elly sat up, bracing herself on her elbows, blinking into the early morning light. The motel room looked worse in daylight: the carpet was dingy and gray, the flowered coverlet more garish, the stains on the ceiling more apparent. Will got out of bed and darted into the bathroom before she could say anything. She sat up fully and pushed over the covers, swinging her legs over the side of the bed. She had to pee. She watched the bathroom door, but several minutes passed and Will hadn't come out.

Damn.

"You about done in there?" she called.

She heard Will mutter, then his voice grew louder. "Give me a minute. Christ."

"Sorry, I'm desperate."

It felt like an age before Will emerged wearing only his boxers, his hair and face damp, rather than the few minutes it surely was. Elly darted up and into the bathroom, closing the door. She sighed in relief.

"You okay if I shower?" she called out, feeling self-conscious.

"Go ahead," she heard Will say. "I'm going to get coffee."

She heard the door slam, and she poked her head out of the bathroom. Will was gone. She grabbed her overnight bag and went back into the bathroom, locking the door.

The water was lukewarm, but it refreshed her anyway, washing off the stale feeling she always got from driving long distances. When she emerged, fully dressed and ready, and combing her hair, Will had returned, and he drank from a extra-large Tim Hortons cup. A second smaller cup sat on the nightstand.

"Got you some," he said, the words sounding like more of a grunt than anything.

"Thanks." Elly packed away yesterday's clothes and perched on the side of the bed, taking up the coffee. It was hot and had caffeine, and that was all that mattered.

They sat quietly watching the news on TV until Will had finished.

"Ready to go?" he asked, tossing his cup into the small waste bin and rising.

"Definitely." Elly rose, grabbed her bag, and followed him from the room. She trailed him to the motel office, where he turned in his key.

"What do I owe you for the room?" she asked.

"Don't worry about it," Will said. "You can buy me a few drinks at Parry's next weekend. Let's go see this trailer of yours."

Elly tossed her bag into the backseat as Will eyeballed the trailer hitched to her car.

"It'll do," he said, "though it'll be tight. Glad you brought rope and stuff."

"I did what I could."

"If you'd been in Calgary, I'd have gotten you to go get the bike trailer I have at my place," Will said, "but that would've been asking a lot to do that much driving." He sighed.

"I'll follow you to the hospital?" Elly suggested.

"It's hard to miss."

"Yeah, but I've never been here before."

He gave her a surprised look. "Really? Man." He put his hands in his pockets. "Be ready in a couple."

He strolled over to his bike and Elly watched him put on all his gear, his movements methodical and spare. When he looked about ready to start the bike, she got into her car and started the engine, letting it warm up a bit. He rode over to her on his bike, idling by the driver's side window. Behind the smoky visor, she couldn't even see his eyes, but he nodded at her and she nodded back. He went ahead and she followed him through town to the hospital.

In the hospital's small waiting room, he paced back and forth. Elly sat calmly in a chair. Will seemed out of place here, in his leathers and smartly cut racing jacket, his helmet hanging from one hand. His lean form seemed to fill the space with his agitation. Her heart beat to match his pacing, but she tried to stay still, letting her tension out by clutching her hands tightly together. Alex would be fine. Only her ankle was broken. Elly shivered. Still, it had been so close.

The nurse had told them Alex was just being discharged and it would be a short wait, but Will couldn't stay still. Finally, Elly saw a nurse pushing a wheelchair down the hallway. Alex sat in it, wearing one of her T-shirts, but with a pair of old scrubs instead of jeans. A brace protruded from under the loose cotton pants. Elly rose.

"Hey, there." She smiled at Alex, who smiled back.

"What are you doing here?"

"Remember, I told you yesterday she was coming out," Will said, stepping up beside Elly.

Alex frowned. "I don't remember much of yesterday," she said.

"Those must have been some great pain meds," Will quipped.

"Are you feeling okay?" Elly asked. She clasped Alex's hand and smiled when Alex gave it a gentle squeeze. Now that she was here, she could take care of Alex.

"I've been better. Fucking asshole, he better not have wrecked my bike."

"You'll need to stay off your ankle as much as possible in the next little while," the nurse said, interrupting. Another nurse came up with a set of crutches.

"We'll be driving back to Calgary," Elly said.

"Not on a bike, I hope." The nurse gave Will a disapproving glance.

"In my car," Elly clarified.

"Make sure to take your pain meds on schedule," the nurse told Alex. "And get in to see the doctor in Calgary we referred you to. He'll take over your care."

Alex nodded, and the nurse handed Elly the crutches. She and Will walked in front of Alex and the nurse, taking it slow.

"I'll go pull the car around," Elly said. She handed off the crutches to Will.

When Elly pulled up to the entrance, Will and the nurse helped Alex into the passenger seat. Will tucked the crutches into the back.

"We'll head to the ferry," he told her. "It's a bit of a drive, but not too bad."

Alex sagged back against the seat and closed her eyes.

"You doing okay?" Elly asked as she pulled out of the parking lot, following Will on his bike.

"No." Alex's voice sounded sharper than it had before. "My whole damn riding season's about done for, thanks to this." She shifted her foot and winced.

"I was so worried," Elly said, her voice shaky. "When Will called, I thought you were dead, or in a coma or something." She shivered, though the morning sun warmed the car.

Alex snorted. "I'm tougher than that."

"It flashed through me that I could have never seen you again," Elly admitted, biting her lip.

"You don't need to worry about me," Alex said, though she sounded a bit spaced out.

Elly's hands clenched on the steering wheel, her knuckles white. She glanced over at Alex, who had laid her head back against the headrest, her eyes closed. What if Alex had been badly hurt? Just the thought was enough to make her stomach flop unpleasantly. It could have been so much worse. She forced herself to focus on the road, but she couldn't stop thinking about how awful it could have been.

The drive to the ferry didn't take too long, though the traffic grew the closer they got to the terminal. Elly found a parking spot off to the side as Will circled round, pulling his bike in behind her.

"I'll wait here," Alex said. "Just make sure my bike's okay."

"I will." Elly killed the engine and got out of the car just as Will walked up.

"We'll go see the manager," Will said. She followed him to the ferry terminal, and after a short wait, the manager led them to a nearby shed.

"Appreciate you holding it," Will said to the man, holding out his hand. They shook.

"No problem at all. Absolutely criminal what happened. Your friend all right?"

"She'll be okay, but she has a broken ankle."

The man winced in sympathy. Will took the handlebars of the bike and pushed up the kickstand. He brought it out of the shed and they slowly walked back toward the car.

"I hope you're strong," Will said as they walked. "It's going to be tough getting the bike up into the trailer without a ramp."

"We'll manage," Elly replied, though she wasn't sure if they could.

At the trailer, they eyed the distance between the bike and the wooden base. Will cursed under his breath.

"It's not going to work, is it?" Elly couldn't see how they'd manage to lift the bike up. She was strong from the farmwork she'd done, and carrying heavy trays at Parry's, but not that strong.

Will put down the kickstand and let the bike rest while he paced in front of the trailer. "I can't believe you don't have anything lower," he said, and though the words were under his breath, she heard them easily, as he'd intended her to.

"This was the best I could come up with. If you don't think we can do it, then we'll have to leave the bike."

"Alex would kill us if we did that," Will retorted.

"She'd just have to deal," Elly snapped back. "Not like she'll be riding it for a while, anyway." She took a deep breath. Calm down. Alex was fine.

Will gave a derisive snort. "We can't leave it. She sold her Harley for this, and saved up. It's not just any bike, Elly. Only someone who had no appreciation for motorcycles would say something like that."

"I have appreciation for them," Elly protested. "But I wouldn't be pining if my bike had to wait somewhere due to an accident or something. It's just a bike, not a person."

Will shook his head. "You have no clue. And I have no idea what Alex sees in you."

Elly stared, her mouth open in shock. Will paced to the edge of the trailer, estimating the height from the ground.

"Fuck you," she said finally, when she was able to speak.

"Honey, you're not my type," Will shot back. "And I didn't think you were Alex's either, you know."

He straightened the bike and put up the kickstand.

"Come get up into the trailer bed," he said. "I'll lift the bike up and you can drag it in."

Elly crossed her arms and gave him a stony glare.

"Please?" he asked, softening the tone of his voice.

"Not without an apology," she retorted. "That was a really shitty thing to say."

"Look, Elly, I'm sorry."

He didn't sound particularly apologetic, but Elly considered Alex, waiting in the car, in pain. They had a six-hour drive back, and it was going to be a long day.

"Fine." She hoisted herself up onto the trailer bed and turned to face Will. He crouched, adjusted his grip, and hefted the bike, letting out a grunt. Elly caught the front wheel, then stepped forward and grabbed the handlebars.

"Fuck." Will gasped, his cheeks flushed. "You got it?" The bike wobbled, and Elly widened her stance.

"Yeah."

Will stepped back, bending nearly in half, his hands on his knees. "Gimme a sec." He breathed deep and, after a minute or two, straightened. "Right. I'm going to hoist up the back, and you drag it into the trailer as I go. And neither of us needs to drop it, all right?"

"Got it."

Will counted under his breath, then crouched again and lifted. Elly backed into the trailer, pulling the bike with her, her hair flopping into her eyes. Will pushed, she pulled, and finally the bike was in.

"Ropes are on the backseat," Elly said. She held the bike upright, unable to reach the kickstand from where she stood, nearly pinned to the edge of the trailer.

"Right." Will went around and opened the back door, coming out with the ropes and the tie-down. Between them, they managed to get the bike standing upright, the rope laced through the bars on the side of the trailer.

"Go slow," Will said as Elly hopped down to the asphalt. "I'm hoping that'll hold, but I'm no seaman with fancy knot skills."

"I'll do my best." It looked sturdy enough. Elly closed the tailgate on the trailer. "You're going to stick with us, though, aren't you?"

Will grimaced. "Through the mountains, but once we get to Crowsnest Pass, you're on your own. I've got work tomorrow, early."

"Does Alex have work?" Elly asked.

Will shrugged. "I think so. She didn't say."

"I'll have to call Derek."

"He'll be pissed, but there's not much he can do. And Alex will be pissed too. She hates missing shifts. Especially since it's a weekend. Lots of money in it."

"Without the doctor's say-so, she probably shouldn't be on her foot at all," Elly reasoned. Will snorted.

"Good luck getting her to obey a command like that," he said. "She's always on the go."

They stood awkwardly as their conversation petered out, and finally Will broke the silence. "There's a good restaurant in Cranbrook on our way. We should stop for breakfast."

"All right." Her stomach growled. "We'll see you there."

"Look, El, I'm sorry." This time he did sound like he meant it. "Things have changed between Alex and me, and it sucks." He shrugged, looking away, moving a few steps.

"Oh." She wasn't sure what to say to that.

"Anyway, I'll check the ropes when I get there," he added over his shoulder as he strode toward his bike. He took the helmet from the handlebar and pulled it on.

Elly returned to the driver's seat and started up the car. Alex opened her eyes, looking groggy.

"We on our way?" she asked sleepily.

"We are," Elly confirmed. "And your bike's in the trailer, safe and sound." She wanted to say something about Will, but Alex closed her eyes again. Elly put the car into gear and began the drive home.

Chapter Eighteen

Alex shifted in the passenger seat of Elly's car, bumping her ankle. Pain shot through her leg and she winced.

"You okay?" Elly asked, glancing over before looking back at the road.

Alex seemed to recall Elly asking her that several times over the past while, though it all blurred together for her. "Are there any more pain meds?" Alex asked. She didn't have any pockets and she couldn't remember what had happened to the plastic vial from the nurse.

"I put them in the glove compartment so we wouldn't lose them," Elly said. Alex leaned forward and opened the compartment, fishing around and finding the blue vial with the white lid. She grabbed the bottle of water propped between the seats and gulped down a pill.

"How much longer till we get home?" she asked. All she wanted was to lie in her own bed, sleep, and wake up to find out it was all a bad dream.

If only.

The next couple of months were a write-off for riding; she wouldn't be able to get back onto the bike until her ankle healed and she could use the foot brake easily. Two glorious summer months, and she'd be stuck at home, or in a car. Emotion welled in her chest and she pressed her lips together, looking out the window at the foothills.

"A few hours. I'll need to stop at the next town and get out and stretch my legs." Elly rubbed her eyes. "I could use a nap, but a walk will help me stay awake."

"You work tomorrow?"

"Yeah. And I need to call Derek when we stop, too, and let him know what's happened. He'll have to schedule someone in the bar to cover your shifts."

"He'll manage," Alex said. "There's always someone. And I'd bet Eric will pick up the slack."

"Good to hear. And when we get back, you'll need to get in to see the doctor."

Elly sounded like she had everything all planned out. It was mind-boggling. "And he'll just tell me what the one in Nelson did—that I'll have to take it easy for months." Alex knew she sounded bitter.

"It's only a couple of months," Elly said.

"Only?" Alex repeated, her voice rising sharply. "Only? It's an entire summer, wasted."

"I'm glad it wasn't worse. God, Alex, I thought I'd lost you."

Heather wouldn't have cared much if she'd gotten injured, Alex thought, and definitely wouldn't have come to the hospital. It was more devotion than she could take. You only did that for someone you loved, maybe even someone you wanted to spend the rest of your life with. Alex swallowed and picked up the water bottle again, taking a swig.

Out of the corner of her eye, she saw Elly shudder.

"I hate worrying over you."

"I can take care of myself," Alex said. Her eyelids drooped, and she blinked hard, trying to stay awake.

"You don't need to always take care of yourself. That's what a lover, a girlfriend, is for." Elly swiped at her cheeks with one hand, her lips pressed tightly together. Alex pretended not to see them, pretended not to have heard Elly's words.

Lover. Girlfriend.

It was too much.

Alex heard the growl of Will's motorcycle as he passed them in the left lane, and her heart clenched. Lucky bastard, out there instead of stuck in this car.

Will pulled into the small parking lot of the gas station in Cranbrook. Elly pulled in alongside him, and as soon as she'd stopped, Alex undid her seat belt and pushed open the door, stepping out onto the cracked asphalt. Awkwardly, she reached back for her crutches and hobbled around the car to check on her bike. Or so she told herself. Getting out of the car was the main thing. Will was already there, checking the ropes one more time, though they'd held this far.

"The Ninja's doing just fine, babe," he said, patting the rear wheel of the bike. "She'll get home in one piece." He glanced at her and frowned. "What's eating you?"

"Girls," Alex bit out.

Will snorted. "All of them, or just one?"

"Just one."

"What's got you so panicky, babe?" Will looked puzzled. "The painkillers aren't doing anything weird, are they?"

"It's like Heather," she said, her voice low. Will frowned.

"Heather? I don't think so. That bitch wouldn't have dropped everything to come out here, not ever. Jeez, those painkillers must be something special."

"She's not my girlfriend like Heather was." Alex wasn't even sure if she was making sense, but it was freaking her out. She didn't want someone worrying about her, or needing her to be around, to be strong.

Will raised a brow. "Babe, you totally need to sit back down. If you don't think Elly's your girlfriend, then those drugs are wicked strong and you're about to fall over." He took her arm and led her back to the car, to the open passenger door.

"All good?" Elly asked.

"The bike's secure," Will said. Elly got out of the car, leaving Alex sitting there, Will standing by her door. She came around the hood.

"I'm getting a snack—anyone want anything?"

"I'm good," Will said. "I need to take off, anyway. Gotta get home."

"No, I'm fine," Alex said, not looking at Elly. If she looked at her, she'd lose what little composure she had left.

"Right." Elly turned and headed toward the gas station.

"Get some rest, babe," Will said, leaning on the door. "It'll be clearer when you're not so stoned from the meds."

"I'm not stoned," she said, feeling irritable. He didn't understand. "She's not my girlfriend."

"Just you and me, eh, Bellerose?" Will said. He gave her a gentle hug. "I don't think that's the way it is anymore. Think about that. But first, get some rest. Text me when you get home. I might be asleep, but if I'm not, I'll text you back."

"I promise." Alex lifted her head and Will kissed her cheek, his gloved hand tilting her chin up.

"Later, babe." She watched as he strolled back to his bike, pulling on his helmet as he went. Within a couple of minutes, he had burned out of the parking lot and was barely a black dot in the distance.

Alex leaned against the seat while she waited for Elly to return, breathing in the cool country air.

"Ready to go?"

Elly stood at the driver's side door, holding a Slurpee. Her expression was concerned, and Alex didn't like anyone looking at her like that.

Alex felt her cheeks heat, and to cover her awkwardness, she closed the passenger door. "Yeah, I'm ready. The sooner we get home, the better."

Elly slipped into her seat and started the car, waiting as Alex shoved the crutches into the back. "You should call Derek before it gets too busy at Parry's," Elly reminded her. "I'll keep driving. The sooner we get back, the better."

"Good thinking." Alex leaned between the seats and dragged her jacket from where it lay, fishing her phone from the pocket. It still had juice. Derek wasn't going to like her news.

❖

Elly pulled up outside Alex's place, her eyes burning from lack of sleep. She'd had the sun hitting her rearview mirror for the last bit, and she wished she could crawl into bed. Beside her, Alex dozed, her foot stretched out before her, the scrubs riding up to show the plain gray brace. From what she'd heard of Alex's conversation with Derek, he'd been pissed, and Alex had been snarky right back at him.

She worried about Alex. Did she have the savings to be out of work while she healed?

Elly turned off the car. Alex didn't wake, so she squeezed her hand gently. That didn't work, so she tweaked a lock of Alex's hair. "We're here," she said.

Alex stirred, blinking. "What?"

"We're home," Elly said. "Well, you are."

Alex rubbed her eyes. "Oh."

Elly opened the door and stepped out. She grabbed Alex's saddlebags from the backseat, one in each hand. Opposite, Alex rose wobbly to her feet, bracing herself on the crutches. She slung her leather jacket over one arm and took out her house keys. Slowly, they made their way up the front walk and up the concrete stairs to the door.

Elly set down the saddlebags. "Here, let me do it," she said, holding out her hand. Alex passed over her keys and Elly unlocked the door, letting Alex go in ahead of her. Alex went into the living room and sagged down onto the leather sofa with a relieved sigh.

"Home sweet home."

Elly left the saddlebags inside the door. She leaned on the doorframe separating the living room from the entryway. "I should get going," she said, stifling a yawn.

Alex frowned. "What about my bike?"

Elly groaned. She'd almost forgotten. "I can't take it off the trailer tonight," she said. "Will and I could barely get it up there. Between us, we couldn't do it."

"We can't just leave it," Alex argued.

"I can leave the trailer here," Elly said, "but that's it."

"We need to get it down, and into the shed," Alex insisted.

"With what magic?" Elly snapped, her exhaustion getting the best of her. "I can't lift it, and neither can you. It'll keep, Alex."

"It needs to be in the shed," Alex repeated. "I don't want it getting nicked."

"It'll be fine overnight," Elly replied, her patience at an end. "Besides, you need to rest. Let me get you some water, and then I'll help you get into bed."

Alex rose, standing shakily on one leg, her hand on the arm of the sofa. "It's my bike, El. It needs to be in the shed. And I don't need taking care of."

Elly rubbed her eyes and took a deep breath. "Do you have a lock for it? Or a chain? I'll take it round to your parking pad in the back and chain the trailer to the fence, and lock up the bike. But that's the best I can do."

Alex winced and sat back heavily, her face going pale. "In the second bedroom," she managed, sounding as if she was holding back a cry of pain. "There's a chain and padlock on the shelf, and my disc lock should be around there too."

❖

Alex watched Elly walk down the hallway, and she leaned back on the sofa, resting her head and closing her eyes. The painkillers were starting to wear off again, but she didn't want to take any more. Not just yet. Her mind was finally starting to clear. Elly was here, and Will wasn't. Will, her best friend and lover, had abandoned her. She pressed her lips together. Will would crack a joke, take her mind off the injury, and he'd understand about the bike. Elly was too worried, too clingy, and she just didn't get it. That bike was worth the world to her.

The clink of a chain made her open her eyes.

"This one?" Elly asked, holding up a stainless-steel chain. "I couldn't find a key, though."

"On my keychain. Wherever I put it." She couldn't remember, and she fumbled with her jacket.

"Oh, I have it still." Elly pulled the keychain from her pocket. "Got it."

"And the disc lock?"

Elly turned her hand, showing the disc lock hanging from its neon orange reminder cable. "Got it. Where does it go, exactly?"

"On the disc brake, front or back wheel." Alex shifted, determined to rise. "I'll come with you."

"Stay there," Elly said, holding out the hand with the keys. "I'll manage. I'm worried you'll make your ankle worse if you don't rest. Go lie down, and I'll be back shortly, and then I'll make you a cup of soup."

Elly left and headed down the front steps. Alex grabbed her crutches and rose awkwardly to her feet. She could make her own food. And she hated soup. She hobbled into the kitchen and opened the fridge, digging out an apple and sticking it on the counter, then grabbing two eggs from their cardboard carton. They slid in her hand but she managed to set them down on the ring of one of the stove's burners before they slipped farther and broke.

Alex took a couple of deep breaths and leaned against the counter, wiping her damp forehead with the back of her hand. She could do this. She wasn't going to be a burden on anyone; she'd always been independent, and she still would be.

Her vision blurred, and she shuffled over to the kitchen table, sinking onto one of the chairs. Maybe she couldn't do this. Alex put her head down on the table, the smooth wood cool on her cheek. She'd push through this, like she always did. She just needed to man up.

The painkillers must have confused her, or made her sleepy, because suddenly Elly was there in the kitchen with her, her hand on Alex's shoulder.

"Alex? You all right?" Elly's voice sounded thick, shaky, and Alex blinked, lifting her head. She blinked again, and focused on Elly.

Elly's eyes were red rimmed, her cheeks blotchy. She swiped at her cheek with one hand.

"El?"

"Sorry," Elly whispered, but the tears kept coming, and she kept swiping them away. "I just…" She took a deep breath and sat down in the chair across from Alex. "I just had this vision of what it'd be like if you weren't here"—she wiped at more tears—"and if you'd been seriously hurt, or…" She swallowed. "Or worse, then I'd be devastated."

Alex reached out and clasped Elly's hand. "El, it's all right." Elly was usually so calm, so strong, and to see Elly like this was starting to worry her.

"It's not all right," she said, her voice thick with tears. "You'd never have known how much I love you, if you'd died. And I would have regretted it forever." The words came out in a rush, and it took Alex a moment to process them.

Love?

Elly loved her?

She thought of how strong Elly was to say it, of how she'd not said it back. She never said it to anyone, not since Heather had thrown it back in her face.

Love? Who'd love you? No one, except me. But if you don't want to be with me, then what?

Elly wasn't Heather.

But reminding herself of that didn't help. She wasn't loveable, she knew it. That's why she'd gone through a string of foster homes, why her partners were only friends. None of them had ever pushed for more, and sometimes she wasn't even sure of Will. They were friends too, good ones, and he understood. Foster care hadn't been kind to him either. He'd never had a Heather. Heather had loved her so much, or so she'd said, and then thrown it away. It didn't matter that it was five years ago. It could have been yesterday.

"I didn't die, El," Alex said finally. Elly was hurting, and she'd hurt even more if Alex didn't stop this. "We're not good for each other, El. You worry about me too much, and you have too much on your plate to be spending time doing that."

Elly sniffled. "What do you mean?"

"You have the farm, and your friends, and you won't stick around Parry's for long, not like me. You should find someone that's like you, someone who deserves you."

Elly looked stricken, but Alex willfully hardened her heart. It was for Elly's own good. She deserved someone worthy of her love, someone who had a proper upbringing, who knew what a real family was like, who knew what love really was. She didn't know.

"Alex, I don't understand." She squeezed Alex's hand. "You don't mean it."

Alex extracted her hand. "Thanks, El, for coming to help me when Will asked. We've had a fun time together." She rose from the chair, grappling with her crutches. "I'll let you out. You should go home and rest."

Elly rose too, hesitantly. "But—"

"You need to sleep," Alex said, forestalling her protestations. "And we both sleep better alone."

Elly didn't have anything to say to that.

As Alex closed the door behind her, life seemed to settle back into place, the way it had been. Tomorrow she'd call Will, let him know how she was, and start planning her recovery. There were still a couple of months left in the riding season, after all.

CHAPTER NINETEEN

When Alex came into the bar at Parry's a couple of days later, drawing attention from the staff and regulars thanks to her crutches, Elly ignored her, running food orders to her tables. Charity came out of the bar just as Elly came back up to enter in another order, and caught her by the computer.

"What's up with you? Aren't you going to go say hello to your girl?" Charity asked. She grabbed a tray from the shelf underneath the computer, letting it hang from two fingers by her side.

"I'm busy," Elly said. "I have a full section."

"They can wait a minute," Charity replied. "Go on."

"No, that's all right." Elly shook her head. Charity frowned.

"What's up with you?"

"Nothing."

Nothing at all.

She'd had no word from Alex; no phone call, no text, nothing. And when she'd tried to call, or text, there was no answer. After all that, nothing.

When she drove by Alex's place the evening after they'd gotten back, the trailer had been sitting in front of the house, empty. She'd hooked it up, expecting Alex to come out of the house, but she hadn't. It was like all they'd had hadn't really existed after all. She'd driven away, her heart aching.

"I don't think it's nothing," Charity replied. "What happened?"

"Nothing."

"Seems a whole lot of nothing," Charity observed. Elly finished punching in her order.

"Excuse me, I need to grab drinks for my table," she said. Charity let her go, but Elly doubted she'd escaped questioning forever. She filled the glasses with ice and pop and placed them on a tray, taking them out to the four-top Shay had seated in her section. Two couples, out for a date night, from the looks of them. The girls chattered to each other, but their hands clasped those of their boyfriends, who listened with half an ear to the conversation while they watched the sports on the TV nearby.

Must be nice to have someone.

She'd thought she'd had someone. For once in her life, she thought she'd found someone she could grow old with. Maybe she shouldn't have left the farm, should have kept on at the diner, where she knew everyone and everyone knew her. There was a comfort in that, and it would surely have been better than this. The farm was for sale, and she'd have to make her way in the world without it. There was no going back.

When Elly finished her shift at ten, she peered into the bar before she left. Alex wasn't there. Her spirits sank.

"Looking for your girlfriend?" Eric asked. He smiled at her, but she didn't return it.

"No, just curious." She swallowed against the lump in her throat at the word *girlfriend*. They had been, hadn't they? "Good night, Eric."

"See you." He turned back to open up the dishwasher and pull out the clean pint glasses.

In her car in the parking lot, she turned on her phone. It buzzed with a message, and her heart skipped. Alex. She listened to her voice mail.

Ms. Cole, this is Fay Greene from AMS Designs. Your CV came across my desk earlier this week and I've been meaning to call. I was hoping you'd be available to come to an interview. My number is…

Elly's heart sank. It wasn't Alex. She clutched at her phone, scrabbling in her apron for her pen and notebook. She repeated the message and scrawled down the name and number. It had seemed like a shot in the dark when she'd submitted her CV to AMS. The position was a bit more advanced than she thought she had the skill for, and she hadn't thought it possible.

But here it was.

A chance.

Elly glanced over at Parry's, the neon light above the door glowing a bright red. If she got the job, she wouldn't have to come here anymore or have to think about or see Alex. Alex had been right about that. She wouldn't stick around Parry's for long.

❖

Alex heard the rumble of the R6 even before it turned into her street. She hobbled on her crutches to the door, pushing it open and stepping onto the concrete stoop. Will pulled up in front of her house and cut the engine, rolling the bike back until the wheel nudged against the curb. He dismounted and pulled off his helmet as he walked toward the house.

"Hey there, gorgeous. How's the ankle?"

"Getting better. The doctor says I should still take it easy for a while. But after six weeks, I can start with some really gentle exercise and take the brace off, if it's healing properly by then."

"Did he say anything about riding?" Will asked. "I miss having you around. It's not quite the same, riding on my own. And my friend Reg is out on the rigs, so he's not around, either."

"I can't put weight on it to use the brake," Alex said, "so I can't ride my Ninja."

"What about as a passenger?" Will asked. "You can ride pillion on mine. All you'd need to do is hold on."

Alex sighed, looking beyond him to where his bike rested. "I can't, not yet. Besides, I'd have to take my crutches along, and those won't fit in your saddlebags."

"Soon, then. Six weeks." Will looked disappointed, and Alex's own spirits sank further. "Hey, babe, don't look like that. Time will go so quickly you'll hardly even notice."

Will bent down and hugged her, lifting her off her feet. She nestled her head against his shoulder like she always did, and while it was comforting, it didn't feel quite the same. The old zing of attraction wasn't there. She loved him, she knew she did, but he needed to be smaller, more girlish, more…Elly.

He squeezed her until she felt her breath catch.

"Down, silly," she wheezed, and he chuckled, setting her down gently. He bent and picked up her crutches, which had fallen to the concrete, getting her situated once more.

"What are you up to tonight?" he asked as he followed her into the house.

"Nothing much. Movie, popcorn, whatever. I think I'll end up catching up on all the films I've wanted to watch." It would be entertaining for a couple of weeks, but not for too long. Already she was starting to feel on edge, impatient to get out of the house, to go to work, to be doing something. Staying at home, resting, sleeping… it wasn't her thing. She couldn't remember the last time she'd been so housebound. Perhaps never.

"We could go out, if you want," Will offered. "Parry's, or somewhere else."

"Not tonight," she said. "I was there last night for a few minutes. That was enough."

"See everyone?"

"Most everyone." Not Elly, though. Eric had said she was working, but she hadn't come into the bar. After the other night, Alex hadn't really wanted to talk to her. Best to make a clean break of it, even with the dreadful pun.

"Elly coming round to nurse you?" Will asked, right on the mark.

Alex winced. "No. She dropped me off, and that's it."

"What?" Will set his helmet down on the coffee table and sat next to Alex. "What's going on, babe?"

"We called it quits. It wasn't working out." Alex didn't look at him. Just saying the words hurt more than her ankle. She'd thought she could forget about Elly, but she hadn't. Anyone else, and she'd have been out at the bar, raring to go.

It must be her ankle, and being cooped up. She should be over it by now.

"I can't believe it. You and I get each other, babe. We understand each other, way better than anyone else does."

He sat forward, looking serious, resting his forearms on his thighs, clasping his hands together. Alex had never seen him look so intense. Will was usually a happy-go-lucky kind of guy, cracking jokes and making her laugh.

"I know we've always just sort of had an…understanding," he began, "but it's really more than that, don't you think?"

Alex wasn't sure where he was going with this. "We've always understood each other," she answered. "More than anyone else."

"Yeah, but I don't think that's true, not anymore."

Now it was Alex who didn't know what Will was talking about.

"Babe, I love you," he said, taking her hands. "And I know you love me."

"Are you proposing?" Alex felt her eyebrows rise.

"Oh no." Will chuckled, sounding a bit sheepish. "Suppose it does sound that way, doesn't it?"

"You weren't down on one knee, but it seemed awfully close," Alex teased.

He cleared his throat. "Babe, I think you're making a big mistake. I've seen you with Elly, and I saw how she came right out to help when you were hurt. No one's ever done that for either of us. She loves you, even if you don't love her. But I think you do."

Alex shook her head.

"You can't lie to me, Bellerose," Will said. He took her hand, but she wouldn't look at him. For once, he had no idea.

"I'm not lying," she said.

"Aren't you?" He tugged on her hand, drawing her attention. His blue eyes were warm, but worried.

"No." She met his gaze resolutely, and he sighed.

"If you say so. But I've never seen you give anyone else a ride on your Ninja. Think about it." He rose to his feet. "I'll be around every other day or so, when I'm done work. If you need anything, you let me know, all right?"

"All right."

Will let go of her hand. "Think about it, though, what I said. I'll let myself out. Don't get up."

He left.

Alex took a deep breath and rubbed at the prickling of tears in her eyes.

CHAPTER TWENTY

Elly stepped out into the sunshine and walked slowly down the sidewalk, her low kitten heels clacking on the cement. She shrugged off her suit jacket and folded it over her arm, her hands shaking.

In a week's time, she'd be starting her new job. Junior graphic designer at an IT company. No more hustling as a server, trying to make enough tips to live on, run off her feet by the end of the night. If she could sell the farm, she could buy a condo or a small house, and her life would be settled. Mentally she ran through her list of things to do, and what she'd need to pack up at the farm. She didn't want to start counting her chickens, but she couldn't help it.

Her phone buzzed in her purse and she fished it out.

"Elly, it's Derek."

"Hi, Derek."

She thought guiltily of her new job, and how she'd have to give her notice at Parry's. She hated to leave them short. It went against her nature.

"What's up?" It wasn't too difficult to sound cheery.

"Could you come in early? Amie just went home sick, and Charity's stuck on her own. I can help her out for a bit, but when the early dinner crowd comes in…"

"No problem. I'll be there as soon as I can."

"Thanks, El. I wish I could hire more people like you." Derek hung up, and Elly felt worse. She didn't want to leave him short-staffed, but she couldn't do both jobs.

She arrived at Parry's an hour later, tying on her apron as she walked into the back, hanging up her purse and jacket on a hook near

Derek's office. The door was closed, and she went back downstairs and out onto the floor, where she saw Derek taking an order from a couple seated by the window.

He came to the computer to ring it in. "Elly, you're here. Thank goodness." He smiled at her as he punched in the order.

"I said I would be."

"That's quicker than I thought," he said, not looking at her. He scanned the screen, then hit a button. "Charity's on a break. She's been run off her feet."

"Do you have a minute?" Elly asked. "I need to talk to you."

Derek glanced out into the restaurant, scanning the tables. "I have a minute. Maybe two, tops."

"I have to give you my notice," she said, slipping her hands into her apron pockets, finding her pen and notebook. They gave her something to hold and fiddle with.

"Aw, man," Derek groaned. "El…I thought you were my girl."

"I got another job," she said apologetically. "And I start next week."

"You're not leaving me for the restaurant down the block, are you?" he asked, eyebrows rising, clutching at his heart in mock distress.

"Oh no," she assured him, a smile creeping onto her face at his purposeful dramatics. "I'll be a junior graphic designer."

"Damn." He shook his head. "Can't hold you here now. A fancy office with a basketball court and free lattes doesn't even compete with us."

"There isn't a basketball court," she said, chuckling.

"You should request one," Derek replied. "Seriously though, El, that's awesome. I'm envious. And a little sad." He gave her shoulder a squeeze. "Do you want me to tell the others, or did you want it kept quiet? I know some people just like to disappear."

"I'll let people know," she said. "And I'll work every night for the rest of the week if you need me."

"I wish you were staying," Derek said, hearing her offer. "I want all of my staff to say they'll work every night." He chuckled and headed to the pass-through, where a cook had just called his name. "You're in section three tonight."

"All right." Elly punched in and went to work.

By the end of the night, the entire staff on duty had heard she would be leaving.

"I'm still here till the weekend," Elly said as she slid onto a bar stool in front of Eric where he poured a rye and cola.

"Karaoke time," he said, grinning.

"Oh no. I don't want to sing."

"You'll have to," he said. "It's a tradition."

"No way."

"You can pick the song, but you have to sing," he continued as if he hadn't heard her. "But you won't have to buy your own booze. We wouldn't let you."

"I'm a cheap drunk," she admitted as she counted out her float for the next day and calculated her receipts.

"That's promising. I'll invite all the regulars."

"Not all," she said, looking up at him.

Eric gave her an understanding look. "No certain biker chick, eh?"

She felt her cheeks flush. "Right."

"It's a real shame, you know. I think she did love you."

"I don't think so," Elly said. She didn't want to discuss it with Eric, but he didn't get the hint.

"I haven't seen her like that with anyone," he said. "You didn't see her, always glancing over to see if she could spot you as you passed by. She could hardly concentrate when you were working."

"She already has someone," Elly replied. "And it's not me."

"I think you're wrong."

Elly shook her head.

Eric shrugged. "If you say so."

CHAPTER TWENTY-ONE

A couple of weeks after starting her new job, Elly returned to the farm. She'd hooked up the trailer, which had sat, forlorn and empty, in a parking space behind her apartment building, and towed it back. It would go into the shed until she needed it to haul her stuff to the city. If she sold the farm.

Stopping for a quick break in Claresholm, and grabbing a Slurpee from the convenience store and gas station, Elly checked her phone. It flashed with a message.

Elly, it's Noreen. I have an offer on the farm. Give me a call when you get this.

Elly's stomach flip-flopped and she sat in her car, her Slurpee forgotten in the cup holder. An offer. A buyer.

It was real.

She drove to Cardston directly, forcing herself not to exceed the speed limit, though she wanted to put the pedal right to the floor. She should have called Noreen, but given that she was already on her way…

She pulled up outside the real-estate agent's office and went inside. Noreen was on the phone, but she waved and indicated a seat in front of her desk. Elly sat and tried not to fidget while she waited for Noreen to finish her call.

"I'll be in touch, Walter," she said. "'Bye now." She hung up the phone and smiled at Elly. "I thought you'd call."

"I was already on my way down, so I figured I'd stop in. Is that all right?"

"Oh, of course." Noreen took out a folder. "There's a family in town who came to see me, looking for a farm property to buy. They've just moved here, and they're renting while they look for properties. I took them out to see it, and they just fell in love."

"They've already seen the farm?" Elly was startled. Noreen hadn't said anything about that. She thought of the state of the kitchen, and the clutter.

"Just the outside," Noreen said. "You didn't give me keys to the house, so they just peeked. They're keen to buy, even though it needs some work. Their kids had a riot running around the yard too."

"That's good." Elly rubbed her hands on her thighs, blotting away the sudden dampness of her palms.

"I know the land was last appraised at about $450,000," Noreen said, flipping a page in her folder, "but they can't afford to pay quite that much."

"Hamilton Farms offered half a million," Elly noted.

Noreen made a moue, looking sour. "Hamilton, that jerk. Horse slaughter is absolutely disgusting."

"I wish he'd said something when he offered. I'd never have considered it if he had."

"Typical of him. Anyway, this family said they could afford just under $400,000. Also, they're waiting for the sale of their previous property to be finalized. I know it's not the best offer, but I promised them I'd pass it along to you."

Elly looked down at her hands in her lap. It was less than she'd hoped, but still…

Thoughts of her new job floated to the forefront of her mind. It would be nice to have a proper house in the city, instead of just a tiny apartment. She might even be able to work from home sometimes.

"Take your time and think about it," Noreen advised. "It's a big decision to make. It's your family's land, after all."

"I will. I'm headed down there for the weekend. I should take advantage and pack up some of my things. By the way, did Jack put in an offer?"

"He told me he would, but I haven't gotten anything from him yet. Can you let me know one way or another by Sunday evening on this one?" Noreen asked. "We shouldn't leave them hanging too long."

"I'll know by then," Elly said. "I think."

She rose and said good-bye to Noreen, going back out to the car. She stopped at the grocery store on her way out of town and grabbed a few essentials.

The sun was high in the sky when she made it to the farm, driving slowly into the rutted driveway in front of the farmhouse. She got out, and the breeze ruffled her hair, smelling of dirt, a hint of manure, and the fresh scent of the country. The hedge bordering the yard bloomed with small flowers, and the flowerbeds her mother had kept up were in bright profusion, though they needed some care before the new owners moved in.

The new owners.

Elly sank down on the weathered porch steps. She'd sat here for hours upon hours as a girl, watching the sun set over the hills, seeing her father come back down the road—gravel in those days—in his old truck, her mother singing to herself in the kitchen as she made dinner. But now, it was quiet, empty.

Lifeless.

The land deserved more than this, a lonely existence. She doubted she'd ever be able to live here full-time, but she hated to see it neglected. She leaned against the post.

This was a family house. Kids should be shrieking as they ran down the stairs, filling the house with laughter, their feet pounding on the floor. A shaggy dog should lie on the porch, keeping guard over his people. Their parents would fill the house with love and security, and it couldn't get more perfect than that.

Elly swallowed hard as she rose and unlocked the door.

She'd made her decision, but she'd call Noreen in the morning.

Elly spent the afternoon cleaning, and packing up the bits she wanted to take with her, going through her lists and walking through the house several times. She didn't know what she'd do with the rest, but she hoped she could find a charity to take some of it. She loaded up her car, then came back inside and made herself a quick, simple dinner of eggs, toast and bacon, and tea. She ate at the cracked Formica table, as she'd done so many times before. She'd take the table with her, once she came back with a moving van for the larger pieces.

Once she was done, she cleared up, and then went to sit on the porch with a book she'd found during her packing, an old, tattered romance novel. It had been her mother's favorite, and Elly remembered sneaking it off the shelf when she was eleven, reading it under the covers at night and wondering why her mother loved it so much. She hadn't read it in years, but when she opened the cover, the words were familiar, almost like an old friend.

She read until the light grew too dim and the breeze too cool. Then she went back inside and curled up on the sofa in the living room, pulling the blanket over her legs. As the sun dropped below the horizon, she heard a rumble of thunder. It had been hot that afternoon, perfect weather for an evening storm. She glanced out the window, seeing lightning flash in the distance.

It brought back other memories, more recent ones. Just over a year ago, she'd mistaken the rumble of Alex's motorcycle for thunder. Alex had been drenched from the sudden downpour, running up the porch steps.

Elly didn't regret letting her in, nor did she regret what had happened next. She knew she was looking through rose-tinted glasses, but that night had been so beautiful, romantic and hot all at once. Her chest tightened and she pressed her lips together. That's all it was now, a beautiful memory. Back then, she hadn't known what Alex was really like. Loveable, yet not the white knight she'd imagined. But Alex didn't love her back, and there was nothing she could do.

She set the book aside and went upstairs, getting ready for bed. When she slid between the sheets, she left her window open a few inches to let the cool rain-scented breeze in.

No matter how she tried, she couldn't sleep. She couldn't forget being with Alex. The bed seemed empty without her, lonely and cold. Elly turned over, drawing the quilts up to her chin. She should call Alex, at least to see how she was doing with her ankle. The thought of the accident made her shiver. What if it had been worse? She turned over again, opening her eyes and staring into the darkened room.

Would Alex even take her call?

❖

Saturday night, and Alex couldn't stand being at home alone. If she could have paced, she would have, but pacing on crutches was not nearly as satisfying. And if she didn't have those, she'd be on the bike, or working. She dressed in a knee-length dark jean skirt with her black T-shirt, and pulled on one of her leather jackets. Then, hearing Louise's TV going, she made her way slowly down the stairs to knock at the door.

"Hey, Alex." She looked down at Alex's brace, at the crutches. "Jeez, what did you do?"

"Long story," Alex said with a sigh. "Are you busy, Louise? I'm going stir-crazy here by myself, and I was wondering if you might be able to give me a ride to Parry's. Pretty please? Cabs are so unreliable. I'll buy you dinner, even."

"Sure, just let me grab my coat. I'm just wasting time watching reality TV anyway."

Louise dropped her off at Parry's. "Rain check on dinner tonight, but I'll take you up on it when I'm jonesing for a good pizza from Spiros."

"Thanks so much. I really appreciate it."

"No worries. Make sure you get a ride home, all right? Or get a cab. See you later." Louise waved and pulled away as soon as Alex had made it to the sidewalk.

Alex balanced precariously as she pulled open the door to the lounge, shuffling to the side and limping carefully in.

"Alex!"

Alex lifted her head and saw Jan waving at her, grinning from a table near the bar. She headed that way, avoiding a group of young men who hogged two tables. Jan pulled out a chair for her.

"Looking gorgeous," Jan said, giving her a once over. "Even with the brace."

"Thanks." Alex sat heavily, blowing out a breath. "I am so sick of these damn crutches already."

Jan leaned over, her arm sliding over Alex's shoulders, and gave her a squeeze. "It'll heal before you know it. Can I get you a drink?"

"Just a beer," Alex said. "And thanks."

"You've missed the drama," Jan said as she rose to go to the bar. "I'll tell you about it in a minute." She went to the bar and came back with a pint. "Keith's, just the way you like it."

Alex dug in her pocket for her wallet.

"On me, this round," Jan said, waving the money away. "So, Vanessa broke up with that chick who was the star singer."

"I'd heard that," Alex said.

"Did you hear why?"

Alex shrugged. "I figured since it was Vanessa, it would be because she was tired of her."

"If only." Jan shook her head, smirking. "Turns out that chick was already dating someone. She came into the bar looking for her, and Vanessa had a rude awakening."

Alex winced. "That sucks."

"It was practically a catfight," Jan said. "I thought for sure Eric would have to pull them apart. But they left after Vanessa told her to get out. You should've been here."

"Sounds like I was better off not being here," Alex said. "Wonder who Vanessa will hook up with next."

"Who cares," Jan said. She leaned closer. "What about you? I haven't seen that girl of yours around. Didn't last, did it?" Jan rested her head on Alex's shoulder. "My place is close, if you want."

Alex opened her mouth, then paused. A few months ago, she might have taken Jan up on her offer without thinking. Jan's perfume lingered, a deep musky scent, and Alex didn't find it seductive.

"I'll see how I feel. The ankle still hurts a lot," she said finally, not wanting to reject Jan too bluntly.

"Of course." Jan straightened but kept her arm over Alex's shoulder.

Alex took a sip of her beer, wondering if she should have taken painkillers instead. The Keith's tasted like it always did, but it wasn't doing much for her. She drank a little more.

A friend of Jan's slid into a seat across from them. Alex couldn't remember her name, but she recognized the curvy blonde. She was cute. Just her type.

"You've met Rachel, haven't you?" Jan said.

"Of course." Alex stretched out a hand, and Rachel took it, holding it a bit longer than necessary.

"Weird to see you out from behind the bar," she said, her pouty lips widening into a smile.

"That's what happens when you break your ankle," Jan said,

squeezing Alex's shoulder again. Alex leaned forward a bit, letting Jan's embrace drop.

Rachel leaned over and glanced down under the table. "Ouch. How'd you do that?"

"Bike crash," Alex said.

"You poor thing," Rachel simpered, and Alex tried to look gracious, though she wasn't sure she managed. She didn't want to be treated like an invalid, even if she practically was one.

"I couldn't stand it if it were me," Jan said to Rachel, who shuddered.

"I can't imagine it. I'd have been in agony," Rachel replied.

"It won't take long to heal," Alex said, taking another drink of her beer. It was easier to drink than make inane conversation. She listened with half an ear as Jan and Rachel chatted, shifting her leg when Jan tried to rest her hand there on her thigh, just above the hem of her skirt. She finished her beer and grabbed her crutches, maneuvering to her feet.

"Let me help," Rachel said, rising.

"No, I'll do it," Alex said, knowing her voice was a bit sharp. "This round's on me, anyway."

She hobbled to the bar and swung herself up onto a stool, propping her crutches against the bar.

"Another beer?" Eric paused on the other side of the bar.

"Yeah, please. And pour a drink of whatever Jan's having, and I'll pay."

Eric raised a brow at that but didn't say anything. He took Jan's drink over to the table, then came back and drew a pint of Keith's, setting it in front of Alex.

"Didn't expect to see you in tonight," he said. "Doesn't that lovely girlfriend of yours want to help you out at home? You two should be there all curled up watching a movie or something, shouldn't you?"

"She's not my girlfriend," Alex replied.

"My mistake," Eric said. "Though I could have sworn you two were…" He waved his hand. "And what about Will?"

"He's not my boyfriend, either." Alex frowned.

"Back to being the lone wolf?" Eric asked. A chit printed up on the machine, but he ignored it. "Is that how it is?"

"Maybe."

"Jan's looking at you," Eric observed. "Bet she's hoping the lone wolf won't want to be alone."

"What's up with you?"

"Nothing. Just noticing things. Wanting everyone to be happy, as I always do."

"I'll be happy when my damn ankle heals."

"Is that really what it is?" Eric printed out her bill, laying it on the bar, facedown.

"You kicking me out?" she asked, nudging the curl of paper.

"Nope. But if you hook up with Jan, I might."

Alex snorted. "I don't want Jan."

"Don't you?"

She wasn't a one-woman kind of girl, but Jan held no appeal. "No."

Jan wasn't Elly, but she wasn't about to say that to Eric.

"Glad to hear it." Eric took up the bill, crumpling it and throwing it into the garbage. "I'll run you a tab. Just let me know when you want me to call you a taxi."

"All right."

Eric went back to his work, and Alex looked at her beer. She glanced at the pass-through for the restaurant, hoping to catch a glimpse of Elly. Just a glimpse would do her. She didn't need to talk to her, but if she could sit here and watch her, secretly…

"She's not here," Eric said from behind her. She turned in her seat, nearly upsetting the full tray he held.

"What?"

"Elly's not here," he said. "She quit."

Alex was speechless, and she felt the hurt spreading through her chest, an unexpected sensation. She'd been wanting to see Elly, she realized.

"She got a better job," Eric said. "It's a shame." He moved away, taking the dishes into the kitchen.

Alex pulled out her wallet and set down enough for the drinks. She left her beer sitting there and walked out into the evening, calling for a cab when she hit the sidewalk. No point being here if Elly wasn't here. She didn't want Jan, or Rachel, or anyone. She'd be better off at home.

❖

On Sunday, Elly went to the real-estate agent's office. Noreen had the paperwork already drawn up, just in case, and Elly sat down to sign what she needed to sign.

"Are you sure?" Noreen asked. "I don't want to pressure you."

"I'm sure," Elly said.

"I'll call my sister. She's a notary and can sign some of these forms, and I'll call up Brian Loose and his wife, the buyers." She picked up the phone and dialed, then passed Elly the purchase agreement and transfer forms.

Elly read through the purchase agreement carefully, taking her time. The bell on the front door of the office jangled, and she looked up from the last page of the agreement. A couple who looked about her age stood there, holding hands, looking happy yet nervous.

"Come on over here, Brian, Evelyn," Noreen said, waving them to chairs. "I was just about to call you."

Elly rose to her feet and held out her hand. "How do you do? I'm Elly Cole."

"Brian Loose," the man said, shaking her hand. "And this is my wife, Evelyn."

"Nice to meet you," Evelyn said, taking Elly's hand in turn. Her grip was gentle, warm. "I'm so glad you're willing to sell. The place is just about perfect." She smiled at her husband, who grinned back at her.

"We've been wanting a place of our own," Brian explained. "My parents have a farm in Saskatchewan, but we really wanted to make our own way."

"What did you farm?"

"Wheat and corn, mostly," Brian said, "though I think here we'll get a few pigs and a heifer."

"That sounds lovely," Elly said. "We used to have a few animals, and the barn's suitable for a cow and pigs, and a few horses."

"The kids loved the barn," Evelyn said. "They can't wait to get up there when there's hay in the loft."

"We used to have a swing," Elly said. "You should put one up."

"We will," Brian said.

"The paperwork is ready for you all to sign," Noreen said, catching their attention. They settled into their chairs, and Noreen indicated where they would sign.

"We'll keep your lease with Jack Collins," Brian said as he signed the purchase agreement. "We've been talking to him, and he's happy we won't start up our own work on the land until next season."

"That's good," Elly said faintly. She hadn't even thought of Jack's lease. She'd have to tell him what she'd decided.

"He said he'd wanted the land, but that he couldn't afford it. I think we'll end up good friends. He's a nice man," Evelyn said.

"He is," Elly agreed. "And we'll have to introduce you to his gran, Mrs. Calderwood. Although she might just introduce herself."

The bell jangled again, and Noreen's sister strode in. "I'm here," she trilled, taking off her wide-brimmed hat.

"Excellent timing," Noreen said. "We're just about ready for you. Now, Elly, here's the part you sign on the transfer form."

Elly bent forward, seeing her name on the form, and the list of quarter sections. She took a deep breath and signed.

CHAPTER TWENTY-TWO

When she returned home from her second-to-last physiotherapy appointment, six long weeks of pain nearly over, Alex found Will waiting for her on her front steps. She walked carefully up the sidewalk. Her ankle ached, but the therapist had told her that it was well on its way to being back to normal, and that she needed to give it a workout.

"Hey, babe." Will rose and came down the steps, taking her up in a big hug, lifting her off her feet. She clung to him, hoping he wouldn't drop her, but he set her down gently.

"Hey, yourself," she said. "You've been gone a long time."

Will shrugged. "Had to take advantage of the construction job in BC," he said. "Besides, I got in lots of riding while I was out there."

Alex's shoulders slumped. She had missed almost an entire riding season thanks to her ankle. "Lucky."

"What have you been up to? Back to work yet?"

"A little bit, but only really short shifts," Alex replied. "Eric's having to do most of the heavy lifting, though."

"He can manage. You working tonight? I'll come in."

"Nope, have tonight off, and good thing too." She sat on the stoop, slowly flexing her ankle. "After physio, I'm beat."

Will sat beside her, putting an arm over her shoulders. "Let's go out for dinner, then. My treat. I've missed you."

Alex glanced up at him, and he took the opportunity to kiss her. His lips were warm, familiar, but there wasn't that usual zing. She responded only hesitantly, and when he pulled back, he raised a brow.

"You didn't miss me, did you?"

Having him say the words, Alex realized what she'd been trying to avoid thinking about. She hadn't missed him, not really. She'd missed his company and desperately missed riding, but that was all. She hadn't missed the sex, or the intimacy. But how to tell him?

She didn't have to. He must have read her expression.

"Thought so."

"What do you mean, thought so?"

"Haven't you come to your senses yet?"

"My senses are perfectly fine, Will."

"You sure about that, Bellerose? You back with Elly yet?"

Alex winced and shook her head. She hadn't seen Elly since the accident, and since Elly had quit Parry's, there was no way she'd run into her. An ache in her chest twinged, and she rubbed at her sternum just below her collarbone. She'd been too chicken to even attempt calling, hadn't wanted to seem like a beggar, crawling back.

"Not Elly? What about Jan? Or"—he paused for dramatic effect—"Vanessa?"

Alex rose shakily to her feet and turned toward the door. "No one, actually."

"Did she turn you into a nun?" Will's voice behind her was incredulous.

She shifted back to face him, holding on to the iron rail. "I needed a break from everything," she said, her voice fierce. "And everyone."

"There's a break, and then there's hiding. Guess which one you're doing."

"You're not my keeper."

"Babe, I've been your friend, and your lover, for years. I know you almost as well as I know myself." He paused. "Actually, I probably know you better. I'm way too messed up."

She couldn't help but crack a smile at that.

"Anyway, you're being stubborn. And I don't know what's going through your head, but you and Elly were good together. And she's a good woman. You think Jan, or even Heather, measures up to her at all?"

"No, and that's the problem. She's too good, Will. She deserves better."

"I didn't expect you to play the self-pity card. Let me know when you've come to your senses. See you around, Bellerose," he said, turning away from her and heading to his bike.

She didn't call out to him. What would she say? When he'd gone, the growl of his motorcycle fading into the distance, she went inside. Their history meant a lot to her; he'd been her friend for over a decade, her best mate, but she had changed and he'd noticed. He'd become sensible, all of a sudden, too perceptive for his own good. She knew what she wanted, but it seemed impossible.

Alex walked slowly into the kitchen, her ankle aching all the way, and poured herself a glass of water, swallowing down an aspirin from the plastic container on the counter. Time to put up her feet. She had physio again tomorrow.

❖

The doctor examined Alex's ankle, testing its range of motion and its strength. "I think you're about healed," he said, glancing up at her where she sat on the examination bed. "And if you're careful and keep it short, you can start riding again."

Alex gave a yelp of surprise. She'd almost given up hearing those words and had thought they were weeks away yet.

"You need to take it easy," he added, rising from his chair, "but a short ride or two wouldn't hurt. Keep it quick, just around the neighborhood."

She could ride again. That was all that mattered. "That's the best news I've had in weeks."

"And just your luck, this weekend is supposed to be nice," he observed. "You can go now. I'll have Dana schedule you for another appointment in a couple of weeks."

Alex slid off the bed and onto her feet, bending to put her sneaker back on. "No problem."

"And watch yourself at work. Don't overwork the joint."

"I'll take it easy," she said, doing up her laces. "Derek won't like it, but he'll deal." She straightened and swept her hair from her eyes.

"I'll see you, then." The doctor left, and Alex scooped up her jacket from the visitor's chair and followed.

Once she got home, after putting gas in Louise's car, she pulled up beside her Ninja, its green panels gleaming in the noonday sun. A short ride. Her heart beat faster. She'd make sure it was in proper shape, then she'd take it out tomorrow. She got out of the car and fetched her tools from the storage room.

The bike sat out behind the small garage, which her landlady had rented to someone else, though Alex wished she hadn't. It would have been a perfect workshop, but she'd have to make do with the parking pad. She set down her tool kit beside the bike, then went back for her motorcycle stand. Sometimes she wished the Ninja had a center stand, but she'd deal with it. She put the bike up on the stand and started by checking the bolts. The bike hadn't been driven in weeks. Though a mechanic had fixed it up after the accident and she knew it was unlikely that anything had loosened, still she went through the routine. When she rose from kneeling on the concrete, her ankle ached, and she half hobbled to sit on the low fence that surrounded the backyard.

Slowly, Alex flexed her ankle, and the pain subsided. She returned to the bike, checked the oil, then pulled out the brush she used to clean the chain. It was all old hat to her now, after so many years of riding. When she'd finished all her tinkering, she put her tools away, but when she came back to the bike, she realized there was no way she could get it off its stand by herself. She had done it before, but her ankle throbbed, she was tired, and the bike was heavy.

"Dammit."

If only Elly were here.

Alex sank heavily onto the fence. She thought about calling but left her phone in her pocket. She'd make do.

The minutes stretched out, and still she sat there, thinking about Elly when she really should have been doing anything but. She couldn't imagine being without her bike, but yet, being without Elly, without the girl she'd come to love—she flinched at that thought, but accepted it—had sucked all the color and happiness out of her life.

"Need a hand?" The neighbor from next door, Ryan, came out his back gate, hefting a bag of trash into the black bin.

Alex rose. "Yeah, if you could. I can't get the bike back down on my own."

"How's the leg?" He came over, glancing down at Alex's sneaker-clad foot before looking at the bike.

"Sore, but healed." She walked over to the bike and gestured to the stand. "If you can just ease that up, so the back tire lowers, I'll hold the bike steady." In a few moments, the bike was back where it should be.

"That was easy," he said.

"Easy with two," she replied. "Thanks."

"No worries." He headed back inside, giving her a wave.

Alex sat astride the bike, her left hand squeezing the clutch in. She pressed the starter, letting the engine rumble to life. It sounded perfect, music to her ears, but still colorless. She wanted Elly on the back, wanted to be zipping down the highway, feeling Elly's knees squeezing her hips, knowing that she was there, behind her.

Saturday morning dawned, bright and sunny, the temperature rising as the morning wore on. Alex ate and downed two cups of coffee, then pulled on her leathers and her boots—being careful not to jar her ankle as she did up the side straps—and a brand-new helmet. The bike waited for her, and she started it, letting it warm up for a few minutes before she pulled into the street.

She did a loop of the streets around her house, feeling her way back to familiarity with the bike, testing her ankle on the foot brake. She felt a slight twinge, but otherwise her body felt fine. She headed out onto the road. She didn't have a destination in mind, but when she paused at the intersection that would take her south or north, she went south. She'd just swing by Elly's apartment, show her that she was doing just fine.

Or at least, that was what she told herself.

When she reached Elly's, she pulled into a spot in front of the apartment building and sat idling.

She should go up, buzz Elly. She could say hello.

But then what? Elly probably didn't even want to see her, not after how she'd been, after what she'd said. Will had called her stubborn, accused her of self-pity. She wasn't that sort of woman.

Alex turned off the engine and dismounted.

Chapter Twenty-three

Elly heard the rumble of a motorcycle as she sat on her sofa, drinking a cup of tea and watching the news on her laptop. The rumble grew louder, closer, but it didn't continue on as she'd expected. She finished her tea and rose, walking slowly to the window to peer out.

A street bike with green panels sat in front of the building, and though the rider's features were obscured by the helmet, she knew it was Alex. Hard to mistake that bike, that poise, for anyone else.

She hesitated, debating whether or not to go down to the street to say hello. It would be polite, at least. She snorted. Polite. She was deceiving herself, and she knew it, though she didn't want to admit it. It had been a long summer without Alex, without their evenings together, without the love and camaraderie she'd begun to get used to. She turned and went into the kitchen, rinsing her cup with a bit of water.

The rumble ceased, and her heart sank.

She should have gone out there, should have said something.

Elly stared into the empty cup, her lips pressed together.

She heard the outside door open, footsteps on the stairs, and her breath caught before she could stop herself. It couldn't be Alex. She didn't have a key.

There was a knock at the door.

The cup slipped from her hand and Elly winced as it cracked against the old cast-iron enameled sink. But that didn't matter. She hurried to the door, turning the deadbolt and pulling it open.

It was Alex.

She stood there awkwardly, looking almost sheepish, a frosted-black helmet in one hand, her dark hair mussed, her black-and-white jacket open at the front to reveal a white V-neck tee. She looked just like she had the first time they'd met, on the porch steps out at the farm. Only the rain was missing.

Elly didn't know what to say.

"Hey," Alex said, her voice husky, quiet. She didn't seem quite herself, quite as energetic and cheerful as she usually did. "Can I come in?"

Elly stepped back. "Yeah," she said, her voice cracking.

Alex stepped past her, placing her helmet on the Formica table from the farm, cluttered as it was with Elly's designs.

"That table looks familiar," Alex said as she dragged off her coat and hung it over a chair, the scent of leather reaching Elly's nose. She breathed it in deep before she could stop herself.

"It's from the farm," she replied as Alex bent to take off her motorcycle boots. "I sold it."

Alex straightened, pushing her boots to the side with a foot. "You did?" She seemed stunned. "I thought you'd never sell."

Elly shrugged. "I had an offer, after Hamilton Farms pulled out," she said. "I decided to take it. They're a nice family, the people who bought it. The perfect sort for the place." It hurt to say it, but it was the truth.

"And you're still in this rental?"

"For now. I'm looking at places. I have the money from the sale, though I'm finding it's not going as far as I'd hoped." Elly paused. Why was Alex here? Small talk wasn't like her.

"Cool." Alex ran a hand over her hair, smoothing out some of the snarls. "My ankle's better," she said offhand, walking into the living room. "Sore still, but on the mend."

"And you're back on the bike, I see." Elly followed her, taking the armchair as Alex settled onto the sofa.

"Yeah, for now," Alex said. She clasped her hands in front of her, then glanced up. "But I've been thinking." Elly saw her swallow, saw the deep breath. "I've had a lot of time to think, maybe too much of it, but I needed it." She let out the breath. "I had time to see sense. And Will helped with that. I've missed you, El."

Elly felt the tears prick behind her eyes, and suddenly she too had to take a deep breath. "I've missed you too," she admitted.

"I shouldn't have said what I did, that day," Alex said. "But it scared me, you being so freaked out, and in love. And here I was, just me. I've never really had that with anyone."

"We were getting there. Charity told me that you never let any other girl ride with you, and that night when I stayed over…I wondered if you were starting to get more serious."

Alex shifted a bit. "I get the impression everyone knew except me."

"Well, probably not everyone. But even Eric figured it out."

Alex let out a laugh. "He's not entirely blind. Now if only he and Charity could manage something."

"That might happen. Hard to say at this point." Elly chuckled. "But no changing the subject." She reached out and squeezed Alex's clasped hands. "I wanted to say something more that night when you invited me to stay, but I didn't because I wasn't sure if you'd change your mind. And I didn't want to push you then."

Alex shook her head ruefully. "You pushed me when you said no sleeping together. Probably the most sensible thing anyone's ever said to me."

"Sensible?" Elly knew she hadn't been thinking about being sensible when she'd brought it up. Frustrated, tired of being a friend-with-benefits, but sensible…not really.

"You didn't want me just for how we are in bed together," Alex replied. "No one's done that."

"Not even Will?" Elly was hesitant to ask, but she had to.

"Will and I have a long history," Alex said, "and he knows me well, and I know him well. That was different altogether. If you're worried about him making a fuss, don't be. He's the one who pushed me to see sense."

"I should buy him a drink, then." Relief swept through her. She'd imagined being in competition with Will and knew she hadn't been likely to win that one.

"He'd like that." Alex took Elly's hand between her own. "Should we make it official, now that we've talked it over? You and I are off the market?"

Elly gulped and a shiver ran through her. “Are you sure?”

“I’m sure. I was blind not to be, before.” Alex looked hopeful.

“I don’t know.” She believed Alex, but what if it didn’t last? She acknowledged the thought, then quashed it. She’d give it her all.

Alex stood and knelt beside Elly’s chair. She took Elly’s hand in her own once more, giving it a gentle squeeze, leaning close. Elly faced her, reaching out to cup the back of Alex’s neck. “I love you, El. We’ll take it a day at a time,” Alex said agreeably. “Come with me.”

“Where?”

Alex rose and tugged on Elly’s hand, and Elly stood. “It’s a beautiful day, and I have a spare helmet in my saddlebag.”

“All right. But you’ll drive a bit slower for me, right?” Elly asked, remembering when Alex had pushed the bike to the max, shooting by the other vehicles on the highway like they’d been standing still.

“Not a kilometer over the limit, unless you ask me to,” Alex replied. She headed for the door, pulling Elly along with her. “Grab your jacket, and let’s go. The day’s not getting any longer.”

“Where are we going?” Elly asked as she pulled on her jacket, the leather soft under her fingers. Her heart pounded in her chest, and she could hardly believe this was happening.

“I was thinking Lake Minnewanka. I’ll buy you an ice cream.”

“You’re on.”

❖

Alex drove along the Bow Valley Parkway, Elly perched behind her on the pillion seat. She could feel Elly’s knees tight around her hips, and she knew if she looked back, Elly would be clutching the handles of the seat tight. Everything was right in the world.

In Canmore, she pulled into the parking lot of a gas station just off the parkway and came to a stop. She pushed up her visor and turned.

“All right, still?” she asked.

Elly fumbled a bit with her visor, then pushed it up. Her cheeks were pink. “All right.” She seemed about to say something else, then stopped.

“What is it?” Alex asked. “We can go back if you want.”

“No, let’s keep on,” Elly said. “I’m enjoying this.”

"Now that's what I love to hear." Alex grinned. "It's going to get a bit faster when we hit the Trans-Canada, but that won't be for too long."

Elly nodded.

"And you can loosen your grip," Alex said. "I promise you, we won't tip over. You're going to be stiff and sore tomorrow." She saw Elly shift on the seat and flex her fingers around the handlebars. "Ready?"

"Ready." Elly pushed her visor back down, the sun glinting on the hard plastic. Alex turned her attention back to the bike. It purred under them, ready to go. She shifted into gear and eased the clutch out. Elly's knees loosened around her hips and she smiled to herself. She'd make a biker out of Elly yet.

At the turnoff to Lake Minnewanka, Alex slowed, and they cruised along the climbing road, shadowed by the pine trees. Alex cracked open her visor and took a deep breath. There was nothing like mountain air. She felt Elly shift again behind her and knew she must be starting to get achy. Too long on a bike when you weren't used to it would do that. Alex felt a bit of soreness herself and knew it was time for a break.

They came up and around the top of the hill, starting the downward trip to the snack shack. Ice cream would be perfect today. They passed the lookout area, where two cars were parked, enjoying the view, and continued down the hill and pulled into a parking spot beside a black SUV. She killed the engine.

"Ice cream's on me," Elly said as she slid off the bike, landing on shaky feet.

"It's on me," Alex said. "I brought you."

"You might have, but you drove, so I buy. That's the rule." Elly pulled off her helmet and stuck her tongue out at Alex.

Alex spread her hands wide and grinned. "Who am I to argue?" She followed Elly up the few steps to the snack shack. Soon, they had their ice cream, and they strolled down to the small beach, finding a weatherworn log to sit on.

"This is just about perfect," Elly said, turning her face toward the sun.

"Just about?"

"I can think of something that would make it better," Elly replied. She glanced at Alex, a smile hovering on her lips.

"Me too." Alex leaned forward, and they kissed.

They broke apart reluctantly when they heard a couple of kids shouting as they ran down the beach toward the water.

"That's a start," Alex said, her voice low, clearing her throat as she choked up. She was here, Elly was here with her, and she could hardly believe it.

Elly laughed, leaning against her. "The beach is too crowded for more."

"And we'd get sand everywhere," Alex agreed. "Not fun." She paused, debating her next words. "But there are a few fun things we could do with what's left of the summer."

Elly blushed.

"Those," Alex replied, "but more than that. Have you ever considered riding a scooter? It only goes seventy, max, and you could start slow." She looked hopefully at Elly, watching her reaction.

To her surprise, Elly didn't immediately disagree.

"It's slow?"

"Just residential roads. It's how I started." Alex hooked an arm over Elly's shoulders. "But no pressure, El. Honestly."

"I don't know," Elly said. She pursed her lips, looking out to the water and the small waves that lapped against the shore. "I never pictured myself riding. Would you teach me?"

"I would."

Elly tilted her head up, meeting Alex's gaze. Her cheeks were still pink. "I'll give it a try. But no laughing if I drop the scooter."

"I know you can do it," Alex said. "But if you don't like it, I don't mind having a passenger on my bike. I like having your legs around my waist, after all."

"And other places!" Elly laughed, and it was the best sound Alex had ever heard.

About the Author

Alyssa Linn Palmer is a Canadian writer and freelance editor. She splits her time between a full-time day job and her part-time loves, writing and editing. She is a member of the RWA, the Calgary RWA, and RRW (Rainbow Romance Writers). She has a passion for Paris and all things French, which is reflected in her writing. When she's not writing lesbian romance, she's creating the dark, morally flawed characters of the Le Chat Rouge series and indulging in her addiction to classic pulp fiction.

Books Available From Bold Strokes Books

Pedal to the Metal by Jesse J. Thoma. When unreformed thief Dubs Williams is released from prison to help Max Winters bust a car theft ring, Max learns that if you want to catch a thief, you have to get in bed with one. (978-1-62639-239-7)

Dragon Horse War by D. Jackson Leigh. A priestess of peace and a fiery warrior must defeat a vicious uprising that entwines their destinies and ultimately their hearts. (978-1-62639-240-3)

For the Love of Cake by Erin Dutton. When everything is on the line and one taste can break a heart, will pastry chefs Maya and Shannon take a chance on reality? (978-1-62639-241-0)

Betting on Love by Alyssa Linn Palmer. A quiet country girl at heart and a live-life-to-the-fullest biker take a risk at offering each other their hearts. (978-1-62639-242-7)

The Deadening by Yvonne Heidt. The lines between good and evil, right and wrong, have always been blurry for Shade. When Raven's actions force her to choose, which side will she come out on? (978-1-62639-243-4)

One Last Thing by Kim Baldwin & Xenia Alexiou. Blood is thicker than pride. The final book in the Elite Operative Series brings together foes, family, and friends to start a new order. (978-1-62639-230-4)

Songs Unfinished by Holly Stratimore. Two aspiring rock stars learn that falling in love while pursuing their dreams can be harmonious—if they can only keep their pasts from throwing them out of tune. (978-1-62639-231-1)

Beyond the Ridge by L.T. Marie. Will a contractor and a horse rancher overcome their family differences and find common ground to build a life together? (978-1-62639-232-8)

Swordfish by Andrea Bramhall. Four women battle the demons from their pasts. Will they learn to let go, or will happiness be forever beyond their grasp? (978-1-62639-233-5)

The Fiend Queen by Barbara Ann Wright. Princess Katya and her consort Starbride must turn evil against evil in order to banish Fiendish power from their kingdom, and only love will pull them back from the brink. (978-1-62639-234-2)

Up the Ante by PJ Trebelhorn. When Jordan Stryker and Ashley Noble meet again fifteen years after a short-lived affair, is either of them prepared to gamble on a chance at love? (978-1-62639-237-3)

Speakeasy by MJ Williamz. When mob leader Helen Byrne sets her sights on the girlfriend of Al Capone's right-hand man, passion and tempers flare on the streets of Chicago. (978-1-62639-238-0)

Myth and Magic: Queer Fairy Tales, edited by Radclyffe and Stacia Seaman. Myth, magic, and monsters—the stuff of childhood dreams (or nightmares) and adult fantasies. (978-1-62639-225-0)

The Muse by Meghan O'Brien. Erotica author Kate McMannis struggles with writer's block until a gorgeous muse entices her into a world of fantasy sex and inadvertent romance. (978-1-62639-223-6)

Venus in Love by Tina Michele. Morgan Blake can't afford any distractions and Ainsley Dencourt can't afford to lose control—but the beauty of life and art usually lies in the unpredictable strokes of the artist's brush. (978-1-62639-220-5)

Rules of Revenge by AJ Quinn. When a lethal operative on a collision course with her past agrees to help a CIA analyst on a critical assignment, the encounter proves explosive in ways neither woman anticipated. (978-1-62639-221-2)

The Romance Vote by Ali Vali. Chili Alexander is a sought-after campaign consultant who isn't prepared when her boss's daughter, Samantha Pellegrin, comes to work at the firm and shakes up Chili's life from the first day. (978-1-62639-222-9)

Advance by Gun Brooke. Admiral Dael Caydoc's mission to find a new homeworld for the Oconodian people is hazardous, but working with the infuriating Commander Aniwyn "Spinner" Seclan endangers her heart and soul. (978-1-62639-224-3)

UnCatholic Conduct by Stevie Mikayne. Jil Kidd goes undercover to investigate fraud at St. Marguerite's Catholic School, but life gets complicated when her student is killed—and she begins to fall for her prime target. (978-1-62639-304-2)

Season's Meetings by Amy Dunne. Catherine Birch reluctantly ventures on the festive road trip from hell with beautiful stranger Holly Daniels only to discover the road to true love has its own obstacles to maneuver. (978-1-62639-227-4)

Courtship by Carsen Taite. Love and Justice—a lethal mix or a perfect match? (978-1-62639-210-6)

Against Doctor's Orders by Radclyffe. Corporate financier Presley Worth wants to shut down Argyle Community Hospital, but Dr. Harper Rivers will fight her every step of the way, if she can also fight their growing attraction. (978-1-62639-211-3)

A Spark of Heavenly Fire by Kathleen Knowles. Kerry and Beth are building their life together, but unexpected circumstances could destroy their happiness. (978-1-62639-212-0)

Never Too Late by Julie Blair. When Dr. Jamie Hammond is forced to hire a new office manager, she's shocked to come face-to-face with Carla Grant and memories from her past. (978-1-62639-213-7)

Widow by Martha Miller. Judge Bertha Brannon must solve the murder of her lover, a policewoman she thought she'd grow old with. As more bodies pile up, the murderer starts coming for her. (978-1-62639-214-4)

Twisted Echoes by Sheri Lewis Wohl. What's a woman to do when she realizes the voices in her head are real? (978-1-62639-215-1)

Criminal Gold by Ann Aptaker. Through a dangerous night in New York in 1949, Cantor Gold, dapper dyke-about-town, smuggler of fine art, is forced by a crime lord to be his instrument of vengeance. (978-1-62639-216-8)

Because of You by Julie Cannon. What would you do for the woman you were forced to leave behind? (978-1-62639-199-4)

The Job by Jove Belle. Sera always dreamed that she would one day reunite with Tor. She just didn't think it would involve terrorists, firearms, and hostages. (978-1-62639-200-7)

Making Time by C.J. Harte. Two women going in different directions meet after fifteen years and struggle to reconnect in spite of the past that separated them. (978-1-62639-201-4)

Once The Clouds Have Gone by KE Payne. Overwhelmed by the dark clouds of her past, Tag Grainger is lost until the intriguing and spirited Freddie Metcalfe unexpectedly forces her to reevaluate her life. (978-1-62639-202-1)

The Acquittal by Anne Laughlin. Chicago private investigator Josie Harper searches for the real killer of a woman whose lover has been acquitted of the crime. (978-1-62639-203-8)

An American Queer: The Amazon Trail by Lee Lynch. Lee Lynch's heartening and heart-rending history of gay life from the turbulence of the late 1900s to the triumphs of the early 2000s are recorded in this selection of her columns. (978-1-62639-204-5)

Stick McLaughlin by CF Frizzell. Corruption in 1918 cost Stick her lover, her freedom, and her identity, but a very special flapper and the family bond of her own gang could help win them back—even if it means outwitting the Boston Mob. (978-1-62639-205-2)

Rest Home Runaways by Clifford Henderson. Baby boomer Morgan Ronzio's troubled marriage is the least of her worries when she gets the call that her addled, eighty-six-year-old, half-blind dad has escaped the rest home. (978-1-62639-169-7)

Charm City by Mason Dixon. Raq Overstreet's loyalty to her drug kingpin boss is put to the test when she begins to fall for Bathsheba Morris, the undercover cop assigned to bring him down. (978-1-62639-198-7) boldstrokesbooks.com

Bold Strokes Books

Quality and Diversity in LGBTQ Literature

Drama

SCI-FI

E-BOOKS

MYSTERY

EROTICA

YOUNG ADULT

BOLD STROKES BOOKS

Romance

W·E·B·S·T·O·R·E

PRINT AND EBOOKS